"Darce, it's been a crazy couple of days. We can't—"

"You're right." She nuzzled his chest. "But what if I told you that I've been thinking about this for a lot longer than the past couple of days?"

"You have?"

"Mmm-hmm." She stood on tiptoe, kissed the corner of his mouth. "And I think you have, too."

"God, Darce," he said, and there might have been more but his words were lost as she kissed him, really kissed him, all heat and need and melting into him. She gripped his shoulders and curled against him, kissing him again and again with absolutely no one watching.

"Darce," he said against her neck. "God, Darce, I've wanted you so long, but I didn't— I can't—"

"Oh, yes you can."

His hands landed low, pulling her tight while his hips pushed against hers, and the rush of need had her digging her fingers into his shoulders to keep herself upright.

"We should think this over," he said even as he molded her to him. "Get our heads clear."

"I've done enough thinking. I want to feel."

Dear Reader,

Books are often compared to children. I have found this to be truest when considering how parents must learn that what works with one child won't necessarily work with his or her sibling. Similarly, the process that enabled an author to write one book won't always come in handy when it's time to develop the next one.

I explored many different ways to tell this story. Some things have stayed constant all along, such as the main characters (three adults, one baby and a dog, though their names sometimes changed hourly) and the primary issue (the sudden reappearance of a biological daddy makes a pair of friends pretend to be lovers). But the *how* of telling the story eluded me until my amazing editor Piya said, "Hmm, what if you tried…"

With that, the true direction of this story was revealed. Darcy, Ian and the rest of the characters were free to come to life, take control of the book and make it fully their own. It seems that in writing, as in parenting, sometimes the best thing to do is to put the pieces in place, step back and prepare to be amazed.

I'd love to hear from you, either through my website (krisfletcher.com) or the group blog run by the Superromance authors (superauthors.com). I can't promise to make the characters behave when you visit, but I can promise a very warm welcome.

Yours,

Kris

KRIS FLETCHER

—

A Family Come True

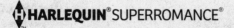

ISBN-13: 978-0-373-60913-0

A Family Come True

Copyright © 2015 by Christine Fletcher

Printed in U.S.A.

Kris Fletcher has never faked a relationship, but she does take great delight in pulling the wool over her loved ones' collective eyes. Ask her about the ancient ultrasound incident. People have almost forgiven her for that one.

Kris grew up in southern Ontario, went to school in Nova Scotia, married a man from Maine and now lives in central New York. She shares her very messy home with her husband, some of their kids and a growing population of dust bunnies.

Books by Kris Fletcher

HARLEQUIN SUPERROMANCE

A Better Father
Now You See Me
Dating a Single Dad

Other titles by this author available in ebook format.

This one is for Larry, who may or may not have been the inspiration for the socks-as-mittens portion of this book, but who definitely inspired the I-love-yous.

Acknowledgments

Renee Kloecker and Jen Talty, who provided peaceful cottage retreats when I needed them most.

My fellow playground mommies, for not being freaked out when I started taking notes on their children's behavior to refresh my baby-deprived memory. Special thanks to my neighbor Carrie, who patiently answered my questions about life with a one-year-old and indulged my need to remember how it felt to hold a little one again.

The usual people who make it possible for me to write a book—Larry, the kids, the Purples, Agent Extraordinaire Jessica Faust, and Piya Campana, the World's Most Patient and Insightful Editor.

CHAPTER ONE

THE MAN HOVERING at the entry to Ian North's garage was very tall, very blond, and very late.

"Hey, Ian. Long time no see."

"Xander?" Ian tugged his work gloves from his hands and set them on the anvil where, moments earlier, he had been happily pounding the hell out of a piece of hot iron while singing along to some vintage Queen. With a glance to make sure everything in his home forge could be safely ignored for a few minutes, he ventured toward his old college roommate. "What are you doing back here?"

Xander pulled sunglasses from his face and hooked them casually over the neck of his silky black tee. "I came to get my dog."

"*Your* dog? Are you nuts?" Thank God Lulu was having a late-afternoon visit to the park with his landlady and her daughter. "She's not yours anymore, buddy."

"Sure she is. I told you I'd be back for her."

"You said you'd be back in a month or so." He crossed his arms and widened his stance. "By my count, two years is a lot longer than a month or so."

Something flashed through Xander's eyes—

something Ian would have sworn was determination if not for the fact that the only times Xander had ever shown real resolve were when sex, beer or his latest get-rich-quick scheme were involved.

"It hasn't been that long. A year, year and a half, max. I'm here, just like I said I'd be." Xander peered past him. "What are you doing back there anyway? Making horseshoes?"

Ian thought of the final touches he'd just finished on a detailed picture frame for his dad. Horseshoes. Right. "Not quite. Now, if the only reason you're here is for *my* dog, you should leave. I'm busy."

"That's it? No 'Hey, Xander. Good to see you!' No 'Jeez, I hope everything was okay.' Not even a simple 'Where've you been?'"

"I don't need to ask." With one finger Ian pushed his safety glasses above his forehead, squinting against the sudden vibrancy of mid-June. In winter, southwestern Ontario was a sea of white, but now the reds of the flowers, the green of the grass and the blue of the sky could be blinding. "I got all the info I needed when the police came looking for you a couple months after you left. Are you on the run or did you land in the pen?"

Xander's face lost some color. Ian cursed.

"Seriously?"

"It was victimless, okay? A little cyber project that got sidetracked. No one got hurt."

"Except the little old ladies you bilked out of their life savings."

"Hey, I don't do that stuff. I just help people find their way into companies. Nothing with actual individuals."

"Yeah, well, it's still— Ah, jeez. You knew you were going to jail, didn't you? That's why you left Lulu with me."

Xander had the grace to look down as he scraped his foot against the cracked pavement of the driveway. "Look, when I left, I knew that the situation wouldn't be good for a puppy. Then things got out of hand and— Anyway, that's all in the past. I paid my debt to society. I'm a changed man and I want my dog."

"Let's review the facts, Xander. Two years ago— oh, pardon me, not that long but I don't feel like doing the math—you asked if you could stay with me for a week. In a moment of foolishness I said yes." Though to be honest, at that time Ian had been new in Stratford, running from a major life curve that had left him shell-shocked and heartsore. Xander's request had been a welcome distraction. "When the week turned into a month, I didn't say anything. When you brought Lulu home, I didn't say anything. When you took off and left me with her and thirty bucks for food—okay, I said some things then, but you weren't here so they don't count. Now, though, you're here, so listen up. She was a puppy when you left. You only had her two weeks. Not yours anymore." He poked Xander in the chest. "Go back to your computer and do something useful, like making some multinationals pay taxes."

But Xander didn't move. "Look, I know I took advantage of you. But I had a lot of time to think while I was away, and I see what an idiot I've been. From now on it's nothing but the straight and narrow for me. I have a job lined up—totally legit— and I'm starting over. Just me, the future and my dog." Xander's eyes darted around the garage, lingering on the steps leading to Ian's second-floor apartment. "By the way, where is she?"

Ah, hell. Ian remembered that tone. Xander's persistence lasted about as long as a boy band's fame, but when he first dived into something he gave it his all. Which meant that right now there would be no changing his mind. Only time and the inevitable roadblocks could do that.

The good news was that if Ian could put the guy off for a day or two, Xander would see something shiny and move on. The bad news was that Lulu and company could return at any minute.

If he could just buy himself a little time…

"She's not here."

"Why not? Is she at the vet? Is she sick?"

"She's fine. She's healthy and strong and she can eat me under the table. She went on an outing with friends." Vagueness was his ally. At least, he hoped so. "She's happy here, Xander. If you want a fresh start, do it right. Get yourself a new dog."

Xander shook his head. No surprise there. "Nope.

One of the things they taught us when I was… away…was about seeing ourselves in our new lives. They had us figure out all the details. Every time I did it, Lulu was in the picture. I don't want any old dog. I need her."

Ian's fear level rose from *Damn, I don't need this* to *Crap, this could get bad*. Xander sounded serious. This might still be nothing more than a whim, but given that Xander was the one who'd bought Lulu in the first place, things could get complicated.

Ian hated complicated.

"Listen, Xander, I'm in the middle of a project and I need to get moving. You should do the same."

Xander shook his head, crossed his arms and leaned against Ian's prized Mustang. "I'll wait."

"I don't think so."

"You know," Xander said with a sigh, "there was a time when you would have invited me in and we could have talked this out over a beer."

"And there was a day when you wouldn't have disappeared without so much as a Facebook post. Guess we're even." He returned to the anvil and made a show of examining the cross-peen hammer he'd been using. Yeah, it was juvenile, but hey, Xander wasn't the only one who could trot out the tough act.

Too bad it didn't work. Xander ambled into the garage, hands in his pockets, eyes darting from the forge to the anvil to the wall of hammers and files.

"You know, Ian, I'm thinking I got us off on the wrong foot here. How about we start over? I walk in and say, 'Hey, buddy, long time no see.' Then you say, 'Xander! Talk about a sight for sore eyes!' And I say, 'Same here. How are your folks? How long have you been playing *Little House on the Prairie*? How's work and your pretty little land-lady and my dog?'"

Pretty little landlady? If Darcy heard Xander describe her that way, she'd be the one hefting hammers. "I have another idea. You see this?" Ian lifted a curved length of forged iron. "I think this would make a great hook. You know, for grabbing your sorry, law-breaking runaway ass and dragging it to the curb before I—"

His words were interrupted by the sound he'd been dreading most—the excited bark of a dog approaching home, followed immediately by Darcy's resigned laughter. Lulu must have gotten away from her again.

Sure enough, a second later the driveway was a riot of movement and sound as a yipping, panting streak of beagle blend raced closer, dragging her leash behind her. And unless Ian missed his guess, Lulu was heading straight for him, with barely a curious glance in Xander's direction.

Mine.

Ian raised his hand. Lulu came to a quivering halt at the entrance to the garage.

"Good girl. Stay."

Xander crouched. "Lulu? It's me, girl! Come here."

Lulu whined and cocked her head but didn't move. Nor did she seem remotely interested in her onetime owner.

Xander pursed his lips—planning to whistle, no doubt—but Ian shook his head. "Save your breath. I've taught her to wait there until I tell her it's okay. Too many dangerous things in here."

"Oh. Right. I never thought of that."

Of course he hadn't. Xander and responsibility were about as well acquainted as rap and polka.

"So, can I go to her?" Xander asked.

Huh. Ian couldn't remember Xander ever waiting for anything, let alone requesting consent. His motto had always been that it was better to beg forgiveness than ask permission. Maybe the time in jail really had taught him a thing or two.

"Hang on. We have a routine."

"Sure. Whatever."

The excited edge to Xander's voice wasn't doing much for Ian's peace of mind, but he pushed himself through the steps. Check the anvil, check the forge, check the—

"Sorry, sorry." Darcy's laughing apology made him spin around to see her stumbling up the driveway, one hand pushing a stroller loaded with toys, the other curled around the baby bouncing on her hip. Lulu must have led her on a merry chase. The neck of Darcy's blouse veered way over to the side, and her shoulder-length, cinnamon-brown hair curled in every direction. She was a flustered mess, but as always, seeing her made him grin. Even despite Xander's presence.

"I thought I had a good grip on Lu," she called as she approached. "But Cady decided Mommy was overdressed and yanked my blouse half off, and I had to either switch the leash or risk arrest for public indecency. But I messed up and she got away and I—"

She stopped just behind Lulu, the hand that had been pushing the stroller rising to shield her eyes as she peered into the shadowy garage. Her cheeks turned as pink as Cady's ruffled sun hat, which had slipped backward, exposing the pale blond head it was supposed to protect.

"Oh. Sorry. I didn't realize you had company."

"It's okay." He walked over to her, automatically taking Cady as she launched herself into his arms.

Xander pushed upright. "Hey, Darcy," he called as he ambled into the light. "Long time no—"

He stopped abruptly. Darcy's eyes flew open and she reached across Ian's chest until her hand landed on Cady's thigh. A small sound slipped free, one he couldn't identify because he'd never heard it before, but his gut told him it wasn't good, especially when she stepped closer to him. His arm went around her shoulders.

Lulu whimpered.

"Darce?" Xander's voice was filled with confusion and uncertainty and something that sounded like shock. This was more than a simple greeting. What the hell?

Xander shuffled forward as if he'd forgotten how to walk. Darcy pressed closer to Ian. His arm tightened protectively.

As Xander emerged into the sunshine, the light glinted off his very blond hair. Hair that was a perfect match for that on the head now resting against Ian's chest. The tiny head of the wriggling child who had just celebrated her first birthday.

Two years ago—oh, pardon me, not that long but I don't feel like doing the math—

All of a sudden the math took on a terrifying significance.

"Ian?" Darcy whispered. "Would you take Cady inside, please? Xander and I need to talk."

DARCY MAGUIRE HAD always considered herself a woman of action. In her life BC—Before Cady—there had never been a disaster she couldn't work around, including the time a blizzard had stood between her mother and a major performance. All that had taken was an hour on the phone, a fistful of money and a snowplow driver willing to serve as a taxi.

If only this could be that easy.

Ian did as she asked without so much as a blink, settling Cady on his shoulder and whistling for Lulu to follow him to the house.

Seeing him holding Cady was a welcome anchor.

The rest of her world might be falling apart at the stitched-with-secrets seams, but her little girl was safe and happy in the best possible hands.

Ian had been blindsided. He was probably going to be hurt that she hadn't trusted him with the truth about Cady's paternity. But as she watched him walk away, she held tight to the fact that no matter how much she might bungle the next few minutes, Ian would make sure Cady was fed and diapered and kept laughing. This one little corner of the world would be fine.

Meaning Darcy had no excuse to put off the conversation waiting to pounce on her.

At the muffled slam of the screen door, she risked a look at Xander. His blue-gray eyes stayed fixed on the steps that Ian and Cady had mounted. She tugged her neckline and hoped everything was back in place. She didn't want to find out she'd conducted the most important conversation of her life with a wardrobe malfunction.

Assured that she was as decent as was possible, she pulled herself upright. "Let's go out back."

Xander dragged his understandably blank gaze from the steps to her. She led him to the yard and the picnic table where two summers ago she, Ian and Xander had whiled away long summer evenings with a few beers and a lot of laughs. Maybe the vibrations of that laughter still lingered here. Maybe they would make it possible for her and Xander to get through…whatever…with the same purpose: to do what was best for her—*their*—daughter.

Dear God, she hoped she could do a better job of navigating Cady through whatever came next than her own mother had done for her.

While Xander straddled the bench, Darcy climbed onto the patio table, settling under the shade offered by the bright blue umbrella Ian had added the previous summer. *Babies shouldn't get too much sun,* he had said when she'd come home from the hospital with her newborn. *And you can't put sunblock on them, but I know you'll want to sit outside with her. I thought this might make it easier.*

Maybe she shouldn't have sent Ian away with Cady. For the past year he had been the one she'd looked to whenever she was sure she was screwing up this parenting gig, which usually happened at least twice a day. Every time he would laugh and tell her she was doing fine, and when she would insist that this time she had really blown it, he would shake his head, grin and say, "Just trust me, Darce."

She really wished she could see him now, rolling his crinkly bronze eyes in the way that meant he thought she was being a total dork but he knew she would figure it out.

"So…" She sandwiched her hands between her bent knees. If she couldn't see them trembling, she might be less nervous. "I know you must have a lot of questions, but this will probably be easier if you let me talk first, okay?"

His slow nod was chased by a swifter shake of the head. "Wait. First. I— Is she— That baby. She's really...?"

His question hung in the air between them, unfinished but no less decisive. Once she answered him, she knew the life she had built—her and Cady with a big side of Ian—was all going to change. And most of it would depend on Xander. Someone not family. Someone she knew far less than she should.

It was a feeling she knew all too well, and it was no more welcome now than it had been in the past. Except now it was worse, because it was going to impact Cady.

She took a deep breath. Facts first. Future later.

"Yes." Damnation, her hands were still quivering. Clamping her knees tighter—*right, Maguire, now you remember to keep your knees closed*—she forced out the words she'd been dreading for the past year and eight months. "Yes, Xander. She's your daughter."

Somewhere nearby a bird let loose with a delighted trill. Talk about surreal. First Xander reappeared, now her life was turning into a frickin' Disney princess adventure complete with animals performing on cue.

"Holy..."

She knew the feeling. On that morning a lifetime ago, when she had finally dragged her gaze away from the test stick in her hand to stare at herself in the bathroom mirror, she had seen that same horror-movie expression now appearing on Xander's face. Yet when she looked closely, she saw in his eyes that same contradictory hint of amazement that had gripped her, as well. That had to be a good sign. Right?

"I did try to find you. To tell you," she added quickly. "But Ian said he hadn't heard from you since you left, and I—"

"Wait a minute." He backed up an inch or so. "We only— It was just that one night. Once."

She didn't need to remind him that one drunken night and one ancient condom didn't always add up to zero consequences.

"And you were with what's-his-name, the jerk who dumped you—"

"Jonathan." Thank heaven she could say his name calmly now, as opposed to the way she had shrieked it, cursed it and blubbered it back then. "I thought that myself at first, but I did the math, checked when he had been out of town and the last time he and I— Anyway, there's no way it could have been him."

"You're sure?"

"Positive. But you're more than welcome to have whatever tests done that you would like. I wouldn't blame you."

The lazy grace she had come to associate with Xander that summer had disappeared. "I don't need— Well, yeah. Maybe I should... Jesus." Long fingers scrubbed his face. "I don't know what to say, Darce."

"It's kind of a shocker, I know."

"Yeah, I guess you would."

His short attempt at a laugh reassured her. At least he wasn't going to pass out. Nor had he run away screaming or shown more than an understandable uncertainty about his role in Cady's conception. So far, so good.

She glanced toward the back door, hoping against hope that Ian and Cady would be watching from the window. Of course, they weren't. Ian most likely had Cady in her high chair, zooming spoonfuls of yogurt toward her mouth while she slammed her "practice" spoon on the tray. Or he would be changing her diaper, making up another installment in the Saga of Lulu and Cady that he was forever spinning for her. Normal. Familiar. Comforting.

Except…oh, that awful blankness on his face when he'd taken Cady from her…

"So, I don't know where you were, but you could teach classes in disappearing, because seriously, I couldn't find you. Ian had no idea, either." Not that she had told Ian why she'd wanted that information, of course. She had told him she was worried about Lulu.

Was that why he had looked so hurt? Because she hadn't told him the truth?

"I thought about hiring a private investigator, but you know, those guys cost a lot of money and

I…well, I had a lot of unexpected expenses, as I'm sure you can understand." Unexpected expenses coupled with a drastic readjustment of her job. Not that she minded, really. Accompanying her mother around the globe had had its moments, but if Darcy had to spend her life catering to a diva, she would take Cady over her mom any day.

"Expenses. Right." Xander's face grew a couple of shades paler. "Oh, shit. I'm going to have to pay child support. And it's all retroactive, isn't it?"

"I don't— Look, that's important, but, believe it or not, it's not my biggest priority right now, okay? So don't freak. I'm not going to sic a bunch of lawyers on you."

His quivering eased the tiniest bit.

"What did you— Jesus, I didn't even catch her name. Katie?"

"Cady. Short for Cadence. Cadence Joy Maguire."

"That's pretty."

"Thanks."

She hazarded another glance at the door. Foolish, she knew. Even if Ian wasn't juggling child and dog, even if she had completely misread him, he would never spy on her.

But, damn, it would be nice to see his face for a second.

"So she—Cady— Damn. I don't even know what I should be asking."

Darcy might be swimming in a sea of uncertainty herself at the moment, but talking about Cady was something she could always do.

"She just turned a year. June seventh. She's right on target for all her milestones. She has five teeth, and another one is trying to break through, so she's a little cranky right now, but mostly she's happy and bouncy. She's a really amazing little thing, and once we made it past those first few weeks, it's been the most exhausting and exhilarating rush I've ever had." All true. She had barely ever imagined herself as a mother, let alone a single one, but now life before Cady was a distant memory.

The drumming of Xander's fingers on the tabletop came to an abrupt halt.

"I want to see her again."

"Right. Of course." This was good. Wasn't it? Every kid deserved to have a dad who wanted to be with her. Some of Darcy's most cherished memories were of her late father. "We'll have to work out some kind of schedule," she said past the lump in her throat. "And I think that while she's so little, you should visit her here, you know? Until she gets to know you and feels comfortable around you."

Xander stared at her as if she had spoken in Shakespearean English. "I mean I want to see her right now."

"Oh." Relief made her laugh sound fake even to her. "Of course. I… Jeez, I guess I've had a few too many sleepless nights. You know, with that tooth coming in."

He wasn't talking about taking Cady on overnights or trips or any of those other scenarios that had made her wonder, wildly, if it was possible to stuff a one-year-old back in the womb. He simply wanted to see her now. One bullet dodged.

But not for long, she knew.

Cady was Xander's as much as hers. He had rights. Moral ones and legal ones. And she would have to honor them.

Are you there, God? It's me, Darcy. I know Xander is entitled to be in Cady's life, but could we maybe spread things out a bit here? One step at a time, with lots of space between them?

Inch by slow inch she pushed herself down from the table, amazed that her feet still worked when she stood on them.

A familiar bark interrupted her worry. Inside the house Lulu pawed at the back door, jumping and whining the way she always did when she spotted the freedom of the yard. Darcy stood a little straighter. Lulu at the door meant that Ian would be right behind her, which meant that Darcy would have someone at her side while she introduced Cady to her father.

Not the answer she'd expected to her semi-serious prayer, but she would take it.

"Just so you know, I wasn't trying to avoid you guys after I left," Xander said.

Ian appeared, slightly stooped so he could hold Cady's upraised hands while she walked. He nudged open the door. Lulu bounded forward, leaping and yipping and rolling in the grass at Darcy's feet.

"You'll find out anyway, but I'd rather you hear it from me. It sounds worse than it really is."

Xander was nattering on and she knew she should be listening, but she had to watch Ian. Because he wasn't coming outside, and he wasn't looking at her. In fact, if the heaviness in her stomach could be believed, he was doing his best to avoid her gaze.

She edged Lulu out of the way and moved toward the door. She could be strong and get through the next half hour, but not until she'd held Cady, not until she'd seen Ian's smile that always made her feel she could handle whatever lay ahead.

"The thing is, Darce, you couldn't find me because I was in jail."

CHAPTER TWO

Xander and I need to talk.

Xander and I.

The words had pounded through Ian as he'd carried Cady into the house, leaving Darcy and Xander alone in the driveway. Alone together.

Xander and Darcy.

He had walked blindly into the kitchen, where he'd come to a sudden stop. Cady had grabbed his chin and Lulu whined at his feet. A distant corner of his brain had whispered reminders about food, water and diapers, but another, more urgent voice had had him perching Cady on the edge of the counter, where he'd held her tight around the waist and stared at her.

Xander.

He could see Xander in her now. The pale blond hair pulled into one ponytail on top of her head like a platinum exclamation point above her rosy cheeks. Legs that were starting to shed their baby fat in favor of lean length. That crooked twist to her lips that he and Darcy had laughed over, calling it her Elvis impersonation. How many times had he picked her up and touched that mouth and sung

"Heartbreak Hotel" to her? Her first real laugh had happened during one of those moments.

Turns out the laugh was on him.

"Mum mum mum." Cady wriggled within his grasp, a familiar unhappy edge creeping into her voice. He shook his head.

The best way to cure your worries is by helping someone else. His grandmother's voice was so clear in his head he almost expected to see her walk through the door. She'd drilled those words into him all his life. He had to admit, she had a point. Doing things for Darcy, especially once he had figured out she was pregnant—well, he'd certainly felt better after shoveling her driveway than he had after time spent mulling the mess his life had been.

Though even Grandma Moxie probably would cut him some slack right now.

"Come on, Cady Bug. I bet you're hungry. How about something to eat?"

He ran Cady's hands under the faucet, making her squeal, then strapped her into the high chair and raided the refrigerator for cheese cubes and tiny cooked pasta, all while maintaining a non-stop monologue. The words didn't matter. As long as he kept talking, she would be distracted enough to stay happy.

"Looks like everything has changed, right, cutie? That's the truth. I always thought that Jonathan the rat bastard was the one who did your mama wrong—oops, don't cry, I won't say the M word again—but I guess I blew that one. And you know how I feel? I feel like a goddamned idiot, that's what I feel like. There's some words to toss out sometime when M-word isn't expecting them. Goddamn. Yeah, that should get a reaction out of her. Maybe even an honest one. Wouldn't that be a change?"

He was overreacting, but so what? Darcy was his friend. Nothing more—but nothing less, either. He would have thought that as her friend, as the person who had brought Xander into the picture, as the one who had fallen in love with Cady the moment she'd arrived—

"Guess I thought wrong. No surprise there, right, kiddo? That's right, shove the cheese into your mouth. Nom nom. Eat with your fists while you can. Those days will be gone before you know it."

He dropped into the chair beside the table, his arms, legs and spirits crossed. Lulu sniffed his knee and let loose with a noise that was somewhere between a whine and a moan. He laced his fingers through her silky fur and scratched behind her ears.

"You know something's wrong, don't you, girl? Don't worry. I won't let him take you."

"Ru! Ru!" Cady slapped her palms on the tray and threw a piece of cheese to the floor. Lulu snapped it up. Cady broke into the chortles that always accompanied the game. Ian was supposed to make sure the food made it into the proper mouth, but at the moment he didn't have the heart.

"Laugh now, sweetie." Despite himself, he angled his head so he could sneak a peek through the lace curtains at the kitchen window. He should have saved himself the effort. All he could see was a fringe of cinnamon—the top curls of Darcy's hair. Curls that Xander had laced his fingers through while—

Ian jumped from his chair and forced his feet toward the hall, the refrigerator, the small pantry stocked with baby food and diet pop. Anyplace where he wouldn't be tempted to watch what was happening in the backyard.

But when he narrowly avoided stepping on Lulu, trailing him with her nose to the ground, he forced his itchy feet to halt. He fell back onto the hard wooden chair. He tipped his head toward the ceiling, where the white blades of the fan stirred the air and his thoughts.

He had to get a grip.

So Darcy and Xander had…whatever. So they had made a *baby* together. It was none of his business. It had happened almost two years ago. It had nothing to do with him.

Except it felt as though it did.

"I frickin' hate secrets." Good thing his only audience was a dog and a baby. Neither of them could point out the irony that he, Mr. Honest-and-Aboveboard, had been keeping a hell of a whopper from Darcy for God only knew how long.

"But that's different." He patted his thigh. Lulu,

who had been gnawing on his shoe, jumped at the invitation and rested her paws on his knee. "It's biology. That's all. I've been alone awhile. Darcy is right here and cute and single… It's good that I've started noticing her. Proof that I'm really over Taylor. That's all. Saying anything to her would have been stupid. Pointless."

Despite himself, he glanced at the window again. "Too late."

IF EVER IAN had doubted that life had a sick sense of humor, it would have been confirmed by the fact that as soon as Cady finished cramming her mouth full of everything within reach, she gifted him with the Diaper of the Decade.

"I think this is the definition of redundant, kiddo." He tossed wipes into the trash while using his elbow to restrain the sumo wrestler formerly known as Cady. "You couldn't have waited a bit longer? Maybe let your shiny new dad do the honors?"

She let loose with a wail of protest.

"My sentiments exactly," he said, though he was well aware that her only concern was her inability to wriggle free. "I know, I know. You want to move."

Come to think of it, that sounded like a fine idea. He'd given Darcy plenty of time to…whatever… with Xander.

"Let's crash the party, Bug."

Lulu barked her agreement and raced into the

hall while Ian grabbed Cady. After a fast detour to the bathroom to wash his hands, they clattered down the stairs.

And there he stopped.

Lulu bounded ahead but Ian stayed out of sight of the back door. The dog yipped and Cady pushed at his shoulders, but still he didn't move.

What if what he felt for Darcy *was* more than biology?

No sooner had the thought brought him to a standstill than he walked away from it double time.

"Get a grip, North."

For one thing, he'd been feeling this…whatever… around Darce for a while. Months, at least. If it really was something more than basic instinct, surely it would have grown or changed or something by now.

For another, he and Darcy and Cady had a good thing going. Yeah, he was pissed right now, but when he looked back on it, they'd done a damned fine job with this friendship. He babysat her kid, she walked his dog, they made each other laugh and had each other's backs. Only an idiot would want to mess up what they had.

Lulu dropped down from the door and gave him a look that could only be described as *get over here and let me out, you useless human*. Cady lunged forward in apparent sympathy.

"Fine. I'm coming, okay?"

So. Biology. Biology stirred with some kind of…

oh, call it confusion…that Darcy hadn't trusted him enough to tell him the truth. A bruised ego, a hell of a surprise, some understandable jealousy revolving around the bundle of drool and giggles squirming in his arms.

"You want to walk, don't you, Bug?" He lowered her to the ground and slipped his fingers into her fists. She shrieked something he couldn't understand, held tight and slapped one foot in front of the other in her version of a beeline for the door while he duck-walked behind her.

"You're getting good at this, kid. Soon you won't need me to hold you up."

What the hell. He'd been debating moving home to Comeback Cove anyway. Maybe Xander's reappearance was some kind of message that it would be okay to go. Ian's work here was done, and all that crap.

They had reached the door—well, as close as they could get to it with Lulu doing her best to claw her way through the window. Darcy's hot-pink top danced at the edge of his vision, but he refused to look at her. He would hand over Cady and take himself and Lulu to the garage, where he could control the fire.

Decision made, he nudged the door open and marched Cady into the sunshine.

"Hello, sweetness!" The forced cheer and slight breathlessness in Darcy's voice made him wonder if maybe he should have checked the backyard action before walking out. His imagination, helpful as always, offered up some vivid pictures of the reunions he and Cady might have interrupted.

Oh, yeah. As if that was gonna help.

"Here you go." He could do make-believe happy as well as the next person. "She's fed and as clean as she ever will be."

"Did you have a good lunch, lovey? Oh, but you must have painted your clothes with it, right? That's not what you were wearing a few minutes ago."

He risked a glance in Darcy's direction. She didn't seem any more rumpled than she had when he'd left. "Nope. Can't blame this one on sloppy eating."

"Uh-oh. Did you get stuck with a blowout?"

He checked on Xander, who was hovering behind Darcy and staring at Cady as if he wasn't sure she was real. That diaper would have grounded him pretty fast. "Nothing I couldn't handle."

"Sorry." Darcy squatted and held out her arms. "Come here, Bug. We, um, I need to introduce you to someone."

For one wild minute he considered grabbing Darcy, calling Lulu and hauling everyone into the house before locking the door—with Xander on the other side. Then Cady released his fingers and lurched into Darcy's embrace.

He was the outsider here. *He* was the one who wasn't part of the family.

He was the one who needed to make himself scarce.

"Well." He stepped aside, patting his leg to call Lulu, who had parked herself between Darcy and Xander. At his signal her ears perked up but she didn't move. It hit him that she was giving Xander the kind of *you should run now* look that he wished he could hand out.

That did it. Next lifetime he was coming back as a dog.

"Okay." He made himself meet Darcy's gaze, forced a hearty grin. "Well. If you're all set I'll get out of your—"

Darcy's eyes widened and her lips clamped tight. Her sideways glance toward Xander was fast but unmistakable.

Holy crap. Unless he missed his guess, this wasn't an entirely joyous reunion. In fact, if he had to pick one word to describe the vibes he was getting, that word would be *panic*.

He didn't know what had changed in the past half hour, but something sure had shifted. Which meant his intentions of firing up the forge and going all Neanderthal on a piece of hot metal were going to have to wait until he was sure Darcy wanted him to leave.

"Come on, Lulu. Let's play."

With that he grabbed a tennis ball from the bucket at the edge of the concrete patio and wandered toward the garden—far enough to give the illusion of respecting their privacy while staying within earshot. Darcy didn't scare easily. Nor did she willingly ask for help. If she was acting skittish, there was a reason.

Not that he thought Xander posed a physical threat. The man had grown into a con artist with delusions of invincibility, but Ian had never known him to be the violent type. He got queasy playing "Grand Theft Auto." And when it came to women, well, given the number of nights Ian had spent sexiled to the futon in their dorm's common room, he was well aware that Xander had something that appealed. No, whatever had happened between Xander and Darcy, Ian was pretty certain it had been consensual.

But *something* had her spooked. So until she indicated otherwise, he wasn't going anywhere.

He tossed the ball. It bounced into the garden, disappearing in the twisted vines of Darcy's snap peas. Crap. Lulu and the garden were a scary mix.

Except Lulu wasn't there.

He swiveled in time to see Lulu bare her teeth and let loose with a deep growl as Xander's outstretched hand hovered in midair a few inches from Cady.

"Lulu?" Darcy's voice echoed his surprise. "It's okay, girl. Xander is… It's okay."

Lulu's response was to snarl louder. Her message couldn't have been clearer. *Stay away. Mine.*

Xander's head twisted from the dog to Darcy to

Ian, then back at Lulu. "Hey, Ian? Could you give us a hand here?"

Well, well, well.

Ian crossed his arms and took in the scene before him. It probably wasn't smart to feel smug over the turn of events, but at this point he would take what he could get.

"What's the matter, Xander? *Your* dog doesn't remember you?"

The flush in Xander's cheeks didn't do anything for his appearance, but it sure made Ian grin.

"Cute. Call her off."

"Sure, sure." He took his time ambling forward and stooped to run a hand down Lulu's back. "Easy, girl. Everything's fine."

She continued to glare at Xander. A fraction of the rigidness eased from her stance, but she didn't move. No doubt she was waiting for some sort of signal. In that case Xander was screwed, because Ian was pretty sure that the only messages Lulu might pick up from him were ones of frustrated protectiveness.

Unless…

Unless maybe he gave Lulu a reason to think that she could stand down because he was stepping up.

He straightened slowly and caught Darcy's attention—not difficult, as she seemed transfixed by the dog. Certain he couldn't be seen by Xander behind him, Ian tapped his chest.

Trust me, he mouthed.

She didn't nod or move, but like Lulu, some of the tension seeped from her shoulders. Message received.

He petted Lulu again, gave her a "good girl" and then—slowly, deliberately—pushed runaway cinnamon curls behind Darcy's ear.

Behind him, he was pretty sure he heard Xander choke.

Darcy's eyes flickered to meet his gaze, her expression changing from confusion to acceptance in the literal blink of an eye.

Lulu dropped to her haunches.

Encouraged, Ian shifted to face Xander while taking a step back and sliding his arm around Darcy's waist. She barely hesitated before snuggling against his side, soft and warm and a whole lot more pliant than was good for his long-deprived body.

Damn. This might not have been such a smart idea after all.

But Lulu had stopped glaring, and Xander's jaw seemed about ready to hit the pavement, so Ian counted this as a win.

"Wait a minute." Xander's laugh brimmed with disbelief. "Are you telling me that the two of you…?"

"I don't know why you seem so surprised." Ian placed a possessive hand on Cady's arm.

"But you said…"

Ian was well aware of what he had said when Xander asked him two summers ago if Ian had any designs on his landlady. Ian's "Are you out of your tree?" had been equal parts *She's involved with someone else* and *I just got dumped by my fiancée, dumbass.*

"Yeah, well, that was then. This is now."

Darcy set Cady on the ground, straightened, then reached around his back and hooked her thumb ever-so-casually in the waistband of his jeans. His pulse spiked. Oh, hell.

She tilted her head to rest against his shoulder. "I didn't have a lot of experience with babies, and Ian had helped with his niece so he kind of taught me what to do, and I started relying on him more and more, and the next thing you know he was spending more time in the house with me than in his apartment over the garage. And then it was like— Well, I guess I don't need to spell it all out."

All true, but damn. When she said it with that little laugh in her voice he could almost believe it himself.

"Yeah. I guess so." Xander shook his head. "Look, it's been a hell of a day, and I've already been here longer than I planned."

That's right, Xander. Leave. Now.

"But I…" Xander glanced at Ian and Darcy once more, and then shifted his focus to Cady pulling herself upright on Ian's leg.

"Could I hold her?"

Ian glanced at Darcy, who bit her lip but gave a quick nod.

Damn it. Why did Xander have to come back and put her through this?

"If she fusses don't take it personally," she said as Ian pried Cady from his calf and handed her to Xander. "She doesn't meet too many new people, so she's kind of shy with strangers."

Xander held Cady at arm's length for a breath or two before pulling her closer. His elbows stuck out at an awkward angle, his knees seemed frozen in position and his face held a mix of terror and reverence.

"But I'm not a stranger," he said, directing the words to Cady. "I'm your dad."

Ian reached for Darcy's hand, lacing his fingers through her clammy ones. Her smile was determined but he saw the fear in her eyes.

Cady reared back, staring at Xander's face without blinking. A hint of a smile lit his face.

"You look like my little sister," he said softly. "Bethie. I guess she's your aunt Bethie."

Ian hid his wince. Darcy—no doubt motivated by her own status as a lonely only child—had mentioned more than once that she wished Cady had a big extended family to dote on her and shower her with frilly pink things and make her feel as though she was the most amazing thing on the planet. Still, he was pretty sure this wasn't the way she would have chosen to add to Cady's relative count.

"So, does she talk?" Xander asked. "Or walk or…? I don't know much about babies, either. Nothing, really." His laugh was a little stronger, if rueful. "Maybe you'll need to teach me, too, Ian."

Darcy opened her mouth, but no words came out. Ian rubbed the small of her back. This had to be killing her.

Ian had been still digging himself out of the mess his own life had become when he'd realized she was pregnant. He hadn't had a lot left over to focus on anyone else's problems.

But then it had become obvious that Jonathan— the supposed father—wasn't in the picture. And Darcy's own mother had reluctantly agreed that pregnancy and a baby were not compatible with the work she needed Darcy to do. Darcy had put on a brave front while slowly developing a crease in her forehead that had rivaled her belly for size.

Still, it wasn't until after Cady's birth that he'd put it all together. He'd come home from work one hot afternoon in late June and found Darcy huddled under the umbrella he'd installed, shaking with silent sobs while Cady slept in her arms. For the first time it had hit him how alone she was, how lost and scared she must have felt.

He had taken the baby and ordered Darcy to get some sleep. And somewhere in the year that followed, he'd figured out that Darcy wasn't the only one who had benefited from his involvement.

His issues didn't matter at this moment. Right now his job was to step up and get them through this. The rest could wait.

"Oh, Cady isn't shy about letting anyone know what she can do," he said to Xander. "She doesn't walk by herself yet, but she pulls up on furniture—"

"And legs," Darcy added softly.

"And then she cruises. You know, pulls herself sideways," he added in response to Xander's blank look. "She can crawl faster than Lulu can run, though she's letting up on that."

"She has a couple of words." Darcy's voice shook a little, but there was an underlying determination that made him want to cheer for her. "She says *Mum mum*, and *Eeeee*, which I—we—think means Ian. And *Ru* for Lulu, though we don't know if she's trying to say her name or imitate the sound of barking."

"You sound like a smart one, Cadence Joy."

The pride and wonder in Xander's voice made Ian pull Darcy tighter against his side. She molded herself to him. He was pretty sure that this time she wasn't seeking to deceive Xander as much as to hold herself up. Didn't matter to him. As long as he was helping he didn't much care about the details.

But he couldn't help but notice how perfectly she fit against him.

Absolutely normal. Proof you're over Taylor. Biology reminding you that you're still alive.

It had been hard enough to make himself swallow that line the past few months, noticing Darcy from a distance. Now, with her warmth and softness glued to his side, he was almost grateful for

Xander's presence. At least with an audience Ian was less likely to throw caution to the wind and do something really stupid.

Cady let out a whimper that he recognized as the prelude to a lungful of protest. Darcy moved out of his embrace. The places where she had pressed against him seemed to blink in shock.

"Here." She scooped Cady from Xander and cuddled the child tight against her chest. "Don't want her getting scared off at the first meeting, right?"

Everyday words, but he could only guess what they had cost her. He wasn't sure if he was more amazed by the casual way she tossed them out or by the fact that she returned to his side. He needed no prompting to nestle her against him once again.

Ah, that's better.

He pushed the traitorous thought aside. Time to convince Xander to leave so he and Darcy could go inside and figure out what to do next. Especially about this fake relationship they had just invented. The one he had to remember was only that—fake.

"So, Xander. What's next for you? Are you staying here in Stratford?" *Say no. Say no.*

Xander's usual confidence switched to uncertainty. "I— Jeez. I have something lined up, a job in cottage country, but..." He ran one finger gently down Cady's arm. "Things have changed."

Yeah, they had. Ian could give him that one. Maybe even a few points for rethinking his plans now that those changes had hit him.

But Ian wasn't backing off until Darcy gave the word.

Cady whimpered and burrowed her head into the cleft between his shoulder and Darcy's. Xander's hand dropped away. Ian wasn't sure if he should feel guilty, victorious or ashamed, so he settled for giving thanks that—for the moment, at least—he was still in the picture.

Darcy spoke up. "She's getting tired. Xander, why don't you give me your number and we'll set up a time to get together again. Let's see, today is Tuesday, so maybe—"

"Tomorrow?" Xander had never sounded so excited about anything for as long as Ian had known him.

Darcy stiffened a little in Ian's embrace. "I've got a lot going on over the next couple days. How about the end of the week?"

A lot going on? Darcy worked from home and had no appointments other than delivering Cady to and from her mornings at day care. He knew for a fact that she had kept the next few days open, because he was her usual hairdresser-and-dentist babysitter, and he was heading to Comeback Cove Thursday morning.

If Darcy was putting Xander off, it meant she wanted time. For what, he didn't know. But he'd be damned if he would let her set up something for the days he wasn't going to be around.

Unless, of course, that was what she wanted…

But no. He hadn't imagined that wariness that had come over her. Until he knew she felt safe, he was going to stick to her like the snap pea vines clinging to Lulu's coat as she slinked out of the garden.

"Hang on, honey." He thought fast. "Did you forget that we're leaving in the morning?"

"I—"

He turned to Xander, watching them with way too much curiosity. "We're going up to see my folks, spend Father's Day with my dad. So it'll be next Monday, Tuesday, before we get back."

"Oh, right." Darcy laughed and elbowed him in the ribs while adjusting Cady. Accidentally? "How could I forget? Like I said, teething, not enough sleep." She shrugged. "It does a number on me."

Xander studied them, skepticism apparent in his crossed arms and narrowed eyes. Ian's stomach clenched. The truth would have to come out at some point, but damn it, he didn't want that to happen until he'd had a chance to talk to Darcy and find out what she needed.

He slipped sideways, turning to slide his hands around a droopy, half-asleep Cady. "Here. I'll take her in while you get Xander's number."

Darcy nodded. "Okay. Thanks."

He paused, considered and then—before he could talk himself out of it—brushed a quick kiss against her mouth.

He kept it light. Fast. Barely long enough to register the hint of ginger on her breath, nowhere near hot enough to account for the rush of *God, yes* that hit him even as he reminded himself that it was all for show. It was clumsy, so awkward that if Xander had been taking notes, he probably would have seen through them in a heartbeat.

But, damn, she tasted good.

And, whoa damn, when her lips parted—purely from shock, he knew—he had to drag himself away.

And, hot damn, but if this was a mistake, it was the best one he'd made in a long time.

CHAPTER THREE

TEN MINUTES AFTER saying goodbye to Xander, fifteen minutes after Ian had bestowed the third surprise in her hat trick of shocks for the day, Darcy pulled down the shade in Cady's room and started the recording of acoustic covers that passed for lullabies chez Maguire. With all the routines accounted for, she turned on the monitor and tiptoed out of the room, closing the door behind her and leaning against it while she breathed.

"Dear God, Maguire, when you mess up, you don't hold back, do you?"

So much for her carefully organized life. So much for those daily affirmations reminding herself that she was strong, she was independent, she could handle whatever the universe threw her way. In a little over an hour, that had all been blown to hell.

Xander was back.

Which she had been dealing with until she'd found out he'd been in freakin' *jail*.

And then Ian had kissed her.

Her fingers rose to her lips and she gave a shaky laugh. Yes, everything else was crumbling around her, but her brain kept tugging her back to that moment in the yard when Ian's mouth had brushed hers. For one second, maybe two or three, her worries about Xander and custody agreements and criminal acts had been banished by the soft play of warm lips against hers. It had been reassuring and comforting, a welcome reminder that she wasn't alone, which was, she was sure, the only reason he had done it. And she really hoped that was the only reason she kept coming back to it. It was nothing more than her touchstone, a moment of peace and sanity when everything else was whirling.

A nice story. Too bad her treasonous brain also insisted on reminding her of the infrequent but oh-so-vivid dreams she'd had over the past few months. Dreams in which Ian played a highly significant and usually shirtless role.

Every time she woke from one of those dreams, she spent the next few days staring at the ground or at Lulu or praying that his work would take him out of town for an extended period. Because, seriously, lusting after her best friend?

At least she'd pulled away from the kiss before her long-denied hormones had kicked in. She could not, would not, upset the balance of their lives more than had already been done. Especially not at a time such as this when she could really use a friend.

But how was she supposed to look at him now?

Not that she had a choice. He was in her kitchen waiting for her, as he'd done so many times over the past year. She had to tell him the truth about Xander and find out what kind of criminal DNA was swimming in Cady's genes, all while feeling as if she'd been plugged into an outlet and was being hit by bolts of electricity at random times and in the worst possible places.

And what kind of parent was she that of all the things that had happened, she continued to fixate on the one that had made *her* feel better for a minute, the three seconds that had served *her*?

Dear Lord, she was turning into her mother after all.

She squeezed her eyes shut and shook away the thought. She would get through this. She would talk to Ian—*talk, Maguire*—and send him to his apartment. She would sit at the computer and come up with a strategy. Later, if she was still this…unsettled, she would put Cady to bed and have herself a private film festival. One featuring Harrison Ford in his prime, fully whipped. Tomorrow, she could wake with a clear head and focus on what mattered—getting Cady through this change without turning her childhood into the same kind of convoluted mess Darcy's had been.

All she had to do was get through the next hour.

LOOKING IAN IN the eye as she descended the stairs took about as much intestinal fortitude as telling Xander that he had hit the conception jackpot, but

Darcy made herself do it. She was rewarded with a glimmer of his usual smile.

Crap. She had forgotten the hurt she'd spotted in his face right after Xander's arrival. The conversation ahead was shaping up to be as complicated as the ones she'd just navigated.

She rubbed her temples. Couldn't anything ever be simple?

"Headache?"

It was as good an explanation as any. "Yeah."

"Need anything?"

This was the Ian she knew—helpful and supportive. The caregiver. The trusted friend, not the Lust Igniter.

"I'll be okay after I grab something to eat. Thanks." She glanced around. "Lulu?"

"I think she's worn-out. Last time I saw her she was heading for her basket."

"I'm jealous."

There was nothing but the usual amount of concern on his face when he studied her. The inner caveman that had shown up while they were outside must have departed with Xander. Thank heaven.

"We should talk," he said slowly. "But if you're not up for it right now…"

"No. I mean, yes." She blinked and dredged up a smile. "I'm fine. But I think, maybe, this calls for a beer. Want one?"

"God, yes."

She pulled bottles from the refrigerator, grabbed

a jar of salsa while she was there. "Can you get the chips?"

He didn't hesitate before opening the correct cupboard and snagging a bag of tortilla chips from the top shelf, where she stored them out of her everyday reach. It hit her as he moved with easy confidence around her kitchen how thoroughly entrenched he was in her life. He knew his way around her kitchen, he dragged the trash to the curb every Thursday, he changed her daughter's diapers, all without asking how or where or when.

She really couldn't blow this.

"Let's go out on the porch," she said when he pulled a chair from the table. The front porch. Public. Less chance of her breaking down. Or, worse, reliving that kiss and feeling tempted to do something truly stupid.

He raised an eyebrow but picked up the monitor and followed her outside.

She set the food on the small wicker table and climbed into her favorite hammock swing suspended from the roof. Ian settled in the oversize chair he had added to the porch last summer, the day he'd announced he was signing up for baby rocking duty.

After a scoop of salsa on a chip and a long, welcome draw on her beer—damn, she had needed that—she was as ready as she would ever be.

"Okay." She ran her nail beneath the label on her bottle. "I have a million questions, and I bet you do, too, but first and most important, thank you. You got me through something I kind of knew would have to happen someday, but I sure wasn't looking forward to it. Having you here made the whole situation— Okay, so it got kind of screwy there for a while, but I—"

"I shouldn't have kissed you."

She blinked. He was jumping straight to that?

"I don't want you to think— I mean, it was all for Xander," he said in a rush. "You know that, right?"

"Of course." *Stop weeping, stupid hormones.* "It's fine. We were winging it, and, okay, maybe I wouldn't have done that, but it worked, and that's what matters."

"Good." He grabbed a chip but instead of eating it, he stared at it as intently as if a secret code were printed there. "I had no idea that you and Xander— But I wasn't planning to pull the whole act out there, especially not if you'd been glad to see him. But when I came outside you looked scared when I said I would leave, so I… I don't know. Reacted."

She thought back, replaying the sudden appearance of Caveman Ian. Now it made sense. "Ohhh. Yeah. I was kind of spooked. Xander had just told me where he spent the last— Jeez, I don't even know how long he was in jail. Or what for." She peeked at Ian. Good. He'd lost the pinched look around his eyes. "Do you?"

"He didn't go into detail, but based on his past run-ins—"

"*Past* run-ins?" It was a miracle she still had enough air to speak given the way her breath had flown from her lungs. "You mean this wasn't the first time?"

"Easy, Darce. He's not a hardened criminal, okay? He had some brushes with the law when we were in university, but never anything that led anywhere. And nothing violent. It's all cyber stuff. Breaking into corporate accounts, things like that. As far as I know, he never does anything against individuals. I'm sure in his mind he's some kind of modern-day Robin Hood."

"Oh." Some of the tension seeped from her shoulders. "Thanks. That helps."

He nodded and stuffed the chip into his mouth. She had a feeling it was her move.

"Here's the story," she said at last. "Xander and I never had a real thing. So you weren't interrupting a reunion of long-lost lovers or anything like that."

The relief on his face told her that he had indeed been wondering. But was he glad to know he hadn't intruded, or relieved that there wasn't anything to interrupt in the first place?

Not that it mattered, of course.

"Remember when Xander was here and you went away over Labor Day weekend?"

"Right. For Hank's wedding."

Now, why did the mention of his brother's wedding make him tense up again? Maybe it had something to do with his ex-fiancée. From what Darcy had gleaned from the bits and pieces Ian had let drop, the ex had continued living in Comeback Cove.

"Well, that Friday night was when Jonathan and I broke up." She snagged a chip and snapped it in half.

"Jonathan." There was a hint of a question in his voice when he mentioned her ex, and she knew what he was asking.

"I know. You thought he was Cady's father. I'm sure everyone thought that, but fortunately—or not—he isn't. That night—well, let's just say it didn't end gracefully."

Call her the Queen of Understatement. On their six-month anniversary she had thought it might be safe to ask what he saw in their future. What she had ended up seeing was his back as he'd run as far and fast as he could.

"Anyway, I made a horrible scene, then came home and went out in the backyard and got rip-roaring drunk. When I got to the maudlin stage and decided I needed a babysitter, I went up to the apartment looking for you, forgetting you weren't there."

"But Xander was."

Oh, if his voice were any more neutral, he would have been beige. "Yep. I bawled all over him, and when I was cried out he said he'd help me get back to my place. I think his intentions truly were honorable, but by then I was starting to sober up and

I didn't want to, so I grabbed some vodka and convinced him to join me. And things kind of... escalated."

Silence hung between them. On the street, a car cruised past, bass thumping out the windows. A kid shouted to a friend on the other end of the block.

"It was one night," she said, leaning forward, praying with everything she had that he would believe her. "One stupid, drunken night when all I wanted was to forget." Forget Jonathan's heavy sigh when she'd screwed up her nerve and had posed the question, forget the disgust on his face when she had started to cry, forget her panicked drunken certainty that she would never be held again. "I woke up the next day and thought of everything that could have happened and had a major freak-out."

"And Xander?"

"Was already gone."

He eased back into his chair. "That's no surprise. I mean," he added hastily, "not to say anything about you. Or your... Crap."

"Are you blushing?"

As if she'd unplugged a dam, he turned even redder. "This isn't the easiest conversation."

No. But considering he had watched her stomach explode during her pregnancy, seen her nursing nonstop in those first weeks when she was too exhausted to make more than a token attempt at covering up and listened to her complain about every oozing, aching body part, his reaction was unexpected. And surprisingly sweet.

"I'm sorry. I won't tease. I know what you mean."

"All I was trying to say is that Xander isn't one for the long haul. As I'm sure you noticed."

Which brought them straight to her biggest fear regarding Cady.

"I don't care that he took off the next day. Frankly, if I had been able to lift my head without feeling like I'd been shoved into a tornado, I might have done the same thing. It wasn't my finest moment." She leaned forward, arms resting on her knees, trying to decide how to ask what she needed to know without revealing too much. "But it's different now. You've known him longer than I have. Do you think he has it in him to stick around, or would he be one of those guys who, you know, only stays long enough to mess up everything?"

Ian studied her for an unnervingly long moment. At times she swore he could read her mind. This was one of the moments when she longed for a way to shield her thoughts from him. It was one thing for him to know that he was her most trusted friend. It would be quite different if he figured out that to her, what they had was the closest thing she could imagine to the family she'd lost when she was too young to appreciate it.

"Ah. Gotcha." At last he lifted his beer for a long draw. She'd seen him do that hundreds of times over the past couple of years. Why, this time, did she have to force herself to stop gazing at the lines of his neck? Why did she find herself swallowing in tandem with him?

Why did she suspect she was now the one blushing?

He finally lowered the bottle. "I don't know," he said. "Back in school, Xander was a goof but basically a straight-up guy. Since then…I don't know. He changed."

Not the answer she wanted, for sure.

"I got the feeling you wanted some time to figure out what should happen next with him," he said. "That's why I said what I did about us going to Comeback Cove."

Oh, holy crap. Yet another twist that had slipped through her grasp. Thank God Cady was safely tucked into her crib. At this rate, Darcy wouldn't trust herself to keep a hamster alive.

"Yeah, about that." She sat back in the hammock, watching him carefully for signs of hedging. "Where did that come from?"

"I dunno. We were pulling off the 'we're a couple' thing, and Lulu growled, and I thought, damn, what if Xander comes back when I'm not around? Remember, I didn't know what was making you so skittish. I thought maybe you were afraid of him for, well, for more than just Cady's sake."

It took a moment for his words to register. "You thought he raped me?"

"Not really. But I thought there might have been some...coercion."

Her indignation melted. No wonder the poor guy had let his inner caveman fly.

"No," she said softly. "Nothing horrible happened." Nothing especially mind-blowing, either, from what she could remember, but no way was she going to say that. Ian was already flashing as red as the fire in his forge. "Things got lousy and complicated, and, yeah, I'm not looking forward to refiguring everything now that he's back. But Cady is the best part of my life. No matter how much I curse my own stupidity, I have absolutely no regrets."

He nodded and rocked back in his chair, but didn't look as though he believed her.

"What?" She snagged another chip. "You're trying to say something but you don't know how. I can tell."

"Jeez, Maguire, can't I hide anything from you?"

Ah, that was more like it. Teasing, complaining, fake indignation—everything she usually associated with Ian. That post-kiss lust—okay, that had been interesting, but she wasn't going to let it ruin their easygoing swing.

"Don't tell me you were serious about me going to Comeback Cove with you?"

She hadn't thought it was possible for him to turn any redder. She was wrong.

"Here's what I'm thinking," he said, setting his

beer on the table. "One, we—I—led Xander to believe we're a couple. So if I go without you it might look strange."

"Because people who are together never do anything separately. Right."

"To paraphrase Indiana Jones, I'm making this up as I go, okay?"

Boom! She had a sudden image of Ian in a leather jacket and fedora, a whip in his hand and a smile that could melt a thousand Arks on his lips.

Looked as if she was going to have to come up with an alternate plan for the evening.

"If you come with me it would give you time to figure out what happens next. Maybe talk to a lawyer. Have you done that yet?"

"No. I should have, I know, but when he vanished off the face of the earth, it kind of slid down the priority list."

He nodded. "You need legal advice, and we need to decide what to do when Xander shows up expecting to see us as a couple. Since I was already planning to go home—"

"Not until Thursday."

He shrugged. "So I'll go a day early. My mother will be ecstatic. At the time, saying that you were coming along seemed like the best solution."

"Hmm." It seemed pretty caveman to her, but, she had to admit, it was nice to know he'd been trying to help.

"Besides," he added so casually that her skin

prickled in warning, "your grandmother is there, and she would love to see Cady."

She'd always known that renting to the grandson of her grandmother's best friend would come back to bite her someday.

"Did Nonny pay Moxie to make you say that?"

"Get real, Darce. You could use some time. I'm going to Comeback Cove anyway. And Helene would give her eyeteeth to have you and Cady under her roof for a few nights."

Did he have to sound so reasonable? Getting pissed off at him would be so much more satisfying than understanding him.

Except he had a point.

She dipped a chip into the salsa, focused on creating the perfect blend of tomato, onion and peppers. It took a lot of effort.

"You gonna eat that or hang it in an art gallery?"

She glared. "Don't interrupt my stalling tactic to discuss your stalling tactic."

His laugh, low and reassuring, was like having someone pour warm water over her—soothing and welcome and oh so comforting.

"I know your intentions are good." She swirled the chip through the salsa again. "But going to Comeback Cove? That seems extreme."

"What's so extreme about it? One phone call, a few hours packing, a few more to drive, and there ya go. Instant breathing space. You have time to sort things through, and when we come back, you'll be ready to do…whatever you decide is right. But you won't be making it up as you go anymore."

He had a point. Again.

"I don't want to upset Cady's schedule. She's already wonked with this tooth. I think she needs to stick to familiar places and faces right now."

"Good point. But you know sometimes a distraction is all she needs to get herself back on track."

Must he always be right?

"What about work? You're not off tomorrow, and I'm swamped."

"Everyone's out of my office tomorrow anyway. Training. As for you—" his eye roll would have made a teenager proud "—you work from home, remember? Take your laptop with you."

"And how much will I get done without being able to drop Cady at day care? I know she's only there part-time, but I get a heck of a lot done in those three hours."

"Hello? Doting grandmother?"

Damn him. "But…Ian, look. You have a close family. It's nothing for you to call and say, 'Hi, Mom. Change of plans. I'm coming home early.' It's not like that for me and Nonny." At least it hadn't been lately.

"Actually," he began, but then gave an impatient sort of shake. "Whatever. It was just a suggestion."

"Wait a minute. Actually what?"

"Nothing that matters right now. You would really rather stay here?"

"Yes, I would rather stay here." At least, rather than go to Comeback Cove. "What are you hiding?"

"Me?"

"Yes, you. You're hiding something and you know it." About his family? Or was it the ex?

Nonny had alluded to some issue back when she'd called to ask Darcy to rent to him. At that point, Darcy had simply wanted someone to keep the grass cut and the house safe when she was traveling for her job as personal assistant to her mother—something that used to happen a lot, since Sylvie juggled careers as an actress, an author and a coach at the Stratford Festival. All that had mattered at that point was that he be polite, solvent and not inclined toward murder. The fact that he was one of the North brothers—part of the big, noisy crew that had both terrified and fascinated her on her childhood visits to the Cove—had been a happy bonus.

It wasn't until he'd been around for a while that Nonny had mentioned a broken engagement. It was only in the past few months that Ian himself had said anything about it, and then only an occasional, casual reference—"Taylor and I went there"—the way he would talk about an old friend. Never any details. And try though Darcy might, she had never been able to get Nonny to spill. It was Ian's story to share, she'd insisted.

Damn her moral code.

He stretched long legs out in front of him. "Sorry, Darce, but when it comes to hiding things you kind of won that round."

Busted. "Okay. I'm not one to talk. If it matters, I can't count how many times I was tempted to tell you the truth. About Xander, I mean."

"I believe you." He paused. "For the record, I was kind of tweaked that you hadn't said anything. Not that you owed me or anyone an explanation, but I thought... Anyway, having heard the whole story it makes sense. In your shoes I would have done the same thing."

"That's good. I'm glad." She smiled before pouncing. "So...actually what?"

"*Actually*, I'd better call my mother and tell her I won't be coming home for Father's Day after all."

"Wait— Who— What?"

He stretched his arms high overhead, reaching toward the robin's-egg blue of the porch ceiling. "You heard me."

"You're not going."

"That's right."

"Because of me?"

"No. Because of Xander."

"But I told you, he never... I mean, damn it, Ian. I appreciate everything you did today, believe me, but I don't need a babysitter. This is my mess and I will get through it."

"I know you will."

"So?"

"So maybe I want to hang around and see what happens."

Oh, no. The caveman was supposed to be gone.

"What are you gonna do, Ian? Shadow me for the rest of my life in case Xander catches me all alone?"

"Nope."

She waited. Nothing else seemed to be forthcoming.

She eyed the beer. Maybe if she shook it up and sprayed him…

"Why are you so determined to do this?"

He shrugged and grabbed the bottle—jeez, it was as if he really could read her mind—and rocked back in his chair. "Honestly? I don't know. But it feels right."

"Because you don't trust Xander? Or— Wait. Do you think I'm dumb enough to get drunk and pregnant again?"

"No!"

The shock on his face reassured her. No one was that good an actor, and, having spent much of her life haunting stages waiting for her mother, she should know.

"Then what's the problem? Ian, I'm a big girl. I don't like this situation, but I'll manage. I know I was a total basket case when I first had Cady, but on the whole, I'm organized, competent and reasonable. I can handle this."

"I think that's it."

"What's what?"

"I know you can handle this. Alone." He leaned forward, quietly serious. "But what kind of friend would I be if I made you do that?"

Oh.

She had no comeback for that one. Maybe because it was so unexpected.

Maybe because she couldn't remember the last time someone had made her feel that her happiness mattered to them.

"Make you a deal," she said softly. "You want to be a friend to me? I'm all for that. But it's about time I returned the favor. See, I have this suspicion that I'm not the only one who's been dealing with things solo for too long."

"What's that mean?"

"It means that sometimes you get this look like…" Almost like the way he had looked when she had handed Cady to him and told him she had to talk to Xander. "Like someone just pushed you over a cliff."

He tipped the chair back. The soft creak of the rocker made her wince and wonder if she had pushed too far.

"Fine," he said at last. "Since you're coming with me anyway—"

"*If* I go with you," she reminded him, though it was pretty much an auto-response. She wasn't at all surprised when he waved it away.

"Everything will come out one way or another. You might as well hear it from me."

He drummed his fingers on the arm of his chair and stared out at the road. She gave him the time it took to eat one chip. As soon as it was gone she stretched out her foot and nudged his leg.

"You falling asleep on me, North?"

"Trying to figure out where to start."

"Well, you know what the song says. Start at the beginning."

"The *very* beginning," he corrected.

"Details, details." She bit her lip, debated and decided to go for broke. "Is it about Taylor?"

"Yeah." But the way he drew out his reply told her there was more to it than that. "Okay." He blew out a short breath as if readying himself for a race. "You know that I spent some time working in Tanzania."

"Right. A year, right?"

"Not quite. Well, it was just before I came home that Taylor ended things between us."

"So much for absence making the heart grow fonder," she said softly.

He grimaced. "In a way that's what happened. Me being away gave her time to realize that her heart was actually fonder of someone else."

The word that slipped out of Darcy's mouth was one she never would have let herself utter in front of Cady.

He shrugged. "It sucked, but it happens. And

even though I didn't think so at the time, we were lucky that she figured it out when she did."

"You have a strange definition of luck."

"Hey, lemons, lemonade. It's over. It's in the past. It was rough, but then it got better."

"And yet you still miss her." Which really shouldn't bother her as much as it did.

"Actually, I don't." He raised a hand before she could give voice to any of the retorts bubbling inside her. "I know. If I'm over her, then what's the big deal?"

"Thank you for being the one to say it. I don't think I could have managed without more swearing."

"Yeah, well, you might want to save the bad words for when they really matter."

"When they really matter? What could be worse than having your fiancée leave you for someone else?"

"Easy," he said. "When the *someone else* is your brother."

CHAPTER FOUR

THE SILENCE THAT greeted his announcement went on so long that he started to think she might have choked on her chip. When he finally made himself look—because, yeah, he hadn't wanted to watch her face while he'd said it—he saw that her mouth was hanging open, her hand on her chest.

Maybe he should have eased into it a bit more gently.

"Oh, Ian."

Her soft whisper hung between them. She probably needed a minute to process it. After all, it had been two years and he was only now able to talk about it.

"I never…" She huffed out a breath that sounded like equal parts disbelief and indignation. "You don't need to tell me anything else. I shouldn't have pushed. But, damn, that was a shitty thing to do."

Maybe it was because he hadn't talked about it for so long, but despite her assurance that he didn't have to say anything, he wanted to explain. "Yeah, well, to give them credit, everybody tried their damnedest to keep it from happening. Taylor even moved to get away from Carter."

"It was Carter?" Her laugh was short and laced with relief. "Oh, jeez. I knew you had gone to Hank's wedding, and for a minute there, I thought—"

"Good God, Darce. I'm no martyr."

"Thank heaven for that. So, she moved?"

"Right. He knew she was leaving, and he agreed. Everybody thought they were doing the right thing, splitting up, trying to keep it from ripping the family apart, but then Moxie put things together. From what I hear, she practically had to push Carter onto the plane herself."

"Wait a minute. They betrayed you, and then your own grandmother— Holy crap."

Everyone in his family had been a wreck. After all, no matter how it played out, one brother was going to end up hurt. But Darcy was the first one focused solely on him. Hearing the indignation in her voice, seeing the way her usually fluid movements were now tight and choppy—well, it was more of a comfort than he would have expected.

"Moxie was right. Not that I was a big fan of the idea when it happened, but... She said it would be worse if Carter and Taylor tried to pretend nothing had happened. Something about resentments building up." He shrugged. "It hurt like hell, but she had a point. Once the truth was out we knew what we were dealing with."

"Well, it must have helped to know that it couldn't possibly get any crappier."

"Yeah, there was that."

She leaned back, arms crossed, watching him. "So if Taylor moved and Carter went after her, why are you living in Stratford now instead of in Comeback Cove, where you could have had the support of your family? How did you end up being the sacrificial lamb?"

"Breathe. It was my idea."

"So much for your 'I'm no martyr' line." She sat up straighter, eyes flashing. "That sucks. As does your family for letting you go."

She wasn't saying anything that he hadn't thought to himself at some point. Funny, though, how much different it felt coming from her.

"Carter and Taylor said they would leave, but remember, we all worked in the family business. I had to think of what was best for Northstar Dairy, too. I had already been gone for almost a year. Everyone was used to that. It made sense for me to be the one to move. Plus," he added, just to prove he was no candidate for sainthood, "Comeback Cove is a small town. My choices were to stay and be stared at or let them stay and, well—"

"Be the hottest gossip in decades?"

"That's about it."

"Good for you."

"I'm not sure that I should be congratulated for it," he said. "But it seemed like the best choice at the time."

"So you decided to move, and you picked Stratford."

"More like Helene told Moxie about you needing a tenant, and it was far enough from home that I wouldn't run into anyone I knew, and I was up for anything that didn't require me to do a whole lot of thinking."

"And here I thought you chose it because you wanted to walk the streets where Justin Bieber grew up."

Ah, the Sass Queen was back.

"So," she said after a moment. "That explains why you haven't gone home much since you moved in."

"Yeah."

"Once in two years, unless I've forgotten something."

He glanced sideways. "Your point, Darce?"

"Well, I couldn't help but wonder why you're going back now."

The truth sat heavy in his gut. Part of him longed to tell her about the charitable foundation Moxie was adding to the dairy—the foundation she wanted him to lead, if he could handle being home. If Xander hadn't reappeared he might have said something, but Darcy had had enough shockers for one day.

Besides, nothing was definite. What was the point of worrying her when he wasn't even sure himself if he could do this?

"It's time," he said at last. "I don't want one piece of my past to take over the rest of my life."

"Very wise."

"Plus, it's Father's Day, and my mom is throwing a big thing for my dad. I don't want to hurt him by being the only one of his kids to not show up."

"Did it ever occur to you that the only reason your mom is doing this is to force you to come home?"

"Of course it is. Ma hates hoopla. You know how she spends Mother's Day?"

"How?"

"She goes to church, then goes back to bed and spends the whole day there, alone. She reads. She naps. She orders pizza for dinner. It's been like that since we were kids."

"Oh, my God, seriously? That sounds like the best Mother's Day ever. What a smart woman."

"A smart, overworked woman who needed a break." Much like the one swaying softly in the hammock across from him.

"Someday I'm going to do that. It sounds like bliss." Her voice switched from wistful to practical in the space of one quick sigh. "But anyway. You. You think you're ready for this?"

"It's been two years."

"I can do math, North. I didn't ask you how long it had been. I asked if you're ready."

Correction: a smart, overworked, *stubborn* woman. "I think so." Especially when sitting on a porch with the setting sun wrapping them in shadows, surrounded by Darcy's laugh and her fierce concern and—yeah—that damned pink top that dipped a little lower than she probably realized.

Taylor was a very distant memory when he was with Darcy.

"I think I'm ready," he said. "But there's only one way to find out for sure."

"You blacksmiths. Always shoving things into fires."

"I'm not planning any long heartfelt talks with either Carter or Taylor, if that's what you mean. I'll settle for being in the same room without going bat-shit crazy."

"I'll pack some of my mom's happy pills, just in case."

It took him a second to process her meaning.

"You're coming with me?"

"Only because I think you'll need the moral support." There was a slightly evil cast to her grin that made him feel as though his beer wasn't sitting well. "And I always thought Carter was a snot-nosed brat who acted like he was better than the rest of you, so I'm going to love being able to mock him silently anytime I see him."

"Darce—"

"Oh, don't worry. I'll behave. The last thing I want is to make things worse for you."

"Damn. I was going to tell you that you didn't have to keep it silent." He shrugged. "Listen, this is nothing compared to you and Cady, but so you know—the whole reason Xander came back in the first place was because he wanted Lulu."

"He *what*?"

"Yep. Something about seeing himself in his new life, walking the straight and narrow with his faithful canine companion at his side."

"You're kidding." For a second the indignant light in her face faded to something more like worry and fear and something else, something that made him want to gather her close and stroke her hair and promise her that everything would be okay.

Lucky for him, the moment passed as quickly as it had appeared.

No MATTER HOW much she longed to sleep in the next morning, Darcy pushed her reluctant self out of bed while the sun was just beginning to brighten the sky. If she was going to have herself and Cady ready for a ten-o'clock departure, she needed to take full advantage of the golden hour before her girlie started moving.

She threw laundry into the dryer, fired up her laptop and tossed jars and pouches of baby food into a bag, all while waiting for the coffee to brew. As soon as it was ready she filled her mug and carried it to the porch for what was usually the best fifteen minutes of her morning.

Too bad she had to spend it calling her mother today.

Sylvie was in London this week, meaning it was already late morning for her, meaning there was a decent chance she would be awake. No guarantee, but the odds were high. Darcy couldn't count how many times in the past year she had given thanks that her own sleep cycle had come from her father instead of her mother.

"Darcy?"

Yep. Mom might technically be awake, but alert and functional were still hours away. If luck was really on Darcy's side, she could get through this conversation before Sylvie woke up enough to become annoyed.

"'Morning, Mom. How're you and the queen this fine day?"

"Don't be an ass, Darcy. You know very well she's touring Japan this month. Why on earth are you calling at such a teeth-numbing hour?"

"A couple of things. The copy edits for the new book came in yesterday. I'll have those turned around within the week, and then I'll send them to you for final approval. If you need me over the next few days, I might be a bit slow in getting back to you because Cady and I are going to Comeback Cove. And I finalized your Sydney itinerary and will send that to you in a few minutes."

"That all sounds— Wait. You're going where?"

So much for that great strategy.

"Comeback Cove."

"For the love of God, why?"

Because my friend needs me. Because I need some breathing room between me and the Amazing Reappearing Biological Daddy. Because the family I idolized when I was a kid has been broken, and I want to help fix it.

Of all the reasons for this trip, there was only one Darcy would even think of sharing with her mother. "Ian was driving up anyway, and Nonny hasn't seen Cady since right after she was born, so it seemed like good timing."

"Assuming there's ever a good time to be bored silly."

Darcy often wondered what on earth her parents had seen in each other. Sylvie was a mercurial, nightlife-loving actress, while Paul had been a quiet, small-town homebody. Sylvie was all about the next excitement. Paul had been all about the moment. Sylvie loved Darcy in a bemused sort of way, as if she were never quite sure where this child had come from and what she was supposed to do with her. Paul had been a hands-on, deeply invested father.

But Paul was dead. Sylvie was not only alive, but provided a major chunk of Darcy's hard-earned income. So on many levels it behooved Darcy to keep her mother placated.

"You know how it goes. Sometimes you have to make these sacrifices for the sake of family."

"I suppose. It was so much easier when your father was alive and I could let him deal with those issues."

Darcy had been called many things in her life, but she was pretty sure she had never before been an *issue*.

"Fine, then. Go do what you must. When will you be— Oh. Hold on a second."

There came the rustling sort of crackle that made Darcy suspect the phone had been relegated to the side of the bed, followed by a lazy "Good morning, Matteo," and something that sounded way too much like a long and welcoming kiss. Oh, goody. There was nothing as delightful as trying to conduct a conversation with Sylvie when her latest boy toy was in the room. All it took was one studly thing to make an appearance and Sylvie Drummond— sometimes known as the most driven woman on two continents—turned into a rather embarrassing pile of goo.

"Mom? Hello?"

"Oh. Darcy." The throaty quality to Sylvie's voice made Darcy want to shove her fingers in her ears and sing *la la la, not paying attention*. "I thought you had hung up."

Yep. Testosterone walked in, five hundred brain cells marched out.

"Sorry. I need to confirm some dates with you. Before you get too busy," she couldn't help but add.

"Of course. Fire away."

Darcy rattled off the requests, knowing full well

from the faraway *mmm-hmms* on the other end that her mother's focus was elsewhere. Sure enough, as soon as she paused, Sylvie pounced.

"You know, dear, why don't you email all that to me? I'll go over it later."

Later, as in sometime when Matteo wasn't around.

It had been this way for almost as long as Darcy could remember. It seemed like mere weeks between the time Paul died and the parade of new friends/uncles/possible new daddies had begun. As an adult, Darcy could look back and see that, yes, Sylvie had gone quite a while without adult companionship, and, yes, it was rather pathetic that she became so dependent on them so quickly. Most of the time Darcy rolled her eyes and gave thanks that she was no longer young enough to have to tag along when Sylvie decided to follow her latest love. Seeing the world was fine and dandy, but Darcy had inherited her father's love of home. She was quite happy to spend her days in her snug little house, just her and Cady. And, usually, Ian. Who had turned out to deliver the kind of kiss that left her wishing it had gone on just a little longer—

Oh, no. Inheriting Sylvie's hair and eyes was one thing. Inheriting her man-induced dizziness was quite another.

"Okay. I'll email you. Better run, Cady's waking up," she lied. "Say hi to Matteo for me. I'll talk to you next week."

She ended the call quickly in case any rogue Sylvie genes were being activated by the contact, distant though it might be.

"At least that's behind me," she said to the robins perched in the crab apple tree next to the porch. They didn't seem remotely impressed with her amazing strength and fortitude.

Though maybe that was because they were mind readers who knew that while a part of her was busy shaking her head over Sylvie, another part was reliving that quick kiss with Ian and wondering about the justice of a world where a grandmother was seeing more action than her daughter ever had.

SOMEWHERE IN THE TALK of Darcy coming along on this trip, Ian had forgotten one major point: the actual car ride.

He gripped the steering wheel and tore his focus from the traffic in front of him to do one of the status checks that had become routine after three-plus hours on the road. Cady: snoozing in her car seat. Lulu: probably asleep in her crate, if the blessed lack of yipping was any indication. And Darcy: swaying in the passenger seat, singing softly to whatever was coming out of the laptop perched on her knee. In denim shorts and headphones she looked more like a college student than a hardworking mother.

For the first time he wondered if talking her into coming along might have been a mistake. Being so close to her in the car was stirring up a crap-load of feelings, most of them pertaining to that stupid kiss. How was he supposed to prepare himself for a seriously awkward family reunion when his eyes kept drifting away from the road and over to where her shorts exposed a whole lot of leg? Long, slightly tan, totally toned leg.

And the humidity had seized control of her hair, making it extra wavy. Each curl was like an individual finger beckoning him closer.

And when she really got into the music, she did some motion with her shoulders that made her breasts jiggle beneath her T-shirt. All in all, being in the Mustang with her was way too dangerous, given that they were on a busy highway and he wasn't supposed to be noticing her.

If he could think of something to get her talking at least the seat-dancing would stop. If only his brain cells weren't being hijacked by his—

Thank God, right at that moment she hit a key with a flourish, punched the air and let loose with a little "yeah, yeah, yeeeeah," before letting out a sigh of what he assumed was satisfaction.

"Ha! Take that you brain-stealing piece of busy-work!"

"What were you doing this time? Something for your mom?"

"Nope. One of my other clients."

"Ah. Another website?"

"Honestly." This time her sigh held nothing but

exasperation. Lucky for him, he could tell it was totally fake. "Author assistants do more than build sites, you know."

"I know, I know. You set up contests, format ebooks and...other stuff." He could go into more detail, but he didn't want her to know how closely he'd paid attention to her work talk.

Come to think of it, he wasn't sure *he* wanted to know how much he'd picked up about it, either. It smacked too closely of being...well...too close.

"Very good. You get an A for listening." She closed the lid on the laptop. "But this time I was planning a social media campaign. Not horribly complicated, but it's a royal pain. I've earned a break. So." She peered out the window. "Where are we? Belleville?"

"Not quite. We just passed the Trenton exit. About halfway there."

"Good." She twisted slightly to look behind her. He glanced her way. Mistake. Between her movements and the grip of the seat belt, her neckline was pulled sideways. He tore his gaze away, but there was no erasing the image of peachy skin and white lace that was now branded into his brain.

Yep. This trip was a serious blunder. Time to remind himself of the real reason she was sitting beside him.

"I think Xander believed the lines we fed him yesterday. About us being—"

"Right." She sounded surprisingly flustered for

someone who had spent the first hour of the drive soothing a wailing child and a howling dog without breaking a sweat. "I have to say, you did a great job. Of pretending, I mean. If the business world ever loses its appeal, have me introduce you to some of my mother's cohorts. They might be able to make use of you."

"Given some of the stories you've shared, I'm gonna say thanks but no thanks." Especially because he hadn't been *acting* so much as indulging his own needs at that moment—not that he would ever tell her that part. "But at some point we're gonna have to come clean with him."

"Yes. We should."

Huh. She didn't seem to have any ideas. Not what he expected from Darce.

"It's your call," he said slowly. "You're the one who has the most at stake here. But I'm thinking, once we get back, we should probably be up front with him."

"Right. I can tell him I was caught off guard by the jail thing, and you picked up on that and wanted to help."

She was saying the right things, but they weren't ringing true. But maybe she wasn't sure how Xander would react. After all, she'd really known him only a few weeks.

"I can explain it to him. He might take it easier from me." And if not, then Ian would rather any anger be directed at him than Darcy.

"You don't need to—"

"Yeah, I do. It was my idea, remember? All you did was play along." And he would forever be glad she had. Even not knowing everything that was happening, it had felt damned right to hold her close, to stand between her and someone who had caused her to look at him with that fearful appeal in her eyes. He might not be able to do a lot for Darce and Cady now—he didn't have the legal knowledge to give her the advice she needed—but he had given her that.

"Still, I think if I explained things from my point of view, he'll understand."

"He probably will. But let me break it to him first, give him a chance to process it. You can go into the details later."

"I don't—"

"Darce. Trust me on this one, okay? It's a guy thing." Mostly his own thing, but let her think it was Xander's ego on the line, not his. That would simplify life for all of them. "He's going to be pissed, and he's going to want to be sure that it was all for show."

"And why should he have any say in that? He's Cady's father, yes, but that's as far as it goes. He has no say as to what I do with my life, as long as Cady is safe and happy."

"He just found out he has a daughter. Yesterday, when you first saw him, your instinct was to give her to me and trust me to take care of her. I took

her inside. I fed her. I changed her frickin' diaper."
And then I went back outside and kissed you, and everything changed, but I'm not going to dwell on that. "Cady is his daughter, but right now I'm the closest thing to a dad that she has. That's going to eat at him. He's going to want to know how deeply I'm tied to you two."

Another reason why they had to end this farce sooner rather than later. The longer it went on, the more Xander would believe in it.

Ian's own beliefs were totally irrelevant.

"I suppose you're right." The laughter had fled from her voice.

"I wasn't blowing smoke last night when I said he's basically a decent guy."

"Except for wanting to take Lulu away from you."

Crap, was that it? "Darce. He's not going to try to take Cady away from you. Even if he wanted to, he just met her and he just got out of jail. He has enough to deal with already. Cady is probably the brightest spot in his life right now, but I guarantee you this, he's smart enough to know he's not in any position to try to be more than a very part-time dad for a long time."

"I know. But…everything is happening so fast, and…"

He waited for one breath, then two. "And?"

"I…" She shook her head. "Nothing. It's just me being—"

Three short beeps interrupted her words and had her diving for her phone. Damn it. Of all the lousy timing.

She pulled the phone from her bag, checked the display and frowned. It hit him that she'd been doing that a lot on this trip.

"Someone text-stalking you, Darce?"

"What? Oh." Her laugh sounded strained. "No, I...well...I don't want to jump to conclusions, but I might have a bit of a problem. With, um, Nonny."

"Is she okay?"

"I don't know."

"What's that mean?"

"It means," she said bleakly, "that I left a message for her last night, but she still hasn't called me back."

CHAPTER FIVE

THANK GOD FOR rest areas.

Darcy stepped stiffly out of the car and allowed herself one blissful moment to stretch every possible bit of her body before she had to dive back into Mommy mode. She reached overhead, clasped her hands, lifted her face to the sun and pulled everything she could pull.

"Dang, that feels good," she said out loud.

She hated being confined. It hadn't helped that the farther they went, the more she'd started to worry. About Nonny's silence. And how Ian was going to readjust to his family. And what Xander's reappearance would do to her family.

The worrying, however, had been almost a relief compared to the other thoughts that had flooded her imagination—thoughts of what would happen if Ian were to stop asking her about things she was already obsessing over. If, instead, he were to lift his hand from the wheel and settle it on her knee and remind her that Cady wasn't the only one who could benefit from some distraction once in a while.

Between the fretting and the lusting, she had a

pretty good idea how it would feel to be a jack-in-the-box, all coiled tight and ready to spring. If she were to take off right this minute, how many laps could she do around the crowded parking lot before Cady started crying?

The thought turned out to be purely hypothetical, for right then her little bundle of joy let loose with an impatient wail. Lulu joined in, setting the entire backseat in chaos.

Darcy glanced across the hood of the car to catch Ian's eye. "Pay you a hundred bucks to deal with them."

"You think I'm that easy?"

"Fine." She huffed out an exaggerated breath and grabbed the handle, giving thanks yet again that Ian had opted for the four-door model. If she'd had to maneuver around a two-door when she was this stiff, she probably would sprain something.

Stifling a groan, she bent and reached for her squirming, wailing daughter. "Shh, Cady Bug. Shh. I know you want to get out of there. Give Mommy a minute."

A sharp bark from Lulu cut through the indignant cries. Darcy looked up to check on the dog and saw that Ian, also bent over on the opposite side of the car, seemed to be focused on her. Or rather, on the spot where her shirt hung free at the neck, giving him a prime view of Cleavage Central.

"Oh, these stupid straps." Pretending to fiddle with the buckle, she reached forward so her arm was closer to her body, pressing the shirt against her skin. Movement at the edge of her vision told her that Ian had backed away and was now staring intently at the latch on the crate's door. She slipped the buckle and pulled her sweaty child free while chattering nonsense to sidetrack anyone who needed it.

"There you go, sweet cheeks." So he'd been given a free show and he'd taken advantage of it. Okay. There was nothing there he hadn't seen during the endless months of nursing.

"Are you ready for a diaper change? I bet you are." It didn't mean anything. They'd been in an awkward position and he was a man, and God knows, even a monk probably would stop and look if a woman's shirt gaped open. Biology might not be destiny but it sure held the upper hand at times.

She slung the diaper bag over her shoulder, closed the car door with a quick hip check, jiggled Cady and finally looked for Ian. Luck was on her side. He was bent over and away from her, clipping the leash on Lulu's collar. Not only did it mean she didn't have to face him right away, but she also had a prime view of his—

"Crap!"

At that his head jerked around. "What?"

"Nothing. Nothing. The diaper bag started to slip." *Smile. Carefree. Don't think about his butt.* "We'll meet you back here in a few."

"Sounds good."

Was he as eager not to look at her as she was not to look at him?

She popped Cady on her shoulder and aimed for the building.

"Darce?"

So close, so damn close to escaping…

"Listen, if you want to get her changed and bring her back to me so you can have a few minutes alone, feel free."

Oh.

She made herself turn around.

"Sure. That would simplify things."

He grinned. "Hey, that's what friends are for, right?"

Yep. Friends. That's what they were.

"Friends are good, right, Cady?" She glanced back to be sure they were out of earshot. "Friends are wonderful. We all need friends. Looking down someone's shirt when she's bending over, that doesn't mean anything. Neither does noticing that someone has a really great butt."

Cady twisted, her palm smacking Darcy in the face.

"Ow! You know, you could just tell me I'm being an idiot. There's no need to get physical."

Physical.

She dealt with the diaper in record time and returned to the parking lot. Ian held tight to Lulu's leash while she barked and ran in happy circles.

"Here you go." She handed the baby over gladly. "There's a line, so I might be a while."

"Not a problem. Take your time."

Damn. Not only did he have a killer butt and arms that were all muscle and sinew thanks to his hours working at the forge, he knew the ultimate way to a mother's heart: giving her the ability to go to the bathroom alone.

"I hope I see your mom while I'm there."

"Why's that?"

"I need to thank her for raising you so well."

His eyebrows lifted. "It's not possible that I'm a great guy on my own? There had to be a woman behind it?"

She hitched her purse higher on her shoulder. "I can't believe you have to ask that. See you in a few. Be awesome, Cady."

She strolled back to the building, reveling in the moments of freedom that lay ahead. Well, as much as a girl could revel while simultaneously trying not to fret. Or drool. Or remember how right it had felt to snuggle against a welcoming body, even if it was only make-believe.

She pulled her phone from her pocket, checking once again for messages or emails. Nothing.

So much for not worrying.

The line had gone down so it took only a few minutes for her to rejoin Ian and company, now standing, crawling and sniffing around a picnic table in the grassy area off the parking lot. He was on the phone but pointed to her cooler and blanket on the table before taking off toward the building.

She spread the blanket on the ground, set Cady in the middle—yeah, that was going to last—and unpacked food. By the time he returned she was doing her best to get some banana into a child who was determined to spend her precious free time cruising and exploring instead of eating.

"Think you're fighting a losing battle there, Darce." Ian tossed a piece of cheese to Lulu, who snapped it up.

"If I were you, I'd focus on helping. Otherwise I'm going to be feeding her while we drive. Do you really want mashed banana all over your car?"

A low blow, she knew, but desperate times and all that crap.

He reached for a tiny square of peanut butter sandwich just as she did. Their fingers tangled in a fleeting caress. For a moment the kiss was back, hovering between them, thick and pulsing and almost visible.

For a moment she couldn't quite draw a deep breath.

She grabbed the morsel and twisted away. "Come on, Bug. Open up. Let's see if Mommy can hit the moving target."

She didn't dare look at him again. Not yet. Far safer to focus on Cady, to call comments over her shoulder, to keep Ian on the fringe of her awareness instead of in the center.

If only *safe* didn't feel quite so much like deprivation...

She was sinking into her own sandwich when he steepled his fingers and tapped his thumbs together. "So," he said. "I have a confession to make."

"That sounds ominous. Did you finally decide that you should let me drive?"

"I called Moxie. To, uh, ask about Helene."

So much for a peaceful few minutes to eat.

"Look," he hurried on, "I know you two aren't as close as you used to be, but I've known her all my life."

"So have I."

"Yeah, but I've spent more time with her. And for her to not answer a call from her only grandchild—well, it's not her. Not at all. I was worried something might be wrong."

She could give him that. The thought of Nonny, hurt and alone, had crossed her mind more than once in the past hours. She didn't want her grandmother to be injured. God, no. But in a way that had been better than thinking Nonny was ignoring her.

"I knew that if anything was wrong Moxie would know, or find out fast. So I called. And the thing is, Darce, Helene isn't home right now. She's on a cruise. To Alaska."

"Alaska?" Dang. She hadn't known her voice could squeak that way.

"'Fraid so."

"Okay. That certainly puts a new twist on things."

She set her sandwich on her plate and tried to think. "We're well past the halfway point in the drive, so it doesn't make sense to turn around."

"Especially since Xander will be there."

So much for her plan to put off thoughts of him until tomorrow. "I guess Cady and I can find a place for a night or two and then take the bus back." Though in a tourist town in summer that might be more than her budget could handle. "Or— Oh, does Moxie have a key? Maybe we could stay at Nonny's anyway."

"I asked. Seems Helene was taking advantage of this trip to have some work done in her kitchen. It's nonstop construction and there's no water."

Didn't it figure? "So, a hotel, then. Maybe Moxie could recommend a place that won't be too expensive and doesn't mind a teething baby."

"She already did." His smile did nothing to reassure. "Her place."

It took a moment for his meaning to sink in. "You mean stay with you and your family? I can't do that. I haven't seen them since...jeez, since the last time I was up there. High school, probably. That's a long time, North."

"Doesn't matter. Moxie is Helene's best friend. You were at the house every summer. I'm living with you. Sort of," he added with an altogether too-endearing blush. "You're practically family."

"Well, not to me."

He sat back, arms crossed, and grinned in a most

maddening way—as though he knew something she didn't.

"What?" Now her stomach hurt.

"What *what*?"

"You have that look. Like you know something I don't know and you're savoring the moment."

He shrugged and pulled an apple from his bag. "Just thinking." One eyebrow quirked. "About what Moxie will say to that."

Her own memories of the formidable Mrs. North, combined with the stories Ian had shared over the years, gave her a moment's concern. But on the other hand...

"Look, I not only was raised by a diva, I spent most of my adult life making sure she got everything she wanted the minute she needed it. I have out-conned hotel managers, stage managers, agents and, worst of all, other divas. And I can do it in three languages. Four if you count swearing in German. There's no way Moxie can make me stay at your family's home."

But, piped up a sly little voice inside her, *if you stayed at the house, it might give you more chances to see Ian and Carter together. See if they need a hand reconciling and all that.*

Not a bad point. She'd be more inclined to listen if she could be sure the voice wasn't being fueled by those sneaky hormones.

Ian bit into the apple, backhanded juice from his chin and let loose a grin. "You know, I think I should call the rest of the family. Maybe sell tickets. This could be the smackdown of the century."

"What smackdown? I don't need to get violent. I'll just say, 'Thank you very much. That's incredibly generous, but I can't possibly.' Which will be even easier if you drop me someplace before you go home."

"Are you kidding? That's like handing my head to her on a silver platter. It's going to be hard enough going home already. I'm not making Moxie pissed off before I even walk through the door."

Guilt tugged at her. She'd forgotten that he was walking back into a situation loaded with land mines.

"And that's precisely why you don't need me around. You and your family need to get past this on your own without tiptoeing around some stranger—"

"Almost family."

"—and her baby."

"Very true. At least, when it comes to you." He pointed to the child clinging to the picnic bench. "It's Cady I really want."

"I'm afraid to ask."

"She's the perfect diversion. If things get too intense, all I have to do is hold her up and make her blow raspberries, and there ya go. Crisis averted."

"Cute and possibly correct. But my kid is not going to be your auto-distraction."

"Not even for a day or two?"

She was on the edge of giving him a resounding *no* when she heard the plea beneath his words. He was only half joking. And being a guy, he probably didn't even know it.

Just like he probably had no clue that the only one he really wanted to avoid was Carter. She didn't think it was simply an oversight that had led him to tell her about Taylor and the broken engagement but never once mention Carter's role.

Unbidden, she remembered Ian walking into the backyard after Xander had dropped his jail bomb. She had never been so happy to see anyone in her life, except maybe the anesthesiologist who administered her epidural. She had desperately needed someone nearby, someone she could trust to keep her steady while the rest of the world swirled around her.

Of course, then he had kissed her and sent things rocking even more, but...

"I don't think so," she said gently. "But how about if Cady and I come along for the first meeting? We can see whoever is there, talk to Moxie, hang out for a while. Then you can deliver us someplace."

He gave her a long look—mentally assessing, she was sure, comparing her powers of resistance against Moxie's powers of persuasion. Let him have his delusions.

"Deal," he said at last. "But you have to promise you won't take the bus back home."

"Ian, I can't stay until Sunday or Monday. A hotel, eating out that much… It's not in my budget." Ironic, given that she had spent such a huge portion of her life in hotels and used to think nothing of them. But that life was long gone.

"Give yourself a day or two. See if you can find a lawyer who can give you some basic information. Then if you're really determined to go back, I'll drive you."

"But your dad—"

"I can drive you home on Saturday and go back Sunday morning in time for the party. It's no big deal."

"Well, yeah, it is. I can't ask you to do that."

"Then stay at the house."

Points for Ian. He'd almost caught her.

"So my choices are to inconvenience your family by staying with them or drag you away when you've just started easing back into the family bosom." Oops. Mentioning bosoms might not be such a good idea given the way he'd been scoping out hers not an hour ago. "So to speak," she added.

"I'd say that covers it."

As if she would do any of that. The bus would work fine. Well, not really *fine*, not with a baby and all her assorted crap. But those were details. Details were her specialty. She could do this.

The only stumbling block was seated across the table, slipping—oh, jeez—a bit of something chocolate into her daughter's mouth.

She couldn't let Ian know. He would insist on coming to her rescue, and she couldn't let him do that. Not this time. This return home was a turning point for him, she knew, and she had a feeling—mostly from things he hadn't said—that there was more to it than a mere wish to begin mending fences. She wasn't going to jeopardize this reunion by pulling him away at a crucial moment.

She would go to his house now and ease that initial meeting. She would be on call for any times he might need a beautiful little bundle of distraction. And on Friday or Saturday she would slip out, texting him once she and Cady were halfway to Toronto.

He wouldn't like it. But she wasn't the daughter of a diva for nothing.

"Okay. We'll go say hi to everyone before we find a place to settle in."

"Moxie will want you to stay for dinner. She already asked if you like chicken and dumplings."

"Really?"

"Yeah. All homemade like you've never had it before."

"It won't be a hardship to say yes to that. But once it's over, promise you'll drive us to a place we can stay. Preferably in town, so I can get out with Cady and see the sights."

He sized her up for a second before leaning back to scratch behind Lulu's ears. "Sure."

"That was too easy."

"Hey, if Moxie hasn't talked you into staying by the end of dinner, you will have earned anything you want."

She allowed herself a small smile, clamping down on the giant grin threatening to make itself known. It had been a long time since she'd faced down an equally determined and devious mind. She was almost looking forward to this.

Though when she considered what could happen if she lost and had to spend the next few days watching Ian—purely to assess his level of Carter tolerance, of course—she had to admit that losing would have its own reward.

DARCY HAD BEEN at Moxie's house many times during her childhood visits, though since she had stopped hanging with the North brothers once she hit high school, her memories were mostly of the bits-and-pieces variety. But once they turned off Highway 2 and headed toward the river, nostalgia began crowding into her awareness. A long backyard, with her dad chasing her. A rope swing hanging from a tree. An old car dashboard and steering wheel, and the way the brothers would fight over who got to play with it next.

And one sharply clear memory that must have come from the summer when she was seven—the first time she'd gone to Comeback Cove without her father.

"Is the kitchen green?"

"Not anymore, unless Moxie has painted it since I left." Ian frowned as he slowed for the corner. "But it used to be. Do you remember it?"

"I remember seeing Nonny in a green room. It must have been a kitchen because there was a counter behind her."

A counter where a pitcher lay on its side while something purple—grape juice?—had dripped over the edge. But neither of the adults had been paying any attention to it, because Moxie had been kneeling beside a chair holding Nonny, who had been making the most terrifying choking noises while she shook with sobs.

That had been the first time Darcy really understood that she wasn't the only one who missed her dad. Until then, the quietness of Nonny's house and the slowness of Nonny's movements hadn't really connected. But after that moment, it made sense.

"You know what I remember most about coming here when I was a— Shh, Cady, we're almost there, sweet cheeks. Anyway, I remember the noise."

The corner of his mouth lifted. "Funny. My big memory is Ma forever telling us that it was time to play the Quiet Game."

"I think that was my mother's favorite game, too." Not her dad's, though. He'd always done whatever it had taken to make Darcy laugh. That moment when Cady had let loose with her first real giggle had made Darcy miss her father in a way she hadn't in years.

"Your mom had a legitimate excuse, poor woman. Four little boys racing around… But even though you guys scared the bejeebers out of me, it was fascinating, you know? I was used to a house where it was just me. Then Nonny would bring me here and it was all noise and pushing and boogers and other gross stuff."

"We were really well-behaved most of the time. We just pulled that act when you came to visit, so you would go home and take your girl cooties with you."

"Sure, North. Tell me another one."

"Can't. Ma will paddle me if I tell family secrets."

She rolled her eyes, but inside, she gave thanks. He'd seemed to be drawing in on himself the past hour or so. Hearing him joke and tease was a relief. She ached to think of what this trip must be costing him. But no matter how hard, he needed to be here, doing this. Families such as his weren't meant to be pulled apart this way.

When they turned into the driveway and approached the big old Victorian with its turret and peachy gingerbread-trimmed porch, she bounced in her seat.

"Oh, my gosh. It hasn't changed at all!"

"Not on the outside much, no, though Moxie has done a lot with the gardens and the yard lately. She's redone practically every room inside."

"Don't tell me that running Northstar Dairy

and keeping your family in line left her time to be bored."

"Nah. After Hank's first wife left, he packed up Millie—she wasn't even two, I think—and they moved in for a few years. Moxie tore down some walls and changed things to make a nice little suite for them."

"Let me guess. Once that was done, it made something else look shabby so she kept going."

"You got it."

They pulled in behind a vintage MG, blazing red against the gray fieldstone wall and green grass.

"Looks like someone is home already," she said quietly.

"Moxie. She takes Wednesdays off now." He killed the engine but made no move to exit the car.

She patted his arm—quickly, to be on the safe side. "You ready for this?"

"Yeah. Sure." But his smile didn't touch the lines around his eyes.

"You don't have to do this. You would be well within your rights to say, 'No, they need to make the first move.'"

There were two sides to every story. She knew that. But it was hard to understand how Carter had allowed the situation to develop in the first place, why Taylor hadn't nipped the growing attraction in the bud, how his *mother* could have allowed him to leave when he'd been so hurt. Sure, he was a grown man and they couldn't have forced him to stay if he didn't want to, but come on.

She'd spent many a lonely childhood day wishing she could live with the Norths, many a long night wondering if her family would have been more like theirs if her dad hadn't died. What had happened to that loud, smelly, loving family?

It was a good thing she was going to be staying elsewhere while she was here. She might have a very hard time keeping silent if she spent too much time with the North clan.

"Ian?"

He shook his head, gave a small, unconvincing laugh. "It's okay."

"Really?"

His answer was to open the door. "Here comes Moxie. Let's go."

Darcy glanced through the windshield, but her perusal of the apple doll of a woman hustling toward the car was interrupted by a quick squeeze of her shoulder.

"Thanks, Darce."

She turned to smile, to reassure, but he was out of the car already, striding toward his grandmother with open arms.

"Just as well," she said to Cady, who was kicking her feet and making her unhappiness known. "I might have done something stupid like give him a kiss for luck."

Stupid, but undeniably enjoyable.

She bit her lip against the shiver making its way down her spine, hopped out of the car and opened the rear door. Three buckles later, Cady was free, bouncing against Darcy's chest in a physical appeal to be let down and allowed to explore.

"One minute, Bug. Let's get Lulu out of there."

But Ian was already returning to the car, pulling the crate to the ground. The dog exploded from her prison in a blur of tan and black, disappearing behind a bush, yapping all the way.

"Come on." He took her elbow, turned her away from the car. "Moxie's dying to see you."

"You mean to meet Cady," she said, but she fell into step beside him and approached the older woman.

In Darcy's mind, Moxie North had always had white hair and wrinkles. The wrinkles might be more plentiful now, but the smile hadn't changed. One part welcome, one part censure and two parts curiosity, Moxie moved with a lightness of step that made Darcy vow to pull out her dusty yoga DVD as soon as she got home.

"Mrs. North, thank you so—"

"You're not a child anymore, Darcy. Call me Moxie." Sharp eyes subjected Darcy to the kind of once-over that was usually delivered by border guards. "You grew up nicely."

"Um, thank you." Moxie's words should have come out as a compliment, but Darcy could swear there was an accusation lurking beneath them. Of course that could simply be her own guilty conscience reminding her that she hadn't visited Comeback Cove in years—a fact that was weighing more heavily on her mind with every minute of Moxie's scrutiny.

"And this is your little one." Moxie's features relaxed as she bent slightly to look Cady in the eye. "Hello, sweetheart. You're a cute one. Yes, you are. It's Cadence, right?"

"Cady, yes. Cadence Joy."

"Nice. Any special meaning to it?"

"Cadence because I like how it sounds, and Joy because that's what she brought into my life."

Moxie nodded her approval. "I like it. Beats the hell out of saddling a kid with some warhorse of a name like Maxine, just so's a grumpy old aunt might leave you money."

Was a smile the appropriate response? Darcy wasn't sure until Ian snorted.

Cady kicked again, wriggling and fighting to get down.

"She needs to move," Darcy said as she lowered Cady, who squealed and started bouncing the moment her mini Mary Janes hit the ground.

"It's good for her. Let her walk as much as you can. She'll have enough years of sitting ahead of her." Moxie's voice softened. "Helene is going to kick herself from here to Sunday for missing you."

Now boarding the train for Guilt Station.

"I'm sorry about that. I had hoped—"

"Hope doesn't cut the mustard, Darcy. Your grandmother's not getting any younger. You need to get your cute little behind up here more often, especially now that you have a young one. She needs to know her family before her family's gone."

Moxie's tongue always had been sharp, but the years seemed to have polished it to a fine precision instrument.

"I—"

"Don't give me any twaddle about trying or doing your best. Swear you'll come back before winter sets in."

Okay. Time to set some boundaries.

Darcy looked up with as much dignity as she could muster, given the way she was bent over and duck-walking to accommodate Cady's need to explore. "I do realize I've been gone too long, and I intend to remedy that. But I won't swear to a promise I'm not sure I can keep. Traveling is difficult right now. However, it seems to be a bit easier for Nonny, who is always welcome to come to my place."

The choking noise coming from Ian was matched only by the slight widening of Moxie's eyes, accompanied by a slow nod.

"Well. You *have* grown up."

"You strike me as a woman who appreciates the truth, Mrs. North. I don't think you deserve anything less."

Ian snickered. "Knew I should have sold tickets."

"Quiet, you." Moxie patted his arm briskly.

"You're in my good books right now. Don't mess up. Why don't you put those muscles to work and bring in the bags so you two can get settled before your folks come home?"

And that was her clue. Darcy didn't dare meet Ian's eyes as she began. "Actually, Mrs. North, Cady and I…"

She wasn't sure what made her stop. Ian hadn't said a word, hadn't moved a muscle. But something made her pause and look his way. His face was very still but there was no hiding the sudden dread in his eyes as he focused on a navy blue Saab turning into the driveway.

"Oh, hell in a hand basket," Moxie said. "Some people have the devil's own timing."

CHAPTER SIX

DARCY'S STOMACH DID one of those dives previously reserved for pop quizzes, blue lights in the rearview mirror and late periods.

"Is that…?" she began. Ian nodded and breathed in.

"Might as well get it over with," he said with a shaky kind of laugh that wouldn't have fooled a baby.

Darcy scooped up Cady, who had crouched to examine some fascinating bits of gravel, and handed her to Ian. He looked at her blankly for a second before smiling.

"Yeah, I think you're right." He settled Cady on his shoulder and strode toward the car.

"He spend a lot of time with your little one?" Moxie asked as she headed toward the car, which had come to a stop.

"Almost as much as I do. He's been there for her right from the start, and he's fabulous with her. Sometimes I swear if he made milk, Cady would love him as much as she loves me."

"Huh."

And what did that mean? Darcy was pretty sure Moxie was drawing all kinds of unfounded conclusions.

But this wasn't the time to dwell on that, for Cheater and Backstabber were hopping out of their car. Even though Cheater was a stranger and Darcy hadn't seen Backstabber for almost twenty years, it was ridiculously easy to spot the anxiety beneath their smiles.

Go ahead. Worry. You earned it.

"Ian!" Carter's voice was awfully hearty. "We didn't think you'd be here until tomorrow!"

I just bet you didn't.

Moxie made a strangled sort of sound. Darcy caught her eye and was rewarded with a quick shake of her head.

"Things changed."

Good. Ian sounded steady. Giving him Cady had been inspired. A baby in the arms was the best tension reliever in the world. Except maybe hugs. And kisses. And—

Oh, Lord, she was *not* going there.

"Hi, Ian." Taylor seemed slightly breathless to Darcy, but then again, maybe she always sounded like Betty Boop. "Who is this little sweetheart?"

Darcy knew a cue when she heard one.

"Hi." The smile she pasted on her face couldn't have been any faker than the ones on the couple in front of her. "I'm Darcy, and this is my daughter, Cady."

"Oh. Well. Hello! I'm Taylor."

"Darcy?" Carter took a step back. "Helene's Darcy?"

"One and the same." For one brief moment, Darcy allowed her inner Sylvie full rein. "And, Carter, I could swear you haven't changed a bit since we were kids."

Did he catch her implication? The slight flush on his cheeks would indicate yes. Huh. For someone who had never aspired to follow in her mother's footsteps, Darcy was pretty proud of the way she'd gotten her meaning across with nothing more than a social pleasantry.

Yeah, stuff that in your pipe and smoke it, Brother Dearest.

Taylor's gaze ping-ponged from Ian to Darcy and back again, no doubt trying to figure out how they belonged together. Let her wonder. It wouldn't hurt for Miss Cheater to have a few seconds of being the one not in the know.

"Well," Ian began, only to have his words drowned out by Cady's abrupt shriek in Lulu's direction. The sudden arrival of the dog was a welcome interruption. It also gave them a reason to talk and exclaim and try to pet the whirling dervish, but that was okay by Darcy. Ian deserved the chance to catch his breath and steel himself for whatever might come next.

No sooner had the Lulu talk petered into awkward silence than Moxie fixed the newcomers with an eagle eye. "And what are you two doing here at this time of day? It's too early for you to have left work already, and I don't remember hearing about any time off."

"We…" Carter began. He cast a fleeting look toward Ian, who was still not saying much but gave an impression of relaxation as he made exaggerated faces at Cady.

"I had an appointment," Taylor said. "At the, uh, eye doctor. You know, drops in the eyes and all that. I wasn't sure I'd be able to drive once it was over."

Oh, dear heavens. Darcy had seen better acting in third-grade drama festivals.

"Eye doctor," Moxie said. "Of course."

"So how was the drive?" Carter asked desperately.

Taylor stared at the ground but couldn't hide the way her cheeks had turned a shade of pink that would look like hell on Darcy but made Taylor look vibrant. Glowing. Full of life.

"Not bad once we got past Toronto," Ian said.

Oh, God. He was trying so hard.

Taylor's gaze cut quickly toward Ian, then back to Moxie. The appeal on her face was no less poignant for its silence.

Darcy could see it so well. A doctor's appointment together. A few moments of laughing in the car, some kisses to celebrate the news they probably knew already but hadn't dared share yet. A quick decision—*let's go tell Moxie in person*—that had blown up in their faces when they'd pulled in and found the one person who could turn this giddy moment into a guilt-and-anxiety fest without saying a word.

She might have felt sorry for them if she wasn't so thoroughly pissed. Ian had taken a huge step in coming back here. He needed to be reunited with his family, not just on the surface, but for real. How was that supposed to happen if these two kept upping the ante?

Maybe they had thought to share the news with Moxie and swear her to secrecy until after he was gone. Maybe. But now they were here, and even though Ian wasn't giving anything away, she was pretty sure he had figured things out almost as quickly as she and Moxie had. Which meant that his return was now about to be overshadowed and made even more nerve-racking.

Well, screw that.

"Oops. Hang on, Ian. I think someone got a little drool on you." She pulled a tissue from her pocket, stepped in front of him with her back to the rest and dabbed at his clean shirt while catching his eye.

Trust me, she mouthed.

Judging by the way his eyes widened, his memory had jumped to the precise point she had intended—straight to her backyard. Good. That would make it easier to make this look convincing.

"Isn't teething fun?" She dabbed once more, placed her palm on Ian's sun-warmed arm and smiled up at him. "Hope she didn't christen you too badly, hon."

Simple words. Almost as breezy as the kiss she bestowed on his jaw when she rose on tiptoe, a casual whisper of her lips across his jaw. But when she drew in a breath and turned back to face the audience, staying firmly pressed against his side, it was easy to see that she'd accomplished precisely what she had hoped.

Carter and Taylor watched with an intriguing blend of interest and relief. The wariness disappeared from his eyes, the worry from hers. A small smile touched Taylor's lips. Darcy could swear the other woman looked happy.

Okay. Her only intent had been to help Ian as he had helped her, to make it easier for everyone to move on. Cheater's happiness hadn't factored into the equation, but what the heck.

Then she looked at Moxie. Moxie, who watched the entire group with a focus that was almost as unsettling as the way Darcy's lips still tingled.

Of course, that easily could have been explained by the stubble on Ian's chin. It had been a long, long time since her lips had grazed stubble. She'd forgotten how potent it could be, how that slight scrape could linger against tender skin, teasing it to wakefulness.

Yeah. That was the only reason.

The moment was broken by the brisk clap of Moxie's hands. "Well, then. Let's not stand around here with our mouths open catching flies. Taylor, come to the kitchen with me. I need to go over some plans for Sunday with you. Carter, make yourself useful and help carry the bags inside. Put everything in Hank's suite. That will work best, I think." She shot Darcy a glance that could have subbed for an MRI. "Yes, I think that will work quite nicely."

If Darcy had ever wanted to know how it would feel to be hit by a truck, she was pretty sure she'd just gotten a decent indication as the implications of Moxie's words sank in. Her jaw sagged. Panic broke over her.

"Wait," she said. "No, that's—"

Carter spoke over her. "Moxie? Did I get that right?"

"You need me to break it down for you, Carter? Walk to the car. Grab a suitcase. Haul ass up to Hank's rooms and set the suitcase down."

Still pressed against Ian's side, Darcy had no problem feeling the deep breath he took. Kind of like the way someone might gasp before a wave crashed over them, she thought wildly.

"Mrs. North, hang on, Cady and I are staying—"

"Right here with us. It's what your grandmother would want." Moxie surveyed them all in a manner that could only be described as regal. "And since I know how fun it is to be in a strange house in the middle of the night with a little one, especially one who's teething, I'm not going to make life difficult for everyone by pretending I can't see what's as plain as the noses on all your silly faces. Now let's get moving. It's almost time for *Big Bang Theory*."

With that, she turned and marched toward the house. Taylor shook her head.

"Every time I think I have that woman figured out..." With a shrug, she smiled at Darcy. "It was very nice to meet you. I hope we'll get to spend some time together while you're here." She tapped Cady's arm. "You, too, sweetheart."

She departed with a quick wave, following in the direction Moxie had taken. The three remaining adults watched her departure in silence. Darcy, for one, needed a moment to process the neat way Moxie had twisted the entire situation with one statement. Thinking about that sure beat kicking herself for the way her impulsive good deed had circled back to bite her in the butt.

Ian glanced her way, his expression the careful shade of blank that he had worn when Xander was around. Oh, she had messed things up but good for him.

"Ian," she began, but a quick tip of his head in Carter's direction told her that he didn't want to discuss it now. Okay. Maybe she hadn't blown it completely. Maybe, just maybe, she had given him a leg up in the reunion stakes. Since that was all she had intended, well, perhaps this could work out somehow after all.

Yeah, and maybe Xander would fade back into the woodwork and her mother would swear off boy toys and Cady would miraculously cut all her teeth without shedding another tear.

"I'm not sure I believe this." Carter sounded as if he was doing his best not to laugh. "Did Moxie say she was putting the two of you in the same room?"

"Looks that way."

"Is this the same woman who threatened me with a belt when she caught me kissing Carole Merriweather in the kitchen after graduation?"

Ian shrugged, then did a double take. "Wait. You and Carole Merriweather?"

"For about three days after high school." Red rushed to stain Carter's cheeks. "I-it was at least a year after you dated her."

Holy crap. So Carter and Ian had dated the same girl in the past? The North brothers really had to reevaluate their definition of sharing.

Ian, however, didn't seem as flabbergasted as Darcy felt. He simply lowered Cady to the ground before heading to the Mustang and opening the trunk. Lulu trotted behind him. Darcy hesitated before joining the parade. She had a feeling that right now the best place for her was right at Ian's side.

"Here." He handed his suitcase to Carter. "Take this before Moxie comes out swinging."

"Good plan."

Darcy watched in amazement as Ian continued to haul items—hers and Cady's now—from the trunk. She bit her tongue until Carter was out of earshot before letting loose.

"Okay, for the record, I'm not staying here, and I'm definitely not sharing—"

"I know."

That helped. But why was he playing along?

"I know this is my fault," she continued, "and I'm sorry, but everything was so weird and all I could think of was how it worked with Xander, and I hoped, maybe, everyone could breathe and move on if they thought we were... But that's as far as it goes. I never intended for this." She gestured toward the neat line of bags, where Cady was happily drooling on a suitcase while Lulu did her best imitation of a bomb-sniffing dog.

"I know why you did it," he said. "It's okay. If you hadn't, I probably would have."

Only because things had been so strained, she knew. So her lips could stop tingling any moment now.

He bent to pull a rock from Cady's hand. Without looking up, he said quietly, "Taylor's pregnant, isn't she?"

Oh, hell. He had figured it out. "That's my bet." Her heart ached for him. "Are you okay?"

He seemed to be thinking over his answer. "Yeah," he said as he straightened, and she couldn't help but notice the edge of surprise in his voice. "Yeah. I would have thought... But it's okay. It's good."

Relief rolled through her. "I'm glad."

"Me, too."

Lulu, evidently bored with all the standing and talking, whined and ran toward the house.

"Think she's telling us to get moving?" Ian grabbed the portable crib.

"Probably." She sighed and looked toward the house. "Okay. I'm the one who messed up. Do you want me to go in there and tell the truth?"

"We probably should." But he sounded no more enthusiastic about the idea than she was. The memory of that awful tense silence made her shudder.

"Maybe," she said slowly, "maybe we could hold off on spilling the beans for the moment..."

"Until Taylor and Carter are gone?"

"That's exactly what I was thinking. Cady, don't eat that." She knelt to pull another rock from Cady's fist. "Let Carter and Taylor have their time, then come clean with Moxie after they leave. It will mean a little embarrassment down the line, but given the circumstances, I think they would understand."

If they didn't, she would happily remind them that they were the ones who had turned the family into Awkward Central in the first place.

And maybe she could find a way to get Ian and Carter alone together, if only for a few minutes. Because as furious as she was with Carter, Ian was the one who needed to talk to him, to put things on the table and find some new ground.

No matter what, Carter still was a member of the family. If he hadn't been drummed out by now, it wasn't going to happen—especially with a baby on the way. The only way Ian could resume his rightful place with the Norths would be to make it clear to everyone that he was not only over Taylor, he was over Carter.

Ian slapped his thigh for Lulu. "Okay. If you're okay with this, it works for me."

"Then let's do it. Go along with the line for now, tell the truth once they're gone, find a place for me and Cady."

His usual grin tugged at his lips. "I'm still selling tickets for that one. Especially now that Moxie can play the 'you lied to me' card."

"Excuse me? Weren't you listening when I told her that I wasn't going to promise to come back here before winter?"

"That was good, I agree. But she wasn't even trying then. She was just taking your measure, seeing what she had to work with."

"Well, she had better measure high, because much as I like you, Ian, there's no way I'm staying here tonight." Tingling lips be damned.

"Not that I'm on Moxie's side, Darce, but seriously?" He grinned and grabbed a bag. "This, I've got to see."

IAN HAD SPENT a good deal of time over the past months wondering how it would feel to walk back into the family homestead. He never had expected to do it while dodging a fur ball, lugging a portable crib and jiggling a baby who had decided that his nose made a great teething toy.

"Ow!" His howl of pain was muffled by Cady's chin in his mouth. "Cady, no!"

He came to a dead stop in the hall. He didn't dare go farther, not with Lulu doing laps around his legs and his vision blocked by a tiny face. Darcy was behind him. Her laughter pealed around him.

"Hang on," she gasped. "I'll be right—"

A few maneuvers and an unsettling amount of giggles later, he was free—not that Cady seemed too happy about it.

"Shh, killer," Darcy said. "Mommy will find you something else to bite on."

"Don't mind me. I'll just stand here and bleed." He was pretty sure he was speaking to the walls at this point—hard to tell, what with the way his eyes were watering—but apart from wondering if his nose was still intact, he was surprisingly cheerful. He was in the house. He'd survived the first reunion with Carter and Taylor. He hadn't even been thrown by the probably pregnant thing.

Maybe he could do this after all.

"Hey, Ian. You need some ice for where that mean old baby bit you?'

That was Carter, and the son of a bitch seemed to be laughing as he walked down the stairs.

"Very funny." Ian blinked to clear his vision—damn, those little teeth were sharp—and focused on the dog. "Lulu, sit."

She did, for about a half second before popping back up to sniff Moxie's feet.

"That dog is going to have to learn some manners if you expect her to stay in this house, Ian."

God help Lulu if Moxie decided to reform her.

"Lulu will be fine once she gets the feel of the place."

"Well, we'll give her a little longer." Moxie gave him a sideways look. "'Course, training a dog is a lot like teaching a baby, and it doesn't look like you're earning any gold stars for that right now, either."

"Hey," he began, but Darcy cut him off.

"Ian is amazing with both Lulu and Cady. They hang on everything he says. He can make Cady stop crying just by walking into the room, and as for Lulu, well, you should see how he's trained her to follow his instructions when he's working around the forge. He keeps her perfectly safe with nothing more than a word. Believe me, once Lulu has a chance to run off the trip, he'll have her behaving perfectly."

Her smile was meant to soften her words, he knew, but his mouth wasn't the only one left hanging slightly open at the way she'd rushed to his defense. It was almost enough to make him hope she lost to Moxie when it came time to confess and find another place to stay.

Almost.

But as unexpectedly comforting as it was to

have Darcy running interference between him and everyone else, she was right. They couldn't share a room. He couldn't even think about sharing the big king bed that he knew was in Hank's suite. *That* thought made him even dizzier than he'd felt when Cady's teeth had sunk into his nose.

"Now," Darcy continued, bright and sunny as always despite the child crying in her arms, "if someone could direct me to the kitchen, I think we'll all be safer from Hannibal Lecter here if I get some food into her."

"It's this way," said Taylor, pointing down the hall. "Do you need any of these bags?"

"The pink diaper bag, please. Ian, are you and Carter okay with everything else?"

Wait a minute. Darcy had had her claws pointed in Carter's direction since last night's confession. And now she was suggesting that they do this together, just the two of them? His arms tensed. Sure, things were easier than he'd expected, but that didn't mean he was ready to be alone with Carter. Maybe Darcy had meant...

But no. This would have to happen sooner or later. If he moved back and took the job, he would have to work with Carter regularly. Might as well start off the way he intended to go, as the saying went.

"We're fine," he said at last. "You go ahead and take care of the Bug. I've got this covered."

He grabbed Darcy's bag. Carter hefted the crib.

"Correction. *We've* got this covered."

Oh, crap.

With a last glance at Darcy—who seemed far too willing to be swept into the kitchen on a wave of estrogen—he whistled for the dog.

"Upstairs, Lulu," he said to the panting bundle of fur. She immediately trotted ahead of him.

"Whoa. Darcy wasn't lying. She really does listen to you."

"You don't have to sound quite so amazed." Ian kept the words light but refrained from adding the *dumbass* that he would have tacked on without thought in the old days. Not yet.

"Still can't believe Moxie unbent enough to put you both in here," Carter said as he set down the crib at the entrance to the room.

"Yeah, well, you never can predict what people are going to do, can you?"

He'd meant it to be innocent. Truly. But the way Carter grimaced was proof that he hadn't interpreted the words that way.

"Ian," he said, his gaze fixed on the patch of sunlight streaming through the stained glass window on the landing. "I-it's good to have you back. It's been killing Mom, having you gone, especially the way things, you know, shook out. Dad doesn't say much. Sometimes, though, I know he's thinking… Anyway, I know it had to be hard for you to come back, and I just want to say, you know, if you need us to stay away, or lay low, whatever, say the word. Whatever we can do to make this easier for you."

Well, that wasn't a speech Ian had expected to hear. And even though he knew he should do the big and generous thing and assure Carter that all was well, he found he wasn't quite ready to say those words. Maybe because it was too early in his trip. Maybe because hearing Darcy rush to his defense had felt so good that he wanted to see if it would happen a few more times before he did the Mr. Forgiving thing.

"Thanks," he said after a second. "I'm okay. You don't need to do anything different because I'm around."

"If that changes—"

"Right. I'll let you know."

Carter's grin was more like his usual one. "'Course, I have a feeling that if I step out of line, even by mistake, Darcy will grab me by the ear and drag me down to the river and boot my ass into the water faster than I could say I'm sorry."

Now, there was a picture Ian liked. A lot.

"I think you might have that one right," was all he trusted himself to say, before adding, "What's up with Hank and Cash these days?"

Discussing their brothers was safe. Still, Ian didn't linger, but walked slowly to the stairs as they talked. Misery wasn't the only emotion that loved company.

"Cash—who knows? He's always at work or out

with a tourist, but Ma thinks he has a secret life. You know, an online girlfriend, an illegal hobby, whatever."

Great. Just what this family needed—more secrets.

"Hank, though, no mysteries there. He doesn't have time. Running the cabins keeps him hopping. But he's happy. Marrying Brynn was the best thing he ever did. He even laughed out loud the other day."

"I thought the youngest kid was supposed to be the wildest. When did he turn into the boring one?"

Carter snorted. "I don't know how to tell you this, Ian, but rumor has it we're *all* boring ones these days. I mean, look at us. Kids and wives and—"

Carter must have realized that he was heading down a road best left untraveled, for when the sudden silence made Ian glance over his shoulder, he saw his brother frozen on the stairs, his mouth clamped shut and his expression unreadable.

Ian drew in a deep breath, hoping to channel some of that okay-ness that he'd felt earlier, but it seemed to have slipped out the door. Maybe he just wasn't ready to be buddies with Carter again. Maybe he wasn't over things as much as he'd thought.

Maybe he and Darcy should speed up the confession before everyone got too comfortable and forgot that, in some ways, the past wasn't all that long ago.

CHAPTER SEVEN

DARCY HAD GROWN UP learning to read emotions and react accordingly. She had made a career out of anticipating her mother's needs and ensuring they were met even before Sylvie articulated them. But she had no idea how to read and measure someone who was doing the same to her, and who had a good forty-plus years experience in doing just that.

Taylor had politely asked about the drive and the baby while leading Darcy into the sunshiny kitchen overflowing with light wood cabinets, white furniture and touches of bright yellow. But no sooner had Darcy opened the container of Cady's favorite chunky beef and vegetables—the mess Ian referred to as the Hangover Special—than Taylor turned green, excused herself and dashed from the room.

"Wuss," Darcy proclaimed in a soft voice to Cady. Usually she had nothing but empathy for the less-than-joyful symptoms of pregnancy, but this time she felt that excessive nausea, bloating and fatigue were simply karma. "Maybe we should make sure we slip her a diaper or two, huh, Bug?"

"I don't remember you having such a vindictive streak when you were a girl."

Crap. Busted.

Moxie approached with her arms crossed and the ultimate poker face.

There were two ways to play this. Darcy could choose to fall over herself with apologies and justifications—or she could make her position clear from the start.

"I don't think it's vindictive to want to see some balancing of the scales."

"Is that what you're here for?"

Darcy shrugged and focused on fastening a bib behind a bobbing neck while keeping little fists out of the bowl. Not an easy feat with one hand.

"I'm here because my grandmother isn't home. Other than that, I have no agenda."

"Really?"

"Really." The Velcro closings on the bib finally connected. Darcy spooned up some food and slipped it into Cady's mouth. "Here you go, big girl."

"Interesting that after all this time, you suddenly show up with Ian."

How to handle that one without telling the truth? "As I said outside, I know I should visit more often, but I'm sure you understand that it was easier to make the trip with someone else."

"I'll grant you that one." Moxie lowered herself into a chair across the table. "But I get the feeling there's more to it than that."

It would be wrong to tell this woman, who was

opening her home to Cady and her, to mind her own business. There was drawing a line, and there was plain rudeness. Not that Moxie seemed to be differentiating between them, but still. It was always better to take the high road.

Darcy decided to let the implied question pass unanswered, focusing instead on Cady, who was doing her best to dive off Darcy's knee and bury her face in the bowl of slop.

"She wants to feed herself," Moxie said.

"I know. At home I let her have her own spoon and some finger food, but I didn't want our first minutes here to end up with your kitchen decorated in beef glop."

The corner of Moxie's mouth twitched. "This room has seen worse than that over the years. I'll have Ian bring the high chair up from the basement. She's a fine baby. She shouldn't have to stifle herself for us."

"Thank you." The mention of a high chair and all it implied created a lump in her gut, but nothing could be done about it at the moment. She hoped to hell that Taylor and Carter weren't planning to stay a long time tonight. The sooner she and Ian could get the truth on the table, the better for everyone.

"Could you grab that pack of wipes from my bag and hand me one, please?"

Moxie rose from her chair and did as requested, lingering for a moment and making fluttering motions with her fingers. Cady's eyes followed the movements in fascination.

"Anything you need, let me know. I don't want this little one having a hard time because you don't want to speak up." Moxie tapped Cady's cheek with one finger, earning a wide-eyed stare. "And I know it's rough when they're teething. Don't you worry about keeping people awake in the night. My room's down here, and as for Ian's folks, well, I think it'll take another decade or two for Robert and Janice to catch up on the sleep they lost when the boys were little. You wouldn't disturb them unless you marched into their room and dropped the baby on the bed beside them."

Darcy repressed a shudder. "Not planning on doing that, thank you."

"There's a mini fridge in your rooms. I'll put some juice and such in it. If you're up with her in the night and need anything else, there's tea and cocoa in that cupboard." Moxie pointed above the double sink. "Cheerios down there if she wants a snack, and you can help yourself to anything in the fridge. Or freezer. One good thing about working at a dairy is we always have milk and ice cream in the house."

"Sounds lovely. I hope we won't need any of it, but it's good to know just in case."

"Prepare for the worst, hope for the best. That's the way to go." Moxie returned to her chair. "Now, then, how long have you and Ian been together?"

Crap, crap, crap. Where the heck was he?

"I—"

"Because it's interesting that he never mentioned it."

Ooh, that one she could handle. "Given the way his last relationship blew up in his face, I don't think it's unreasonable at all."

Moxie shook her head. "You don't mince words, do you?"

"Actually, I'm usually very mild-mannered."

"Are you, now?"

Cady chose that moment to smack her hands together, sending bits of glop flying through the air. Darcy would never have imagined she would welcome being showered with goo, but it seemed there was indeed a first time for everything.

"She has your eyes." Moxie, who of course was untouched by the spray, sat back and grinned. "But her mouth...not yours. Does she favor her father?"

Good Lord. Was there any topic that Moxie couldn't twist into a land mine?

"So, did Nonny go on this cruise by herself?"

Was that a chuckle?

"Nope," Moxie said at last. "There's a group from church that went together, and a few others from the senior center. I thought for sure she would have told you about it."

"She might have mentioned it." Probably had, too. But Darcy spoke to Nonny so infrequently these days that it could have been months since their last real conversation. Part of it, of course, was simply the hectic pace of Darcy's life now that Cady was on the scene.

But Darcy couldn't deny that lately, every interaction with Nonny was spent braced for—not attack, never that—but there had been a major shift in their relationship ever since the call when Darcy had said, "I'm pregnant," and Nonny had uttered a low, disappointed, "Oh, Darcy."

Yep, that had been just the response she needed when she was already dealing with guilt and worry and other fun.

But there was no way Darcy would dare say anything against Nonny to Moxie, of all people.

"I wish I had remembered about this trip." She dabbed at Cady's chin. "But it sounds like something she's dreamed of for years. I'm sorry to have missed her, but I would have hated to make her lose out on this."

"Oh?"

"Well, yes. I mean, she's the reason I came." One of the reasons anyway.

Moxie made *Eensy Weensy Spider* motions with her fingers, prompting Cady to stop eating and stare. "Since you seem to appreciate plain talk, Darcy, that's what I'm going to give you. I think Helene told you all about the cruise. Lord knows it's all she's talked about for months. You might think you didn't know about it, but I'm betting if you stopped and thought a minute, you'd remember something."

Darcy stopped waving the spoon in front of Cady's face and gave Moxie her full attention. "Are you saying that you think I chose this time deliberately, because I knew Nonny wouldn't be around?"

"I wouldn't say it was deliberate. But I wouldn't say it was a total coincidence, either."

Thank heaven Taylor returned at that moment, a little whiter but smiling nonetheless. "Well, I'm back. Did I miss any excitement?"

Only if she thought the Inquisition was nothing more than a fact-finding mission.

"All better?" Moxie asked.

"Fine." Taylor reached toward Cady before hesitating, her hand hovering in the air. "Oh, listen, I don't... I'm not contagious or anything. I swear she won't catch anything from me, but you know, I had something for lunch that didn't sit quite right and—"

"Taylor." Moxie's smile was probably as close to indulgent as she ever came. "You don't have to spin stories. We understand perfectly. Congratulations, child."

"Oh." Some of the color returned to Taylor's cheeks. "Oh. I... Well... When we pulled in and saw Ian, I..."

Darcy probably should add her own good wishes, but, honestly, she wasn't feeling that generous yet.

The best she could manage was a semi-sincere, "It gets better."

She really should have stayed home and dealt with Xander herself.

"Well, Cady." Time to switch to distraction mode. "Looks like you had a great time smearing your food. I think we should change you into something not so disgusting."

"Good thinking." Moxie tapped Cady's nose. "Your room is up the stairs, second door on the—"

"I'll take her."

Of course Ian and Carter showed up now. Men. Could they never time things properly?

Cady squealed and held up her arms. Ian reached, did a double take and retreated.

"Forget it, Bug. Let's keep the mess confined to one adult for now."

"Oh, thanks, hon. You really know how to make a girl feel pretty."

His grin was entirely too wicked. "Don't worry, Darce. On you, even the Hangover Special looks good."

He was playing the part, she knew, embroidering the fabric of the farce. Still, his words left her feeling a little lighter and a lot less uncertain.

"Is there a broom handy so I can sweep up the mess?"

Moxie waved a hand. "Not to worry. Carter, get your arse in gear and clean this up. You two run along and get that girl presentable."

Ha. Darcy bit back a snicker at the expression on Carter's face as he took in the mess on the table and floor. Maybe there were some perks to being here after all.

"HERE YOU GO."

Holding Cady at arm's length, Darcy brushed past Ian and into a room that could only be described as beckoning. A white comforter atop a king-size maple bed and white eyelet curtains at the bay window were warmed by splashes of poppy red in the quilt folded at the foot of the mattress, the throw pillows resting against the mound of fluffy white ones, the cushion on the window seat.

"There's a bathroom through there." Ian pointed to the door to the left. "But come here, because I think…"

She followed him through a narrow space that felt like a former closet, now set up as a kitchenette with a few cupboards, a microwave and the fridge Moxie had mentioned, opening into another room that obviously had been a nursery at one point. Either that or Hank had a thing for butterflies and teddy bears.

"Wow. What a great setup." Her gaze lingered on the rocking chair, the toddler bed, the ducky-adorned chest of drawers. "Maybe you should stay someplace else while Cady and I set up shop here. Where's Lulu?"

"I put her on a long leash on the clothesline. Figured she should run some more." He opened the top drawer of the dresser. "Ah, just as I thought," he said, pulling a foam rubber pad from the drawer and setting it on top of the dresser. "Voilà. Instant changing table."

"Perfect." She set Cady on the softened surface. Predictable wails followed. "Shh. You're fine. Someday you'll learn to eat neatly and then we won't have to change your clothes after every meal."

Ian tapped Cady's nose. "Don't listen to her, Bug. Sloppy eating is one of the biggest joys in life."

"Very funny. How long do you think Carter and Taylor will stay?"

"Honestly, Moxie's probably going to invite them to dinner."

"Really? On your first night home?"

He handed her a wipe. "Moxie is from the 'rip the bandage off in one yank' school. She won't push anyone into anything she doesn't think they're ready for, but she doesn't coddle, either."

"I never would have guessed." She peeled off beef-encrusted rumba pants and handed them over. "So, speaking of yanking things, how did you survive your first time alone with Carter?"

"Fine."

Okay. Clipped tones, crossed arms—yep, someone was definitely holding back. A change of topic might be in order.

"By the way, the pregnancy cat is sort of out of the bag."

"Yeah?"

"Yeah." She grabbed one flailing arm and attacked it with a wipe. "I think the pretense was mostly for your benefit."

He blew out a long breath. "I figured. Did you say anything?"

"Nope. I was too busy dodging Moxie's questions and staying in character. Besides, that should come from you, not me."

"I think it falls in the fake-girlfriend job description."

"Uh-uh. I deal with my family. You deal with yours."

"But yours is out of town."

"Sucks to be you."

His retort was cut off by three short beeps from her phone. She blew a kiss on Cady's tummy, tucked her fresh clothes back in place and handed her to Ian. "Can you walk her for a minute?"

"Sure." Her pinkie brushed his palm. The contact lasted maybe one, one and a half seconds, but it was all it took to send her tripping back to the kiss in the yard, the laughter in the car, the way his hand had curved around her waist when she launched them on this foolishness today.

For a moment or two her breath didn't seem to want to follow its usual pattern.

She stepped back, moving toward sanity and away from areas best left unexplored, even in her mildest thoughts.

Focus, Maguire. Read the text.

But one look at the message and she was almost ready to take her chances with her runaway libido again.

"Are you frickin' kidding me?"

"What?"

"Xander. He's here. In Comeback Cove."

"What?"

She showed him the message.

"'Hi, Darce,'" he read aloud, his disbelief growing more apparent with each word. "'I was at loose ends and didn't want to wait to see Cady again, so here I am. Don't want to intrude but can we set up a time to meet? And does Ian know a cheap place where I can stay?'"

She shoved the phone into her pocket and closed her eyes, hunting for stability while the world spun around her. Ian's hand on her shoulder wasn't the solution she would have expected, but it helped all the same. She rested her head against his chest. Not the smartest move, she knew, but with panic building, she figured it was better to grab an anchor than let herself be swept away.

"You okay?"

"Honestly? No. This is all… I don't know. Too much. Forty-eight hours ago he didn't even know she existed, and now he's following us up here and asking to see her? It's… I know it's probably better for him to be interested in her than to brush her off, but, really, this has me rattled." She pushed out the rest of it. "Especially because he has every right to see her."

"You don't know that for sure."

"I spent a lot of quality time on Google last night, Ian. He has as much right to Cady as I do."

"Even though he wasn't around for the first year?"

"Put it this way. I don't think any judge would say, 'Oh, hey, congratulations on meeting your child and you can now have her every Wednesday and alternate weekend.' But he's entitled to spend time with her and get to know her and work up to those regular visits."

Ian squeezed her shoulder. "It's only for a few days," he said softly.

"What do you mean?"

"He said he has a job in cottage country, remember? Starting next week."

"Oh, wow. I forgot that part. You're right." She stood a little straighter, peeled herself away from Ian's side. She really had to stop touching him. "Okay. That helps. I mean, yes, this is a lifelong thing, but you're right. All I have to do is get through this week, and then we—*I*—will get some breathing space."

"Is that what you want?"

She thought it over. "You know me. I can handle anything as long as I have time to plan. So if all I have to do is muddle through these few days, then I'll have time to sort out what happens next…"

"I can't believe I'm saying this, but do you want me to talk to Carter?"

Carter?

"You said he doesn't do that kind of law."

"He doesn't, but he probably studied family law at some point. If nothing else he'll have a better idea of where to search than we do. Plus, he's here."

"Any port in a storm?"

"I wouldn't put it that way. But Xander's going to expect an answer soon."

Oh, hell, Ian was right. She could only stall so long, especially as Xander needed a place to stay.

And maybe talking about her mess would be like a first stop in discussing other messes. Kind of an opening line, so to speak.

"Maybe, since Carter is still here…"

His nod was short and tight, but it was a start.

"Meanwhile, can you recommend a place for him to crash for the night?"

This was going to play hell with her plan to duck out ASAP. If she stayed someplace else, Xander probably would want to go to the same spot—unless she chose something out of his price range. Trouble was that she couldn't afford much herself. But if she hopped the bus back home it would look as though she was trying to avoid him. Or he would offer to drive her back, which made sense on the surface, but since the mere thought made her start to hyperventilate, she figured it was probably a bad idea.

Ian snorted. "Right now my suggestion would be that he turn around and go home. But I'll ask Moxie."

"Ask me what?"

Darcy jerked farther away from Ian and whirled around, searching for the source of the all-too-satisfied voice.

"Damn it, Moxie." Ian pulled Cady's fists from his hair. "What are you, part cat? How can you sneak up on people like that?"

"What do you think? Years of practice. Now, what do you need to ask me?"

"You mean you weren't eavesdropping through the whole conversation?"

Moxie didn't even pretend to look innocent. "It's my house, mister. If I want to be a good hostess and come upstairs to check on my guests, put some juice and cookies in their fridge, then I think you should be saying thank you instead of getting on your high horse."

"The room is lovely." That, at least, Darcy could say without lying. "I think you've thought of everything."

"Is that so?"

"Here we go." Ian's mutter sent Darcy's suspicion level soaring.

Moxie glared at him. "'Cause it sounds to me like you could use a hamburger or two."

"I don't—"

"To go with the pickle you've got yourself in."

Shouldn't those words have been said with sympathy instead of glee?

"Moxie—" Ian began, but was promptly shushed by his grandmother.

"Now listen. I wasn't trying to eavesdrop, believe it or not, but I heard enough to guess that you're having some kind of legal trouble. Leastways that's what it sounds like if you're looking to Carter for help."

"It's nothing horrible. Really." Because in the grand scheme of things, Darcy reminded herself, it could be far, far worse.

Moxie rolled her eyes as if to say that she would be the judge of that. "I heard you talking about Xander. Is that the fella you knew back in university, Ian?"

"Right. He—"

When he hesitated and caught her eye, Darcy knew he was seeking her permission to continue. Great. Maybe they could take out a billboard that said Darcy Maguire Is Easy When She's Drunk.

She took Cady from Ian. "How about we go downstairs, pull Carter in and do all the explanations at once."

"This had better be good," Moxie said. "I already missed *Big Bang*, and now it's almost time for *Jeopardy*."

"You're getting the scoop before my own grand-mother."

"Is that so?" Moxie's grin was almost frightening. "Well, then, give me a minute to grab some paper and a pen. I might have to take notes on this one."

CHAPTER EIGHT

CRAZY AS IT had been to imagine himself coming home and talking with Carter and Taylor within the first fifteen minutes of his arrival, Ian found this even more unimaginable: sitting in Moxie's sunporch with an untouched beer at his side, watching Darcy calmly explain the Xander predicament to his openmouthed family.

His parents had arrived home as he'd carried Cady downstairs. Once they finished staring, they had fallen all over themselves to welcome Darcy and Cady, especially after Carter made a crack about Moxie getting racy in her old age and putting them all in Hank's suite. Ian thought his mother had been close to whiplash with the way her head had swung back and forth, looking from him to Moxie to Darcy to Carter to Taylor and back again. Then she had taken a deep breath, focused on Cady and broken into the most hopeful smile he had seen in years.

Of course, that would have been a lot easier to enjoy if he hadn't known it was based on a lie.

Ma was already three-quarters of the way in love with Cady. As for Darcy, that was harder to tell, but from the growing respect on his mother's face as Darcy spelled out the situation, he predicted she would be in Ma's good books before sundown. By the end of the visit, Ma would have the wedding planned and be picking out new colors for Hank's old rooms in preparation for the future grandchildren she would saddle with nicknames from her favorite country music singers. She was going to be crushed when the truth came out.

Dad would nod and carry on. Disappointed? Most likely. Like any parent he wanted his sons to be happy. But it wouldn't hit him where he lived.

Ma was a different story.

After Taylor had broken their engagement, after Ian had picked himself up only to be slammed by the second wave of Carter's involvement, after he'd made the decision to come back to Canada instead of staying in Tanzania—after all that he had come back to this house. He'd walked in, Ma had taken one look, and for the first time in his life, he had seen Janice North fall apart. Not for herself. For him.

Ian had thought he couldn't find any new way to hurt, but watching his mother crying over him had pulled new bits of his heart forward to be ripped and freshened his desire to beat the living shit out of his brother. If Carter had walked in at that moment Ian couldn't have guaranteed they both would have walked out alive. It had been the ugliest moment of his life.

And now Ian was going to hurt her.

It wouldn't be as bad this time. She would understand once everything came out. But he felt like ten kinds of wrong to sit and watch and listen silently, knowing what was coming down the pike.

Darcy had stopped talking. At some point in the conversation she had slipped her hand into his. Or maybe it had been the other way around? It didn't matter. It was all part of the act, the story Darcy had instigated to ease him back into his family. Her heart had been in the right place, but he had to stop it before things got out of control. Before anyone else got hurt. Before he let himself get too familiar with the feel of her hand in his.

"So let me get this straight." Moxie, as always, was the first to speak. "You had a pity party with Xander, you got pregnant, he went to jail and now he's back stirring up a hornet's nest."

"That's about it," Darcy said.

"Talk about a smelly kettle of fish." Moxie leveled a finger in Ian's direction. He wouldn't have been surprised if a lightning bolt had shot out. "Where do you stand in all this, mister?"

This was his chance. But even as he loosened his grip on Darcy's hand, Carter spoke.

"Legally, Ian has no say. It's all between Darcy and Xander."

"What about Lulu?" Darcy said, and before he had the chance to second-guess himself, he squeezed her fingers. Only she would remember the dog in the middle of this.

"Whole different issue." Carter frowned. "Since Xander doesn't seem to be pressing that at the moment, I suggest we focus on the fact that he's here and wants to see Cady."

"He can't just walk in and start making demands, can he?" Taylor scooped Cady's rattle from the floor and held it out to her. "Surely Darcy is entitled to want some time for everyone to get to know each other."

"He can't expect to take her for solo visits immediately, no. But he has the right to spend time with her."

Funny how, even though Ian had known that, it was like a fresh kick in the gut to hear it coming from someone speaking from the perspective of the law. Though maybe that was because of the way Darcy's fingernails were cutting into his palm.

"Xander hasn't done anything to make you think he would be a danger to the child," Carter said. "Correct?"

"No," Darcy said slowly. "And to be clear, I don't want to stand in the way of him getting to know her, especially since he'll be a good distance away from her soon. But the way he followed us up here...part of me says, 'Oh, good. He's excited to be part of her life.' Part of me is kind of leery."

Moxie snorted. "You and me both, sister."

"Ian?" Carter focused on him. "You've known him longer than anyone else. What do you think?"

He picked his words carefully, trying to remain objective.

"When he showed up, he insisted that Lulu was the key to his new life. Now I think that's what he sees in Cady. He said himself, he doesn't know a lot about kids, so I think right now she's more a symbol to him than anything else."

Ma scowled. "Not that every parent doesn't think that way at times, but that's no way to begin. He should want to be with her because she's wonderful and amazing and he can't wait to learn everything about her." She bent down to smile at Cady. "Isn't that right, baby girl?"

"Yeah, well, in fairness," Ian continued. "He only found out about her yesterday. It's not like he's had time to get to know her for herself. His showing up here could be just because he wants to do that."

"You said he'll be leaving Stratford next week?" Carter asked.

"Right. At least, I think so." Darcy bumped her shoulder against his. "You were more coherent than I was. That is what he said, right…hon?"

She had added the endearment as an afterthought, he could tell, but it still sent unanticipated warmth humming through him—warmth that couldn't be stopped no matter how sternly he reminded himself this was all for show.

"He didn't mention a date. But I got the impression his time in Stratford is limited."

"So he might be guilty of nothing more than wanting to get to know her while he has the chance," Carter said. "No one could fault him for that."

Dad spoke up for the first time. "You're saying Darcy has to accommodate him."

"It would be the wisest course."

Darcy sagged ever so slightly against Ian's arm. She pulled away quickly, almost before he'd registered the touch, but it had been there. And even though he knew the relationship they were presenting was a sham, the brief connection served as another reminder. The romance might be fake but their friendship was real. She needed someone. He could still be the shoulder for her to lean on, a bridge to carry her through this. For that he was grateful.

His brief peace was pierced by Moxie's sudden cackle.

"I have an idea," she said, and years of past experience had him sitting straighter. It was all he could do to keep from sniffing the air like a groundhog checking for danger.

"You ever hear the old saying about keeping your friends close but your enemies closer?"

Darcy nodded. Probably a mistake, but she didn't know better than to encourage Moxie.

"You—" Moxie pointed at Darcy "—want to do the right thing while watching out for your little one.

You—" now she leveled her finger at Ian "—want to look after your family."

His *what*?

"Whoa," he said. "Time-out. Before we go any further, I—"

But Moxie barreled right over his words. "So I say Xander should come stay here."

There wasn't a boxer in the world who could sucker punch as efficiently as Moxie.

"Excuse me?" Darcy's question was more squeaked than voiced. Across the room, Ma shook her head. Dad wore the bemused grin that meant he'd been bested once again. Taylor stared at Moxie as if she couldn't believe her ears.

Carter simply nodded.

"That could work," Carter said.

"I'm sorry. I don't…" Darcy took Ian's hand once more. "You think that the way to handle this is by bringing Xander here?"

"Isn't that what I just said? Honestly, girl. Helene never said anything about you having trouble hearing."

"That's enough, Moxie."

It wasn't until Ma's eyes widened that Ian truly grasped what he had said. He had reprimanded Moxie, the least milk-and-cookies grandmother who ever walked the planet.

Carter snorted. Probably trying to hold back laughter, the bastard.

"Ian Tyson North, are you going to sit there on

my sofa, in my home, and tell me what I should or shouldn't say?"

"Only if he has a death wish," Carter said in an undertone. Damned lawyers. They always had to add their two cents.

But there was no denying that Moxie had been out of line.

"You have the right to say anything you want," he said quietly. "It's a free country. But it wouldn't hurt any of you to remember that Darcy has had a lot thrown at her in the last couple of days."

"Is that so?" Moxie was giving him the steady, narrow-eyed gaze that had always made him and his brothers say she should have signed on with the local police as their resident Bad Cop.

But he was no lawbreaker. Nor was he her employee or even living in the same town at the moment. Darcy and Cady weren't his *family*, as Moxie had tossed out so casually, but they were here at his instigation. No one was going to make them feel uncomfortable on his watch.

"I see where you're coming from," he said. "But it's not always easy to follow the way your mind works, Moxie. Darcy has every right to want more explanation, and she deserves to get it without being made to feel like she's said something stupid."

"Hear, hear." Dad raised his lemonade in Ian's direction. Darcy squeezed his fingers.

"I'm okay," she said to the room at large. "And really, I am pretty adaptable. But Ian is right in say-

ing the last day or two have left me spinning. I'm
not operating at peak efficiency, so if you would
be patient with me, I'd be grateful."

*That's my girl. Give it back without letting them
know they—*

Hang on. *My girl?* What the hell was he thinking? All the fake togetherness was messing with
his brain. Time to end the act.

He pulled his fingers free. "You know, before
we get back to this—"

"Fair enough."

Good God, would Moxie ever shut up and let
him finish a sentence? And for the love of all that
was holy, could she wipe that satisfied smirk from
her face?

"Here's what I'm thinking." She carried on as
if no one had either rebuked her or dared to speak
without her permission. "If that Xander comes and
stays here, he'll have time with the child and can't
say anything about you not doing your best."

"Which could be important, given the fact that
he didn't know about her for so long," Carter added.
"You don't want anyone to be able to say, 'Oh, she's
throwing up roadblocks, trying to keep him from
his daughter.' The fact that he didn't know of her
existence until he literally stumbled across her—
that could be played against you. It's better to bend
over backward now."

Moxie crossed her arms over her chest. "As I
was saying, he would get to know little Cadence

while you're beside him to keep an eye on things. The rest of us will be here, too, to keep things from being too awkward, and so Mr. Caveman over there doesn't rip any heads off."

Ian shook his head. Was Moxie talking about *him*?

"At the same time," Moxie continued, "Xander seems to be looking at this whole parenthood thing through some rainbows. A few days of changing diapers and getting up at night with a little one who's cutting teeth would help him see what he's really in for."

"Darce?" Ian waited until she twisted to face him. He knew what she would say—it was too much, too fast, too disruptive. He needed her to block out everything else and everyone else and focus on the only thing that mattered.

"Forget Xander and all of us and even you. Think about Cady. This could be your best shot at handling the introductions your way."

She searched his face. Some of the doubt leached from her eyes.

"You have a point." She spoke slowly and glanced around the room. "But I— Dear heavens, you already are going out of your way to take in Cady and me. I can't ask you to house Xander, too."

"Why not?" Dad's voice was as mild as always. "He came to visit a few times when he and Ian were rooming together. This isn't that different."

Yeah, it was. But it was damned decent of his father to put it that way.

That, he realized, was the big reason why he wanted to make this visit work, to make this job work: to be back with the people he knew and who knew him the way no one else ever would. He had good friends in a lot of places. But nothing was the same as being with family, with the people who knew when you were lying through your teeth but understood why and opted to let it go. That only came with a lifetime of togetherness. He hadn't realized how much he had missed it until now, when it was dangling in front of him again.

"This house is big enough that we could take in Xander and half of his prison buddies." Moxie seemed to reconsider. "You did say he was the peaceable type, right, Ian?"

"Cyber crimes only, Moxie. Unless he's changed drastically in the last two years, I can give you my word that he won't steal anything or murder anyone in their sleep."

"Oh, that was reassuring," Ma said drily before pressing her fingers to her lips and glancing apologetically at Darcy. "That was a joke. I'm sorry. I didn't mean—"

"Not to worry." Darcy was starting to sound more like her resilient self. "Contrary to what Ian thinks sometimes, I'm not some delicate hothouse flower." She peeked up at him with a teasing kind of grin that implied all kinds of inside jokes. He'd smiled back down at her before he even knew it. "I find it's better to bring things out in the open than to walk around dodging elephants."

"Then that's settled." Moxie pushed to her feet, the queen dismissing her subjects. "Give Xander a call and tell him there's a room waiting. And let him know there's chicken and dumplings for dinner. As I recall, that was one of his favorites when he visited before."

"Thank you all," Darcy said as the adults stood. "You've made a confusing situation a lot less overwhelming. I'm grateful to all of you and to Ian for insisting I come here."

"Oh, for pity's sake, girl. You're family now. This is just what family does."

Confusion flitted across Darcy's face for the briefest of seconds until she laughed. "Well, then, I guess I'm doubly lucky." She patted his cheek. "Thanks again, sweetie."

He squeezed her hand, bent to pick up Cady's stacking cups and froze.

Xander was going to be staying at the house. Xander, who was the reason he and Darcy were pretending to be involved in the first place. Which meant that the farce might have to be carried on for a bit longer.

Which meant that he and Darcy would be sharing a room after all. A room with one big, inviting king-size bed.

Oh, holy shit.

DARCY WAITED UNTIL Ian returned from getting Lulu before lifting Cady and saying, loud enough to carry, "Oops, I think it's diaper time. Can you give me a hand with her, Ian?"

"Sure thing."

They ascended the stairs silently. Well, except for Cady, who was not happy about being removed from the activities on the main floor and was doing her level best to break her mother's eardrums.

Lulu, that most adaptable of creatures, scooted ahead of them once they reached the top and pattered to the correct door, where she plopped on her behind and gave them a look that said, *Would one of you please put those opposable thumbs to work?*

The minute they were inside the room—with the door closed and, Darcy ensured, locked—she set Cady on the bed and turned to Ian.

"Does the door to the other room lock, too?"

"I'll check."

She pulled her phone from her pocket, debating texting Xander right away while Ian was busy, but decided it could wait a few more minutes. She didn't want the impending conversation to be interrupted by anyone.

She kicked off her sandals and sat on the edge of the bed. The big, cushy bed. The only one in the room.

Oh, God. She couldn't sit here. It was too much of a preview.

But though her legs twitched and tightened, she

stayed put. She would get through this. They were going to talk it over like adults, and they would come up with a solution, and soon this would be nothing more than something to look back on with laughter. Kind of like the time last summer when Ian had walked into the backyard and caught her naked from the waist up because it was a hot day and she thought he was at work and she was too damned tired to nurse discreetly.

Though now that she thought about it, neither of them had ever mentioned that again.

Cady crawled over to Darcy and grinned. Darcy flicked away a line of drool with her thumb before cupping her precious girl's chin in her hand.

"You're worth whatever I have to do to make this work." She wasn't sure if the words were for her daughter or herself, but they made Cady giggle and bounce, which made her own heart a little lighter. So, bonus.

"All set."

Ian's words brought her back to the matter at hand. Damn. She had been so close to forgetting for a moment or two.

"Let me guess." He lounged in the doorway, a hint of a smile tugging at his lips. "You don't trust Moxie to keep from sneaking in and eavesdropping."

"Mostly I just don't want to be surprised again. There's only so many times I can handle life jumping up at me and shouting *boo!*"

"Figured. I bet it's not diaper time, either."

"You know, you could at least pretend I'm a woman of mystery. Stroke my... Praise my intelligence, and all that."

Great one, Maguire. Talk about *stroking* while perching on the edge of the bed they were going to end up sharing after all. When, deep down, she could hear a tiny voice whispering a reminder that she hadn't had anything stroked in a long, long time. One year and nine months, to be precise.

"Sorry, Darce. You have a lot of talents, but intrigue isn't your thing."

"You might be singing a different tune by the end of the weekend." Try as she might, she couldn't keep the words as light as she wished.

"Are you really okay with the thought of Xander coming here?" His teasing tone had departed.

"I don't know. I mean, yes, I'm okay. It's just... everything is happening so fast. It feels like it's all going to spin away from me and blow up into an entirely different universe at any moment." At least, it had felt that way until he had turned her to him and reminded her of what was really at stake. Funny how everything else had seemed to slip away then. "Thanks for your help down there. I was starting to lose sight of the big picture."

"Just doing my job."

Now, what did that mean?

"Will it help if I remind you that Xander is probably even more afraid than you are?"

"Yes. But no."

"You know, with answers like that, you might have that woman of mystery thing going on after all."

Her laugh was shortened by the tightness of her throat. "Nah. That's just the confusion talking."

"How about this?" His foot stretched as if he were planning to move forward, but at the last second he pulled it back and crossed it in front of his other leg. Probably planned to sit beside her and had changed his mind when he remembered the bed thing.

Curiouser and curiouser, Alice in Wonderland would say. Except for Darcy, it was more like *Complicated and complicateder.*

"Let's take this one piece at a time," he said. "Focus on what's in front of us at each moment."

"I'm trying." She made a face. "It would be a heck of a lot easier if the pieces didn't insist on jumping all over each other."

"Yeah, there is that." He finally peeled himself from the doorway, but instead of joining her, he sat on the floor, one hand reaching to pat Lulu and the other stretching to Cady, who scrambled to the edge of the bed and was rewarded with a loud kiss on the cheek.

Lucky kid.

"You've watched me make things," he said slowly. "You know how it works. I have an idea of what I want to create, and I have to keep that big picture in mind, but all I can change is one section—the little bit that's hot and pliable. If I try to shape anything else, it won't work. All I'll do is waste my time and get frustrated. And probably break something while I'm at it."

"You have a point."

"Hey, with Moxie as my grandmother, I had to learn to think on my feet."

"Yeah. I have a whole new appreciation for that, too." She grabbed her phone. "Okay. Let me try this the Ian way. Step one, tell Xander what we've decided."

A few taps later, the text was sent. Sure enough, while a new set of butterflies had taken up residence in her stomach, some of the old ones had definitely left. She set the phone on the bedside table and took a mental step forward.

"So Xander's been shoved into the forge to soften up."

"Now you're talking."

"And we can deal with the next item on the agenda." She forced herself to meet his eyes. "Do we keep pretending?"

"Do you want to?" Mild panic raced across his face. "I mean, do you think we need to?"

Oh, but those were two very different questions. And there was only one of them that she was going to address.

"I'm not sure. But I… If he stays here it would make things easier, in a lot of ways, if he kept on thinking we're together. It would mean we wouldn't have to have a lousy conversation at a really awkward time."

"It would give you some distance."

"Distance. Yeah. That's a good way to put it." With the way the whole situation was flying through her fingers, the truth was she could use all the slowing tactics she could find. "It might even make it easier to explain it to him when the truth comes out. You know, once he sees that his coming here kind of pushed everything up a notch, he might understand why we wanted a barrier. He'll see that we just wanted to be sure he's everything he says he is while he's getting to know Cady."

"Yeah, that might cushion the blow."

"Are you okay with pulling the wool over your family's eyes a bit longer?"

He took Cady's hands and bounced her arms up and down. "It's not the way I would prefer to do things," he said at last. "But if we told them the truth, one of them would let it slip before Xander stepped in the door. Moxie could keep it close. But Ma, Dad…they couldn't do it."

She noticed he didn't say anything about Carter's and Taylor's ability to keep a secret.

At least if she had to stay here she might have more chances to encourage Ian to hash things out with Carter. She and Ian could talk about it at night when it was just the two of them in the room, in their pajamas, in the great big beautiful—

Her phone beeped. Her relief at having her thoughts pulled back from the danger zone quickly turned to a sinking feeling in her gut when she saw the message.

"Xander?"

"Yeah. He loves the idea and will be here in twenty minutes."

"You gonna be okay?"

"Do I have a choice?"

His gaze softened. "There's always a choice, Darce. Sometimes it's between sucky and suckier, but there's always a choice."

Yeah, he had her there.

"Well. We have twenty minutes to figure this out." One piece at a time. Maybe if she got the elephant out of the way first, the rest would fall into place. "First up, sleeping arrangements."

"You and Cady take the bed. I can make up something in the other room."

"With what, the mattress from Cady's crib and the toddler bed? I think you outgrew those long ago."

"There are air mattresses in the garage."

"Seriously, Ian, do you hear yourself? Moxie already wandered in here while we were talking. If you set up a bed someplace else, you know she'll find it."

He grabbed Cady and pulled her onto his lap. "Poor Bug. You're going to have a rough time pulling anything over on your mom when you get to be a teenager."

"The bed is big enough that we can share it without—" *without getting too close, without touching, without rolling over in the night and curling around each other, and* "—without too much awkwardness." She pointed to the quilt folded in neat thirds at the foot of the mattress. "We can roll that up like a jelly roll and put it down the middle. Not because I don't trust you or anything," she hastened to add, even while her conscience pointed out that *his* hands weren't the ones she feared might roam. "But because it will be easier to relax and sleep if we're not lying there worrying about…whatever."

"Makes sense."

Was he blushing? Maybe that was just the reflection of the heat she felt in her own cheeks.

"It's only a few nights. Who knows? After a day or two I might feel ready to come clean with Xander, and then we can stop the farce."

"We'll take that as it goes."

"Right. And I guess we should talk about, um, public displays of affection."

"If it helps, my family isn't super touchy-feely. No one will expect to see much."

That was definitely relief making her sag. Not disappointment. Relief.

"Yes. Good. So, I'm thinking holding hands, a little pat on the arm once in a while, things like that. Enough to get the message across without, well, without going overboard."

"Yeah, that should do the trick."

And it would mean no more kisses. Thank God. The touches in public were challenging enough, but those brief kisses kept calling her, whispering to her long-deprived body, keeping her in a constant state of *what would happen if...?*

Ian's kisses were to be avoided at all costs. Otherwise, there could be a jelly roll the size of Lake Superior between them and she still wouldn't get any sleep.

"I think we're good," he said, but she shook her head—and not just because Cady was chewing on his shirt.

"We need stories."

"Aren't we telling one already?"

"People always expect a story. You know, how did you guys meet? How long have you been going out? What kinds of things do you do together?"

"Those are easy. We met when I moved in. We don't go many places because we're mostly home with Cady, but we go to the park and stuff. We've been going out— Okay, we can't say too long, otherwise Moxie will give me hell for not bringing you here earlier. So, six months?"

Dear Lord. It was so obvious he was a man.

"Six months is okay," she said. "But the rest needs work."

"Like what?"

"Like…we take Cady and Lulu to the playground. Cady giggles when you push her in the baby swing. Lulu runs around like a maniac and jumps in and out of the pond when the weather is warm enough." All those everyday, ordinary family-type moments that she loved.

"That's not a story. It's the truth."

"Which is why it works. Remember what I said to Xander before you—" *before you kissed me and turned everything inside out and upside down; not that it matters all that much, really* "—I mean, just after we started pretending?"

Judging by the way he suddenly couldn't meet her eyes, his mind had gone right back to the same moment.

"You said something about me helping you, and me spending more time at the house."

"Right. It was pretty lame, to be honest, but it was all I could come up with on the spot. We need to embellish things. Not much. Stick to the truth as much as possible, but add details to make it realistic."

He didn't roll his eyes, but she could tell he was tempted.

"Trust me on this, okay?"

"Whatever." He turned and stretched toward Cady, who was crawling full speed toward the bathroom. He snagged her by the foot and dragged her back toward him. "Sorry, Bug. You're not leaving without a grown-up."

As expected, Cady let out a wail that caused Lulu to raise her head in instant Vampire Slayer mode.

"Oh, poor baby. How ridiculous of us to want to keep you safe." Darcy slid to the floor and imitated Moxie's *Eensy Weensy Spider* motions. Cady stared in fascination, one chubby fist in her mouth.

"Ooh, this works well. I'm going to have to get Moxie to teach me more of these." Darcy wiggled her fingers, eliciting a giant grin. "Now, as for how we got together—"

"Uh-oh."

"What? Oh." His meaning came clear the next time she inhaled. Diaper time. "You know, now that we're together and everything, maybe you should—"

"Go feed Lulu? Great plan. You two have fun."

"You are such a coward, North."

"Some call it cowardice. Some call it self-preservation. Later!"

Lulu scrambled to her feet and trotted behind him. The door closed, Cady let out a howl at being left behind and Darcy sighed.

"Just once, I'd like to spin a story that didn't have a crappy ending."

CHAPTER NINE

IAN SLIPPED OUT through the back door to avoid running into any family members as he headed for the yard with Lulu in tow. Darcy was right. He was a coward through and through. Not because of the diaper—he'd handled more of those than any childless single guy should ever have to deal with—but because Darce had been pushing into conversational areas he didn't want to explore. Not yet. Not here. Probably never.

How long have you two been together?

She was right. They needed to prepare for the usual questions. But as he whistled for Lulu to follow him toward the river, he admitted that the real reason he hadn't wanted to create stories with her was because stories had this nasty habit of pulling the truth into the spotlight. Truth was the last thing he wanted to hold up for scrutiny right now.

No, right now he was going to throw a stick for his dog and have a few minutes of solitude to clear his head before the pretense had to begin in earnest.

It was a good plan. So of course it couldn't last.

No sooner had he located the perfect throwing stick than the whine of a tired engine had him looking toward the road. Sure enough, Xander's battered old Honda bounced down the driveway. Not a good sign, seeing how the driveway was freshly paved and free of potholes. He would have to take a look at Xander's car before Cady was allowed in it. Darcy wouldn't know what to look for.

Neither did he, really, but that was beside the point.

The squeak of the car door as it opened wasn't very reassuring. Neither was the way it seemed to drop and sag at an angle that he was pretty sure the designers had never intended. But the tightness it caused in his gut was nothing compared to the way his entire intestinal tract twisted as Xander emerged with a nervous smile on his face.

He believed Xander had the right to be in Cady's life. He truly believed Cady should grow up knowing her father.

But he was slightly surprised to admit he also believed he wanted to make some things very clear to Xander before anything went any further.

"Hey, Ian. How's it going?" Xander reached for the sky. "Damn, that's a long ride. I think it'll take me three days to stop feeling like I'm still in the car. How did Cady do?"

"She's a trouper," he said, a little stiffly. "Only cried when she got tired or hungry."

"She must get that from Darcy, 'cause God knows, I'm the world's lousiest— Hey, Lulu. Come here, girl!"

Lulu, who had come running the minute the door wheezed open, dropped her stick and stood on guard—eyes narrowed, ears back. There was no welcome in her bark.

Xander stayed behind the safety of the car door. Well, at least it was good for something.

"I always heard that dogs never forgot folks. Guess that was wrong."

"Or maybe she does remember you." Ian ran a hand down her back, feeling the tightness of her muscles. "She was a wreck after you left, you know."

Xander blinked. "What?"

"She spent days sitting by the door, waiting for you to come back. She knew me, she felt safe with me, but she knew that she was your dog. It took months for her to get over you, Xander. Months."

"Look, I'm sorry about that, but I—"

"Xander." Ian leaned on the wheezing hood of the car. "Swear to me you'll do better by Cady than you did by Lulu."

Xander's face lost a little of its carefree shine. "You saying you don't think I'm going to do right by my kid, Ian?"

"I'm saying that, for Cady's sake, I hope you aren't starting anything you don't intend to see through."

He expected Xander to defend himself. Instead, he looked down at the ground, curling his fingers around the top of the car door.

When he looked up, there was no shame or bluster in his eyes. Instead, Ian saw the one thing he hadn't seen in Xander for a long time: honesty.

"I screwed up. I know it. But here's a couple of other things I know. I'm not leaving her. And I'm not going to mess up again."

Lulu bumped against Ian's leg.

"And while we're laying our cards on the table, Ian, let me say this. I get that you and Darcy are together, and I know you're a big part of Cady's life. I'm good with that. I don't have any intention of trying to come between you two." He fixed Ian with a steadfast gaze. "But I'm not going to take a backseat to you, either. I figure you treat me with respect, I do the same for you, and Cady gets two guys in her corner."

Well, hell. Maybe Xander really *had* turned things around.

Ian allowed a cautious nod. "I can work with that."

But Xander's focus had already shifted to a spot behind Ian and a giant smile erupted on his face.

"There she is!"

Ian didn't have to turn to figure out that Darcy and Cady must be approaching.

Xander pushed past him. "Cady! How's my girl?"

His girl. And damn, but it seemed as though Xander just might possibly be worthy of her.

The car door still hung open, taunting him with

its lopsided list. Since his choices were to deal with it or interrupt the family reunion, he opted for the inanimate and gave it a shove. It moved forward a few inches before stopping.

He knew the feeling.

Steeling himself, he shoved his hands into his pockets and started down the pansy-lined path toward the happy trio. One glance at Darcy's face and he mentally amended his description. She was smiling, but he easily recognized her polite face. Worry stirred with protectiveness inside him.

He reached absently for Lulu, who was hovering near his leg, and sank his fingers into her fur while ordering himself to watch the events unfolding before him. A few steps ahead, at the spot where the path widened and curved out to the house, Darcy curled at the waist, Cady's fingers in her fists, doing the awkward hunch-over walk that kept Cady upright. And Xander…

Xander watched Cady with a wonder that sent shame flooding through Ian. Wariness and uncertainty were one thing, especially given Xander's track record, but Ian hadn't let himself go beyond those. Xander had had a hell of a surprise dumped on him. He could have bolted as far and fast in the opposite direction as possible. Instead, he'd run the other way. Closer to his kid.

Xander deserved a chance.

And if Ian was any kind of friend—to Darcy,

Cady or even Xander—he needed to get his butt in gear and help make that chance a fighting one.

DARCY GLANCED DOWN the path at Ian, willing him closer, but still he hung back, sneaking peeks from the corner of his eye.

Maybe he thought she and Xander and Cady wanted some privacy. Maybe he didn't want to intrude on daddy-daughter time. All well and good, but they were supposed to be a couple. If he didn't haul his ever-so-enticing arse over to her in the next, oh, thirty seconds, she was going to have to be blatant and obvious, maybe grab him by the collar and plant a kiss on him that would leave them both reeling.

Hmm…

"So," Xander said. "I hope you don't mind me blowing into town, but like I said, you know, loose ends for the next few days. I figured this was my best chance to get to know her." He nodded toward Cady. "She sure is a cutie."

"She always has been. Once I— Once we get back home, I'll put together a collection of pictures from when she was younger."

"I wish I hadn't missed that."

How was she supposed to answer? The truth was, even at the most terrifying moments, she had never wished for Xander to magically reappear and start playing daddy. She had wanted nothing but stability and security for Cady, and there was little in her experience—with either Sylvie's circle of men or Xander's own actions—to make her expect him to contribute to either of those qualities.

No, the only one who had surprised her had been Ian. He had turned out to be the most solid rock she could have imagined. But it wasn't until this moment, sending him mental *come here* vibes, that she saw how much she had let herself depend on him—and not just for rent money and a hand with child care.

Ian was giving her a hand. Being a friend. He was very generously buying her time to ease this transition. That was all. She was grateful, and she would take him up on it, but she couldn't let herself fall into believing that either he or the situation was anything more. That was the first step down the Sylvie path.

Xander crouched in front of Cady, both hands extended. "Hey, pretty girl. Can I help you walk?"

Cady eyed him and his outstretched hands. Darcy held her breath. Just an hour ago, she had insisted in front of assorted Norths that she wasn't trying to discourage Xander from knowing his daughter, but now, with the reality upon her, she was having a hard time believing herself.

She lifted her head and scanned the yard once again, realized what she was doing and gave herself a mental slap upside the head. But that didn't stop her from letting out a small sigh of relief when Ian caught her eye, quirked a brow and hustled down the path.

He stopped beside her, seeming to assess the scene. When he reached and gave her shoulder a quick squeeze, she allowed herself one second of leaning into that comfort. Surely she could have that little bit.

Ian let go. His hand hung in the air for a second before he knelt beside Xander, who looked at him with upraised eyebrows.

"It's easier if you're standing," Ian said quietly. "In front of her until she gets to know you. Then you can walk behind her. It's hell on your back, but she loves it."

Darcy breathed in, short and fast, as she grasped what was happening. Ian was taking this on himself. He had seen how torn and lost she was, and he was stepping in, stepping up, taking some of the burden from her.

Ian shifted, easing himself back toward Lulu. "The other thing she likes is high fives," he continued as Xander rose. "Like this." He held his palm upright in front of Cady's face. She made a gurgling noise and reached forward to smack the proffered palm with a loud *whee!* She barely seemed to notice when she almost lost her balance. She would have kissed the stones if Ian hadn't done a fast save with a hand to her tummy.

As quickly as Ian reached for Cady, that was how fast Darcy's memory flew to another time and place. She probably had been about three or four years old, walking atop a narrow rock wall. Her dad had walked beside her, saying something about the flowers. A missed step, some wildly flailing arms, and then Daddy had grabbed her hand and everything had been steady again.

"Easy, Bug!" The determined lines creasing Ian's face melted into his usual Cady-indulgent smile. "I know it's fun, but it's not worth landing on your pretty little kisser."

Sylvie hadn't been the world's most stereotypical mother, and Darcy might have issues with the way her mother had allowed both of their worlds to be tossed around by the whims of whatever man she had been with, but in one area she had come through big-time: she made sure Darcy knew how awesome her dad had been. Seven years wasn't much time to build up a lot of memories. Sylvie had supplied them. She had always been able to come up with a Daddy story when Darcy needed one.

Watching Ian with Cady was almost like being given the chance to see how her dad must have been with her.

Cady stared at Ian as if trying to decipher some secret message, bounced up and down, and raised her free hand.

Given the angle, Darcy was pretty sure Xander couldn't see the way Ian's fingers twitched before he took a quick breath and glanced up at Xander.

"Give it a try."

The words were casual. The impact on her was not. Ian was known. He was trusted. He knew Cady as well as she did. But Xander... God help her, but all she could think was that he had the potential to play havoc with Cady's life the way Sylvie's men had done to Darcy.

She and Ian exchanged a fleeting look. His expression was reassuring. If only there were some way to do a certainty transfer.

Cady's hand did a kind of up-and-down motion in the air, as if she were trying to make up her mind as well, but Xander had no doubts. He held his palm in the approximate position Ian had done.

"Hey, cutie. How about a high five for your dad?"

Darcy bit down hard on her lip.

Cady bobbled again, tipped her little head so her topknot tipped to the left and slowly reached forward to tap Xander's hand.

EVERY TIME IAN thought that this trip home had already grown as unbelievable as possible, the stakes ramped up again. Like now. Sitting down to dinner with his folks, his meddling grandmother, his former fiancée, his brother who had married and knocked up his former fiancée, his fake lover, her baby and the baby daddy. They were a freakin' reality show in the making.

With seating arrangements sorted, the blessing on the meal invoked and the salad passed, Moxie folded her hands beneath her chin and looked to the pseudo-family end of the table with the kind of smile that the North brothers knew meant pleasure for no one but her.

"Well, Xander. Been a long time since we've seen you. Never woulda thought that you'd be back under these circumstances."

Xander turned the slightest bit pink but met Moxie's gaze head-on. "That makes two of us, Mrs. North."

"Huh. Can't imagine you're too surprised by some of those events. Unless someone planted little receivers in your brain and sent messages about breakin' the law into your head while you were sleeping."

At Ian's right, Darcy wheezed. On his left, Ma covered her eyes and muttered something that he was pretty sure was an appeal to the Almighty.

Xander didn't flinch. "I made a lot of lousy choices and hurt people in ways I never imagined. I'll be the first to admit that I was an idiot. But those days are behind me now, and I'm looking forward to a fresh start with a new job and my amazing daughter. Now, did I hear that the dairy recently celebrated one hundred years in business?"

Ooh, smooth.

Moxie gave Xander a watered-down version of the evil eye—no doubt because she knew exactly what game he was playing—but Ma jumped into the breach with tales of ways they had marked the anniversary. Ian stayed silent. The big event had happened right after he'd returned from Tanzania, short weeks after the Carter-Taylor situation had erupted. He had walked through the weekend in a haze of jet lag and heartbreak—not a recipe for retaining many details.

But it kept the conversation going and meant nobody was interrogating him. It also gave him the chance to do something he'd needed to do since their arrival.

He needed to be sure Taylor was happy.

He stole a few glances at her as she followed the conversation with Carter's arm bumping against hers, her face alight with a smile. Had she ever been that relaxed, that lit up, while she was with him? He couldn't be sure. They had been good together, but watching her he realized that something was different about her now. She had been nervous around him when he'd first arrived, sure, and the whole hijacked-pregnancy-announcement thing probably had thrown her, but even with that, she seemed more—well—*relaxed* was the only way he could describe it.

If that was indeed what he was seeing, then he knew in his heart she had been right to end things.

Carter, though...

Darcy, who had been slipping bits of gravy-soaked food to Cady, extended her fork over his plate. "Mind if I steal your peas? Little Miss Piggy has decided she loves them."

Sharing food—yeah, that was definitely a couple kind of thing. Nice way to get the message across.

"Go for it." And, because he was trying to be better, he leaned forward to catch the attention of Xander, seated on the other side of Cady. "I think she has your metabolism, Xander. She eats all the time."

Xander was silent for a moment as if waiting for the other shoe to drop before finally nodding. "Hey, when the food is this good, who can blame her?"

"That's for sure." Darcy sounded bright and perky. All for show, he knew, given the way her fist clenched the fork like a dagger.

"So, Ian," Moxie began, and his appetite disappeared. "What exactly do you do at your job?"

Moxie knew the answer. She had grilled him on the subject during every phone call. Probably ferreting out information to use to lure him back home, but it had given them something to discuss at a time when a hell of a lot of topics had been off-limits. So, if there had been a hidden agenda, he could live with that.

"Different things on different days," he said slowly. "That's one of the reasons I enjoy it."

"Here's what I want to know," Xander piped up. "The blacksmith thing. Where did that come from? I don't remember you ever saying you had a burning need to shoe a horse. Or are you doing your Superman imitations, like bending steel rods with your bare hands?"

The truth was that he had picked it up on a whim when he'd seen a flyer for a class being offered the autumn right after Xander's visit. His only motive had been to find something to fill the evening hours, to keep him from dwelling on how his life had belly flopped. Finding that he liked it, that he was half-decent at it, had been a happy bonus.

But he couldn't say any of that in this crowd.

He shoved a bite of chicken into his mouth to buy a moment. Darcy must have picked up on the ploy, for she placed a warmly protective hand on his forearm.

"Xander, a word of warning. Don't mention shoeing horses and blacksmithing to Ian unless you're ready for a very detailed lecture." She patted his arm, her voice warmly indulgent. "Long story short, farriers take care of horses. Blacksmiths forge things from wrought iron or steel. Farriers need some blacksmithing skills, but a blacksmith might never see a horse. Ian makes a lot of beautiful pieces with a practical purpose, like candleholders and hooks for hanging things."

"Sounds like you know a lot about it, Darcy." Carter smiled. "Are you a blacksmith, as well?"

Her laugh pealed around Ian. "Me? Heavens, no. I am the least artistic person on the planet. No, anything I know has come from hanging out with Ian, that's all." She punctuated her words with a shoulder bump that left him grinning on the outside but issuing stern reminders to himself on the inside.

Damn, she was good at this.

"Oh." Carter helped himself to a bread stick. "I thought that might have been what drew you two together."

Beneath the table, an elbow connected with his ribs.

"No, sorry. The only thing I make is websites for authors."

"And beautiful little girls," Xander added, grabbing a bit of carrot from the high chair before Cady could send it to the ground. He always had been a fast learner.

"So now I'm curious." Ma's smile was all innocence but Ian knew better than to relax. "Did things just evolve, or was there a moment when you two looked at each other and figured out that everything had changed?"

All eyes and ears turned to Ian. Forks hovered over plates, heads tilted and he saw with dismay that Darcy had been doubly correct. They needed a story. Not simply because folks were curious, but because this particular crowd had a vested interest in knowing he was happy, that he had moved on and that there was still magic in his life.

He really should have listened to Darcy.

"Oh," she said in that overly bright way. "You know how it is. He was in the apartment and I brought Cady home—"

"Christmas," he blurted, and the moment he said it, he knew it was the right answer. Christmas was all about miracles. People expected things to happen then.

"Christmas?" There was a world of questions behind Moxie's short utterance.

"I... Yeah." Memories tumbled through his head, with one outshining the others the way the star of Bethlehem must have stood out in the heavens. "Last year. Darcy decided she needed a real tree."

Her eyes widened but she played along. "It was Cady's first Christmas. I couldn't have anything fake."

"Right. She twisted my arm and made me go to some cut-your-own place. I think there was a bribe involving hot chocolate and homemade cookies. So we got Cady all bundled and drove to this farm—"

"An hour outside of town, and of course it was freezing cold—"

"And when we were almost there, it started raining."

"Pouring," she elaborated happily.

"It was about as miserable as you could imagine. Just when we pulled into the lot, it decided to come down in sheets. We sat there and stared out the window."

"Cady may have learned her first swearwords," Darcy said.

"Darce said to forget it. She'd get a tree from a lot. But I knew she wanted the real thing." He grinned down at her, and it was as if their audience had faded into some fuzzy watercolor background. As far as he could tell, he was back in that cramped car with the rain battering the roof and the windows fogging up, feeling cut off from the rest of the world and not the least bit unhappy about it. In fact, as he recalled, he'd sat there and thought that if the zombie apocalypse had erupted at that moment, his only regret would be that he hadn't kissed Darcy.

"So what did you do?" Taylor's soft question pulled him out of the memory.

What did he do? In reality, he had been so blown away by the direction of his thoughts that he had jumped out of the car, grabbed the saw and cut down the first tree he'd spied. It had been lopsided and way too tall, but none of that had registered at the time. All he had been aware of was the sweet smell of fresh-cut pine and a fear that had chilled him even more than the rain—the fear that he was straying way too close to a line that should never be crossed.

But this audience needed the happy ending.

Stick to the truth as much as possible, Darcy had said. It made everything easier.

Maybe that was true for details. But feelings— nope. Totally different story.

"Well, boy, don't leave us hanging," Moxie said. "What happened next?"

He looked at Darcy. Mistake. With her eyes wide and her lips slightly parted, he knew she was remembering, too. And if he was going to be totally

honest—because with all the secrets and lies floating around this table, a little honesty sounded like
a great idea—she probably remembered the way
the air between them had seemed to crackle for a
few seconds. The way the world had shrunk down
to the space of the front seat. The way, for a moment or two, they both had known exactly what
was going through the other's mind.

Kind of like the way he could read her thoughts
right at this moment. It wasn't hard. They were
written in the swirl of confusion and wonder in her
eyes, painted in the pink of her cheeks, carved in
the curve of her lips.

A sudden *clang* jerked him back to his family,
to reality. Darcy jumped, too, and broke into nervous laughter as she turned to Cady, busy smash-
ing a napkin ring against her tray.

"Think she's trying to tell you to hurry up and
finish your story, Ian?" Ma's voice had that indulgent tone she only employed in the presence of
babies and puppies.

What was he supposed to say now?

Darcy to the rescue. "I can't do justice to the
story the way Ian can—" she flashed him a smile
guaranteed to set romantic hearts everywhere fluttering "—but I can tell you this. We kind of forgot
about the tree for a while."

Chuckles erupted around the table. Moxie nodded in seeming approval. Carter applauded. Cady
squealed and clapped her hands together as well,

setting off another round of laughter. Ma said something about dessert. Dad rose to clear dishes and the danger passed.

He should have felt relieved. He was, in a way. People were convinced. Xander seemed to believe them. Mission accomplished. Except every time he looked at Darcy, he couldn't help but wonder what would have happened that day if he'd followed his gut and reached for her instead of for the car door.

CHAPTER TEN

WITH DINNER OVER and Xander and Carter on dish duty, Ian made sure Darcy had everything she needed to bathe Cady before deciding he had earned that walk by the river. He dragged Lulu out of the kitchen and slipped out unseen.

He'd located a new stick for throwing and made it halfway across the yard before he remembered an important point about life in the North household: *unseen* and *unnoticed* were at very different ends of the spectrum.

"Hey, there." Ma ambled toward him, her hands in the pockets of well-patched jeans. With a contented smile on her face and a daisy stuck haphazardly behind her ear, she looked closer to his age than her own.

"What's up?" He threw the stick far down the grassy shoreline. Lulu took off at a trot.

"Not much. Just wanted to see how it's going. If you were settled in, if you need anything, what the hell you're doing springing this girlfriend thing on us out of the blue. The usual."

Oh, yeah. Now he remembered why he had

stayed away for so long. It hadn't been all because
of Carter and Taylor.

"Everything's fine. The rooms are great."

"And Darcy?"

"Come on, Ma. If I'd told you I was seeing someone, you would have… I don't know." He shouldn't
have thrown the stick so hard. He could have used
a distraction at the moment. "It didn't feel right,
okay? I didn't want to get anybody's hopes up."

"Ours or yours?"

"Not a fair question."

"I'm your mother. I get to ask whatever I want
and you have to answer."

"I don't recall any clause about that in the Char-
ter of Rights and Freedoms."

"It's in the fine print. Seriously, Ian. A little
warning would have been nice."

"I'm sorry about that part." At least that was true.
"This thing with Xander kind of forced our hand."

"Understandable. But if Helene had been home,
and Darcy and the baby had gone there, would you
have opened up to us then?"

"Hard to say."

"As I suspected." She whistled and pulled a dog
biscuit from her pocket, waving it in the air. Lulu,
who had been ambling in their direction, kicked it
up a notch and raced back.

"Why do you have dog treats? You don't have
any pets?"

"Carter and Taylor have one."

"They do?"

"Yep. I think it was Taylor's way of easing him into the realities of feeding and walking and poop."

"How's that working?"

She shrugged. "You know Carter. Brilliant in the office, clueless in real life. I hope he watches you with little Cadence. He's going to need all the fathering help he can get."

Oh, hell, there it was. Janice North claimed to be down-to-earth and practical—and in most matters, she was—but when it came to her sons she had a fanciful streak wider than the St. Lawrence.

Maybe he could distract her.

"I thought that wasn't public knowledge yet."

"There's public, and then there's a woman who survived multiple pregnancies watching another woman racing for the bathroom every twenty minutes. I know how to connect the dots. When were you going to tell us about Darcy?"

"When it felt right. You know, Hank is right here in town. He can give Carter the heads-up on being a dad."

"Yes, but he hasn't dealt with a baby in a long time. Though, between you and me, I have my suspicions about Brynn."

"You think she's pregnant, too?"

"Not positive yet. But if she isn't, I think they might be at the trying stage."

"Well, that would be nice. Cousins the same age.

Now all you have to do is get Cash settled and your work here will be done."

She gave him the look he remembered well from his youth—the one that said he was as dumb as a box of rocks. "Seriously, Ian? You think that's how it works? I see the way you are with Cady. Do you think you could ever stop worrying about her just because she found someone?"

Maybe he should start laying the groundwork for the springing of the truth. "That's not going to be my call. She has a father."

"Don't be an ass. If you love the child, which you obviously do, then she will always have a place in your heart. Furthermore, you're already playing a bigger role in her life than her father is. I know there are reasons for that, and things are shifting. But if you and Darcy are serious—"

"I am not having this conversation."

"Oh, yes, you are. If you two are serious, well, biology isn't always destiny. Xander doesn't know what he's in for yet. Not really. He may turn out to be an excellent father, and if so, bully for him. It's impossible for a child to have too many loving people in her life. But she and Darcy are a package deal. If you're involved with one, you're involved with both."

"Is there a point to any of this? Besides telling me things I already know, I mean."

"Of course there is. I'm too busy to wander off

on tangents without a point." She stepped closer and squeezed his shoulder. "Are you happy?"

Such simple words, but coming from her they carried more meanings than he cared to separate out.

"Yeah. I am."

"Really?" She looked him up and down. Just in case a truth fairy was hiding behind his back, maybe. "Or are you saying that so I won't worry?"

"If I were trying to spare you, you honestly think I would say anything else?"

"Of course not. But I'm well aware that my sons will go to great lengths to keep from worrying me, never realizing that when it blows up in their face, I only worry more."

He bent over in an elaborate search for Lulu's stick before Ma could read the truth in his face.

"Things are good. You don't have to lie awake at night over me."

"So, you are happy with Darcy, even though you didn't see fit to share this relationship with us?"

"Forget the guilt trip, Ma. It's not gonna work."

"So you say. How are you doing with the Xander factor?"

"I'm dealing with it." Though his gut told him that helping Darcy deal was going to be the most difficult piece of this pie. "It's not a great situation, but it's still new. Give us time."

"Fair enough. Let's talk about something that *has* had time. How is it being back here?"

There it was—the six-million-dollar question.

"It's not the easiest thing I've ever done." The short blast of a cruise ship horn pulled his attention to the river and the last bits of daylight dancing on the surface. "But it's not the hardest, either."

Her nod was the short, brisk type that let him know his answer had been measured and found acceptable. "Given the circumstances, that's probably appropriate."

He tossed the stick and waited, pretty sure at least one more question was on the horizon.

"So this job Moxie wants you to take. What do you think of it?"

Bingo.

"It sounds interesting." He walked slowly along the shore, following Lulu's path. Ma matched his pace. "I think it's great that Moxie wants to add a charitable foundation to Northstar. And, yeah, it was a nice surprise when she asked if I wanted to be part of it."

"No surprise at all. Your heart was always more inclined toward helping people than making money, though you did a fine job of that part when you were at the dairy. This would let you blend both."

"Yeah. It has a lot going for it."

"You think you're ready to come home?"

He shrugged. "Can I get back to you on that one? Say, after I've been here longer than five hours?"

"Five hours and a whack of surprises." She

bumped against his shoulder. "You can have another day or so."

"You know what I love about you, Ma? Your
patience. Oh, and your generosity."

"Bite me. What about Darcy?"

"What about her?"

"Would she come with you?"

Yep. One meeting and Ma had them married off,
raising a family and probably picking out rocking
chairs for the porch of their retirement home.

"We're not at the point of discussing that."

"How can you not be— Oh, Ian." Dismay colored her words. "Don't tell me you haven't told her
about it."

"I haven't said anything to her yet. No."

"Why not? You're old enough that I can't say
your age anymore because it makes me feel ancient. You had a lousy curve thrown your way, but
you've come back from it, and, honestly, I think
you're happier with Darcy than you ever were with
Taylor."

Whoa, whoa, whoa. What the hell?

"But you can't keep this from her. Forget that
Moxie could be telling her all about it even as we
speak. This is the kind of thing that—"

"Time-out." His head still whirling from her earlier comment, Ian struggled for sense. "Look, for
one thing, Darcy is a lot more understanding than
you give her credit for, especially when it comes
to privacy and…and things like that." Good God,

she'd practically invented the concept of secrets. "Remember, she wasn't supposed to come on this trip at all. The whole idea was for me to test the waters on my own. If it was going to be too hard to be here, then the topic would be moot anyway."

"So you were planning to come home for a few days, make up your mind and then go back and say, 'Guess what I decided, honey?'" Janice stared at him. "And here I thought you were the smart one."

"You said Carter was the brilliant son."

The whack she delivered to his arm wasn't the usual playful one that she had developed over the years of parenting four sons. This one had some muscle behind it.

"Hey!" He rubbed the spot where her fist had connected. "You been hitting the gym, Ma?"

"Sometimes I swear the only way you boys will pay attention to me is if I smack you first. Now listen. You are a levelheaded man who had his life yanked out from beneath his feet, but who then put that behind him and built something that looks pretty damned wonderful from where I sit. I like all of that. You seem happy again, and I really like that. So don't blow it by turning into an idiot now."

"But I—"

"No buts, Ian." She pulled another biscuit from her pocket and tossed it toward Lulu. "Honey, you're a family man. You always have been. Some people are happiest when it's just them, or maybe them and one other person. That's not you. You've always needed strong bonds all around you. You need to be settled with someone, to have a mess of kids climbing all over you and driving you up the walls, just like you and your brothers did to your father and me."

"You make it sound so appealing." Which, unfortunately, was the truth.

"But, Ian, let's get real. You're not getting any younger. If you want the kind of life that will make you happiest, you need to get it in gear. Kids are a miracle, as I'm sure you've found with Cady, but being the kind of parent they need takes a hell of a lot out of a person. You don't want to be dealing with teenage drama when you're sixty. Trust me on this."

"So I should snap up Darcy and start making babies, just so I have enough energy to keep up with my future potential children?"

"Of course not."

Huh. Could have fooled him.

"You're not ready."

"Are you forgetting what you said, oh, fifteen seconds ago?"

"No, Ian. I'm not senile yet, though God knows how I have any brains left after raising this crew. I don't want you to miss out on something wonderful by dragging your feet, but before you even think about forming a new family, you should make sure you're good with the one you've got."

"Ma, I—"

"No. Just listen for a minute, will you? I believe you're happy with Darcy. I believe you're finding your way back to us. But the fact that you've been doing your level best to keep her in one part of your life and us in the other, that tells me you might not be as ready to move on as you think you are. Add in Xander, and, honey, I'd be lying if I said I think you're in any position to make solid decisions right now."

Much as he wanted to dismiss her words, a tightness in his gut made it impossible.

"You can't drift through this one, Ian, and you really can't run away from it. Make sure you're as good as you think you are before you do anything permanent."

"You feeling philosophical in your old age, Ma?" But he kept the words light, knowing she would understand that he wasn't blowing off her advice. Not by a long shot.

"You know how it goes. You live long enough some stuff eventually starts to make sense." She shuddered. "But don't tell Moxie I said that, okay? I don't want her to know that I think she might really be onto something most of the time."

WITH TWO YEARS of togetherness to draw from, why the heck had Ian chosen the Christmas tree memory, the one most guaranteed to screw around with her mind?

Kneeling before the bathtub, Darcy squeezed

water from a sodden washcloth, sending it dribbling over Cady's head. Cady's sputters and splashes kept Darcy laughing but couldn't hold her runaway thoughts at bay.

Did he have any clue how close she had been to following him out of the car that day and kissing him the way she had hoped to hell he would kiss her? How was she supposed to fall asleep beside him tonight with the echo of those crackling moments in the car pounding through her and nothing but a jelly roll and good intentions between them?

Her frustrated sigh sent bubbles flying. She should have invited Xander to start his Parenting 101 lessons right away and join in bath time. She would have had to give directions and explain things and teach him the words to the tubby songs. Auto-distraction.

But Cady could deal with only so many changes at once. And even though Darcy's head was very aware that Xander was indeed Cady's father, she wasn't ready for him to be the daddy. Not yet. And not here in Comeback Cove, where "Daddy" had a very different meaning for her.

"Ian's dad knew your grandpa, Bug. They were great friends." She squeaked a ducky. "He knew me when I was your age, too. Kind of hard to imagine."

Cady batted at the duck. Darcy wiggled it just out of her reach, laughed at the indignant frown, then allowed Cady to grab it before dancing it away again.

Seeing Robert was almost like getting a glimpse of how her own dad might have changed over the decades. Paul Maguire had been a little more boisterous than Robert—at least in Darcy's memory—but when Robert had smiled over Cady banging things at the table, then slipped her a new napkin ring after Darcy took the first one away, well, for that moment she could have sworn she'd heard her dad's laugh echoing in the room.

"He would have loved you so much, Bug." *Squeak, squeak.* "He would have known how to make this right. He had this parenting thing solid."

Bath finished, she rocked Cady, humming little tunes while dispensing the bedtime bottle, and tried to keep from panicking over the impending bedtime. She had to be practical. Sleep was essential and it was her best defense. The key was to fall asleep before Ian came upstairs. So as soon as Cady was settled, Darcy pulled on her nightgown—giving thanks that she had tossed one in her suitcase instead of relying on her usual soft, ripped and too-short T-shirt—and climbed between line-dried sheets that took her immediately back to those summer visits with Dad and Nonny.

Great. Another topic to keep her awake.

"It's a conspiracy," she whispered into the jelly roll, trying desperately to make her mind blank. To forget Moxie's barbs about Darcy "forgetting" that Nonny would be out of town this week. To forget Xander, here to claim his share of Cady's life. To forget that very soon there would be a long stretch of confusing, delicious and totally off-limits man curled up on the other side.

Whether it was the constant exhaustion that went with motherhood or simply her mind ordering her body to shut down while it could, somewhere along the line she fell asleep. She wasn't aware of anything else until she was dragged back to wee-hours wakefulness by Cady's soft whimpers.

A quick glance at her phone told her it was a little after one. A longer glance at the other side of the bed told her she was no longer alone.

She swallowed hard while shoving her feet into slippers. The night-light and moonbeams played across Ian's side of the bed, drawing her attention like a dieter to chocolate.

He was sprawled on his stomach with his left arm out to the side and the hand dangling through the air. His right leg was crooked up against the jelly roll. His head rested on the pillow, dark against the white case, and his soft breathing called to her almost as strongly as Cady's strengthening cries.

Off-limits, Maguire.

She slipped through the kitchenette, closed the door, stepped over a drowsy Lulu and lifted Cady from the crib.

"What's the matter, sweet pea? Is it that tooth again?"

One dose of medicine later, they were settled in the oversize rocker. For a second or two she debated trotting up the stairs to the attic room and waking Xander, plunging him headfirst into Parent Boot Camp. After all, wasn't that why he was here?

But as Cady nestled warm and trusting against her shoulder, she knew she couldn't do it. Being hauled out of bed at this hour sucked, true, but cuddling her daughter in the muted glow of the night-light, listening to the soft creak of the chair, feeling Cady's breathing slow and her little body grow heavier as Mama made everything better... Nope. Even if Cady had been comfortable enough with Xander to invite him to take over, Darcy wasn't ready to share the shadowed peace of this moment. Especially not while wearing jammies, and especially not with Xander.

Ian, on the other hand...

Darcy hummed tunelessly, patted Cady's back and admitted the truth.

Ian did things to her.

Things she hadn't felt in a long, long time. During the day she could convince herself it was simply prolonged celibacy making her feel this way, but at night the truth came creeping. She liked him. Liked being with him and laughing with him. Liked kissing him. Really liked knowing that if she needed help all she had to do was say the word and he would be by her side.

Though how could she like something that made her so damned scared?

"Oh Cady Bug," she sang to the slightly mangled

tune of "Danny Boy." "Dear Cady Bug, please go to sleep now—"

A smothered snort from the other side of the room interrupted her song.

"Ian?"

"Please tell me this is a dream," he said. "Because if you're really singing that, I might have to report you for child abuse."

"Everyone's a critic," she said as softly as possible.

He peeled himself from the door and crossed the room. Funny how it felt so much smaller when he was in it. "The tooth?"

His voice was rough and thickened by sleep, and, oh crap, she was melting all over the chair.

"I think so. She'll be asleep again soon. Sorry we woke you."

There was just enough light for her to make out his shrug. "No problem. Do you need anything? Water, a pillow…"

A massage that didn't stop at the neck or shoulders sounded mighty attractive.

"I'm okay, thanks."

He studied her while she rocked. "Aren't you cold?"

Dear Lord, no.

For a moment she allowed herself a lovely fantasy—that when it came time to climb back into bed, Ian would reach over the jelly roll and take her hand, stroking it with his thumb, encouraging and inviting but leaving the next step up to her. The next step, of course, would find her vaulting over the quilt and dive-bombing him into the mattress.

"Go back to bed," she said gently. To bed, to sleep, preferably before she got there. "I gave her some meds. She'll be out again in a few minutes."

Instead of doing as instructed he shuffled to the window, pulled back the curtains and peered outside. She couldn't imagine what there was to see at this hour, but maybe it was a protector thing, like with dogs.

As if on cue, Lulu whined softly and pawed the air. Yep. The great defender, standing on guard for thee.

Ian, however, was still at the window. Maybe he'd fallen asleep standing up. Maybe he was counting the stars.

Maybe he also was doing his best to avoid the bed. Because as weird as it had been to slip between those sheets earlier, knowing he would be joining her, it was going to be a whole different story now with both of them awake. And aware. And—crap—more than a little aroused, at least on her part.

Nope. Definitely not happening.

She eased to her feet. Cady stirred but didn't protest. A few steps, a pat on the back and Cady was down for the count. Probably chasing Lulu through some dreamscapes.

Darcy shivered. Damn. She really wished Ian had gone back to bed when she'd told him to go.

He had left his perch by the window and waited at the door to the kitchenette. She padded past him into their room, resolutely averting her eyes from the bed as she grabbed the monitor from her side and tossed it into her workbag.

"What are you doing?"

It really was unfair the way his voice got lower and rougher when he tried to speak softly. It scraped against parts of her that hadn't been scraped in a long time.

"I'm wide-awake, and I have a lot to do, so I'll go downstairs and sneak in an hour or so of work. Where can I set up camp without disturbing anyone?"

"You should sleep."

Yeah, as if that was going to happen.

"Hey, us working moms have to grab the moment when it presents itself."

"I hope you don't expect me to buy that line."

Her hands slowed as she zipped the bag. "You could at least pretend. Help me save face and all that."

"Darce." His hand hovered over hers. He was so close, damn it, standing beside her wearing nothing but sleep pants and an undershirt—which she strongly suspected he wore only out of consideration for her—and oozing temptation. Warmth radiated from him. *Cozy,* it seemed to whisper. *Snuggleable. Doable.*

She had to get out of there.

"Darce, listen. I know it's weird sharing the bed and all, but the only way it's going to get easier is if we just, you know, do it."

Her head snapped upright. Her jaw sagged.

"Shit." He covered his face with his hand. "That came out really, really wrong."

Oh, the rightness of that wrongness...

"Don't worry about it." *Keep it brisk, Maguire.* "We're in an awkward position here. Practically anything we say can be turned into a double entendre."

His mouth quirked. "Like *awkward position?*"

"Did I... Oh, jeez. I did say that, didn't I?"

His only answer was a mildly repressed snort. She pulled her bag to her chest—all the better to shield herself with—and sidled toward the door.

"Yeah, this is why I think it would be best if I went downstairs. Work. Warm milk. All those good things."

"And this is why I think you should come back to bed. You can't hide the whole time we're here."

Did he have to see through her so easily? "I went to bed early. I can nap when Cady does if I need to."

"Or you could bite the bullet, get back under the covers and get through this."

Her foot slipped back. "Not that easy."

"Of course not. But it will just get harder—"

She coughed.

"Damn! I mean, the longer you put it off, the more difficult it will be."

He had a point. Worse, he was as stubborn as she was. The more she argued, the deeper he would dig in his heels. Maybe the best course of action would be to get into the bed, wait for him to fall asleep and slip out. She could do that.

"Fine." She grabbed the monitor, set the bag by the door for ease of escape and flounced over to her side of the bed, where she yanked back the covers, issued a stern warning to her libido and dropped to the mattress.

"That was quick."

"That's what she said," she retorted without thinking, then stuffed her fist into her mouth. Stupid, stupid, stupid—but her inner adolescent burst into giggles.

Ian eased into his side with much more grace. Probably trying to keep from jostling her. Little did he know that an earthquake couldn't shake her as much as the sight of his head against the pillowcase.

"There. You survived."

"But I'm not asleep yet."

"Give it time, woman. Count sheep. Distract yourself."

"Close my eyes and think of England?"

"What?"

Oh, crap. She couldn't have kept her mouth shut?

"Victorian era advice to brides on their wedding night," she said as tonelessly as possible.

Over on the other side of the jelly roll, Ian was silent...until he burst out laughing.

"Seriously?"

"You think I would make up something like that?" Especially when they were the only two people awake in a dark house surrounded by the lingering echo of his Christmas story and a thick fog of awareness.

"No. No, I guess you wouldn't."

His laughter faded to occasional snickers. She stared into the darkness, listening to him breathe, willing him to fall asleep the way she had with Cady so many nights. Too bad she had yet to perfect the technique.

Maybe if she pretended to be nodding off...

"Darce?"

Her fingers curled into the pillow. He wasn't simply asking if she was asleep. There was an extra edge in his voice that had her instantly on alert.

A smart woman would ignore him, maybe fake a snore. Of course, a smart woman never would have got herself into this predicament in the first place.

"What?"

"Listen, Darce...there's something I should tell you. Since we're both awake anyway..."

Sheets rustled. The echoes of his movements vibrated through her, and she opened her eyes in time to see him push up on his elbow and stare down at her. His hand rested on the quilt, a breath and a dare away. She sucked in oxygen and stopped deluding herself.

If he kissed her—if he said he wanted to ditch the pretense, make the relationship real, have hot sweaty sex until the sun came up—she was going to say yes.

But the words that cut into the night were none that she could have predicted.

"Darce, the real reason I came up this weekend is because I'm moving back home."

CHAPTER ELEVEN

WHO COULD HAVE guessed that one little sentence could carry such a giant load?

Saying the words, pushing them out despite the tight dryness in his throat, brought a rush of relief that caught Ian off guard. He'd known it wouldn't be easy to break the news to Darcy. Given the intensity of the silent sigh that slipped through him, he must have been dreading it even more than he thought.

Half a heartbeat later, the relief disappeared under a new wave. Worry over Darcy and Cady. Guilt over the thought that he wouldn't be around at a time when she might need him most.

Then a black hole of lonely opened inside him and sucked everything else into its maw.

How the hell did he think he could leave?

"Oh. Oh, of course."

There was no question in her voice. No disbelief or automatic denial, no *Wait, I need you*. The only emotion seeping through the cracks in the deliberate flatness of her voice was dull acceptance. Almost as if she'd been expecting this.

"It's not definite yet," he added quietly. "But Moxie wants to establish a new arm to the business, a charitable foundation, and she wants me to head it up."

"Oh. Wow. How, um, how perfect for you."

"Yeah, I thought so, too." Or at least he had until he heard that forced brightness behind her words.

She sat up, arms hugging her knees, her hair hiding her face. Not that he could see much of her anyway with just the night-light, but still, he missed the tilt of her chin, the flash of her smile.

"So that's why you came back now. You wanted to test the waters."

"In a nutshell, yeah."

"I see." She curled in on herself a bit more. "Well, I guess I don't have to worry anymore about how you're doing, being home."

"Does it help if I say that having you along made it a lot easier? And not just because of the pretend stuff."

He wasn't going to let himself think about the parts he wished weren't an act—the parts that involved touching. And holding her against his side while Cady snuggled into his shoulder. And sharing secret smiles with her when the others weren't looking.

"Glad as I am to have helped, right at this minute I kind of wish I hadn't been so successful, you know?"

"Yeah. I do."

Did he dare touch her? It might not be the smartest move, given the way he had to drag himself away every time it happened. But this wouldn't be about him. It would be about easing some of the tightness in the stiff line of her back, the way she hunched over as if trying to hold herself in one piece.

"Darce." His palm stalled above her shoulder.

Coward.

Steeling himself against the soft strength that was such a part of her, he let his hand settle and squeeze. Her initial flinch changed into something a lot more welcoming as she leaned into his palm. Her hand grabbed his. Her fingers wove through his.

"When will you leave?"

"I don't know exactly yet... I'll give you at least a month's notice for the apartment, but I imagine I'll be out by Labour Day."

"Oh."

"I'm sorry about the timing. With Xander, I mean."

"Don't worry about that. You got me through the worst parts. It's all details from now on, and you know me, I can step-by-step my way through anything."

True. She would get through whatever came next. But that didn't make him feel any better.

"You won't be getting rid of me completely, you know. I'll still come back for visits, watch the Bug grow up, all of that." He hesitated as an unforeseen complication to that plan made itself known. "Unless…I mean, with Xander on the scene now if you think that might be too confusing for her…"

"Stop that." Her fingers pulled free. "You have been part of her life since before she was born. She needs you."

As if to emphasize her words, a small whimper sounded over the monitor. Darcy sat straighter, poised to act. He stopped her with a hand on her back.

"Easy. That was Lulu."

"It… Oh. Jeez." Her laugh was closer to a sigh. "No wonder it sounded deeper than usual. Guess I really am tired."

She dropped to her pillow, flat on her back. His eyes had adjusted to the dim light and it was easy now to see the way she stared at the ceiling, her head rigid on the pillow, the dark pattern of her nightgown against the white sheets.

There was nothing seductive about her pose. If anything, her fingers clutched the sheets almost defensively, as if she were using them as a shield, which heaped another log on his guilt fire. Her hair stuck up on one side and sort of mashed against her head on the other, and the penguins frolicking across her nightgown were more likely to induce laughter than lust.

But, God, if only he could push the damned quilt out of the way and hold her…

"You really missed them, didn't you?" Her voice was small and wistful. Damn it. He shouldn't have told her this way.

On the other hand, now everything was out in the open. If there had been any chance of them turning make-believe into reality, well, it was so far off the table now that even Lulu wouldn't bother chasing it.

But none of that answered her question.

"Yeah. I did. I want to be part of a family again."

Moxie's line about Darcy and Cady being his family taunted him. He pushed it to the back of his brain.

"And...how are things with Carter? Did you talk any more with him tonight?"

"We're getting there."

"But you—"

"Give it time, Darce."

"Time. Right." She rolled onto her side, turning her back to him. "I think I can sleep after all. G'night, Ian."

"'Night."

He closed his eyes. Too bad it didn't block out the truth he'd been too slow to see—that leaving the everyday life he'd built with Darcy and Cady was going to be even harder than coming back to Carter and Taylor.

Though maybe that hadn't been an oversight.

Maybe it had been self-preservation.

He was leaving her.

An hour after Ian dropped his bomb, Darcy accepted that her ability to fake herself into sleep wasn't remotely as successful as her ability to fake a relationship. She eased out of bed, grabbed her supplies and almost ruined the whole maneuver by screaming out loud when something brushed her leg. Thank God she realized it was Lulu before she woke the whole house—or, most important, Ian.

"You are one lucky pup," she whispered as soon as she and Lulu were in the hall with the bedroom door closed softly behind them.

Moving slowly she took herself to the sunporch, where the clan had gathered the previous afternoon. She sat on the glider where she and Ian had presented the Xander case to his family—had it really been only about twelve hours ago?—and rocked slowly back and forth, trying to lose herself in the rhythm of the creaks.

They had been a team sitting here. She and Ian, working together. Almost like a family.

And now it was all going to change.

The laptop lay untouched at her side. Who was she kidding? Even if she tried to address her to-do list, she would end up typing *he's leaving, leaving, leaving* in the middle of some code. Work was going to have to wait until nap time, until she'd had a chance to slap some kind of bandage on the hurt.

Because, oh, yeah, she definitely would have become adjusted to this by afternoon. Sure she would.

The worst of it was that she couldn't blame him. The job *did* sound perfect. He *did* belong with his family again. Yes, she had been pissed with them all when she'd learned how they handled the Great North Love Triangle, and Carter and Taylor were still on her list of those she would consider sacrificing to the zombies, but now that she had met them, seen the way they came together to help her—okay. Maybe they hadn't handled the mess the way she would have wished, but she was pretty sure they had done the best they could at the time, when emotions had been running high and logic had been gasping for breath.

So, yes, he had every right to want to move home. She hoped she had sounded cheery enough after he'd broken the news. She didn't want him to go, Lord no, but she couldn't make him feel any worse about leaving. He'd dealt with enough the past couple of years. Her job was to let him know he'd be missed but that he had her blessing and understanding, that they would be glad to see him whenever they could swing a visit. Falling apart could wait.

She opened the laptop, ordering herself to ignore the sudden blurriness of the screen. She couldn't do anything that required concentration, but she could do something. Check some links, reply to emails, make a grocery list for when she got home…

Home. Where she would need a new tenant. Maybe a woman this time. Someone who traveled a lot so there would be no danger of getting friendly, letting herself rely on someone else, starting to feel like…

She blinked and wiped her face. Damn it. She was *not* going to cry over this. They would still see him. It wasn't forever. Not the way it had been when her dad had left.

But it wasn't going to be the same.

And, dear Lord, she was going to miss having him around.

Lulu yawned and rolled over. Darcy scrunched her bare feet into the dog's warm side.

"He's going to take you, too, isn't he, girl? Cady is going to…"

Oh, Cady.

"I promised her I wouldn't be like my mom," she whispered to Lulu. "I promised her I'd keep things steady, like when my dad was around. But now it's all going to hell anyway."

No. She had to find the silver lining. Surely there was one. Wasn't there a rule about that?

Okay. For one thing, she…well…she could have her garage back. No more hammers pounding at all hours, no more hot forge, no more parking her car outside in the snow. True, he had always cleaned it off and warmed it up for her all through winter, but whatever.

That was one. And…um…

"Ooh," she said to Lulu. "No more wondering if I'm going to run into someone doing the walk of shame across the backyard."

Not that there had been much chance of that. Other than a handful of times soon after he'd moved in, the only person doing that particular walk on her property had been, um, Xander.

"But only that once," she assured Lulu, who thumped her tail on the floor. Female sympathy. Power to the woman.

Of course, if things had turned out differently tonight…

Wait a minute.

"Hey, girlfriend." She dropped sideways onto the glider and whispered to the dog. "If the big reason I couldn't do anything with him was because I didn't want to mess up a good thing…but everything is seriously messed up right now anyway…is there any reason why I shouldn't jump him?"

Lulu cocked her head as if she were thinking it over. Darcy followed suit, turning the idea over in her mind, examining it from every angle. She needed to be rational about this.

Everything was changing already, whether she wanted it to or not.

They were already sleeping together.

People already thought they were involved.

She knew him. She liked him. She trusted him. And, yeah, she wanted him.

"A year and nine months is a long time to go

without," she said to Lulu, who whined. Oops. Maybe not a good plan to discuss her sex life with a dog who was a virgin.

"Though who knows what's happening when you take off at the dog park."

She bent down once more and scratched behind Lulu's ears.

"I feel like I've been thrown on a roller coaster backward and blindfolded," she said. "If everything is getting turned inside out anyway...would it be so wrong to grab this one little corner of my life and try to turn it into something awesome?"

Thump thump thump went the tail.

"Three thumps?" Darcy thought for a moment, then grinned. "Thump thump thump. Go for it." She ran her hand down Lulu's back. "Girlfriend, I like the way you think."

IAN WOKE TO early-morning light that revealed an empty space on the other side of the bed and a hollowness in his gut that he knew had nothing to do with hunger. And that was before the memories jumped him.

Ma was right. He'd had to tell Darcy about the move, though not for the reasons Ma had intended. But, God, he wished he'd handled it differently. Throwing it out like that, no warning, no explanation...

If he believed the stuff he'd learned back in psych class, blurting out the job offer was probably a defense thing. After all, they had been alone, the rest of the house had been asleep, they had been in a bed with all those double entendres stirring up thoughts that were too damned vivid for anyone's good—yeah. Freud or whoever might have been right about that one.

All he could do now was move forward and hope to hell he didn't cause her any more hurt. Which he would have if he'd done as he'd wanted and leaned over the stupid jelly roll and kissed her until she had no doubt that convincing other people they were involved was no hardship at all, at least not on his part.

That would have been fine and dandy for a while, but she'd had enough changes thrown at her in the past forty-eight hours. She needed him to be her rock. And what kind of selfish jerk would shift what was between them, even move into friends with benefits territory, when he knew he was only going to be around part-time at most? Yeah, that would be the way to make a woman feel secure, all right. Announce he was leaving town, then jump her. As if he didn't care enough to start something when he was going to have to deal with it all the time, but from a distance, hey, no problem!

No, it was better this way. For her, for him, for Cady and Xander and Moxie and probably even Lulu, though he might be working a bit hard to convince himself of that one.

He peeked in on Cady—still asleep—and looked in vain for Lulu. She must have left with Darcy. Maybe he should take advantage of the peace and shower away his regret.

Except when he padded into the bathroom, Darcy was everywhere.

Her purple-and-white travel toothbrush sat neatly capped beside his. Her brush lay on the counter, one lone hair curling from the bristles. A women's daily vitamin bottle watched over his razor.

He sucked air between his teeth as she surrounded him. He'd been in her bathroom at the house many times. None of these items were new to him. But he had never before seen her toothbrush beside his, her moisturizer next to his shaving gel, the hair from her brush reaching toward his comb. It smacked of togetherness and belonging and coupledom.

Worse, it didn't feel at all strange. Seeing her things mixed with his felt like…like when he was working at the forge. That moment when the prep work was behind him and he could see the shape of the finished product, could glimpse how it was going to turn out.

A sour taste filled his mouth. Feeling that way while shaping metal was one thing. Feeling that way about Darcy was another.

He pulled back the shower curtain and was promptly slammed by Torture Round Two—the travel bottles holding her hair stuff, a tube of body-wash, a little pink puffy thing for scrubbing. He picked it up and inhaled, filling himself with the smell of ginger and flowers, the scents he associated with Darcy. All he could imagine was squeezing more of the gel onto the puff, running it down her arms and the curve of her back, swooping it forward and dragging it in a slow, straight line from the hollow of her neck to between her breasts, swirling it around her belly button, sliding it lower, one centimeter at a time until it slipped between her legs and she pressed her naked, wet self against him and he let the puff drop to the shower floor as he fitted her against him and—

Oh, *shit*.

So much for the shower giving him some relief.

He turned on the water and hopped beneath the spray, deliberately keeping it a few degrees cooler than he would have preferred. Hey, it couldn't hurt. A few swipes with a rough washcloth and the generic bar soap Moxie had stocked since he was a kid helped to banish the most blatant sign of his fantasizing. Of course, those thoughts didn't vanish completely, but at least they were pushed down to a sublevel.

He could manage that.

Then he stepped out of the shower, wrapped a towel around his waist—because, like an idiot, he'd forgotten to bring his clothes in with him—and opened the door to find Darcy standing there. As if she'd been waiting for him.

And the buttons on the top of her nightgown were all undone.

SHE HADN'T EXPECTED him to be naked.

Okay, technically, a towel covered the major bits.

She had seen Ian in nothing but shorts or a bathing suit a number of times, but there was a major difference between seeing all that skin when she had vowed to ignore it, and seeing it now. Now, with water droplets clinging to the smattering of hair on his chest. Now, with her breath stuck in her throat and her heart hammering and sweet heat coiling deep and low. Now, when she had given herself permission to toss this one bit of her world into the air and see where it landed.

He spoke first. Good thing, because the connection between her mind and her body seemed to be misfiring.

"Sorry. I should have taken my stuff in with me."

And deprive her of this view?

"Don't worry. I was just wondering…"

She was pretty sure the towel twitched. "Wondering?"

"Wondering…" She inched forward, pushing the words out before she could turn and run. "Wondering how it would feel to kiss you without an audience."

This time there was no question that something

was disrupting the drape of the towel. Her hopes jumped right along.

"Darce, I don't think—"

"I know everything is changing," she said. "And most of it is out of my control. But this…this is mine. Yours. Ours."

"I can't start something with you, Darce. Not now." Damn the man. Did he have to be so noble?

"I don't see it as a start." She stepped closer, slid her hands up his chest. His mouth tightened but he didn't pull away. "I'm thinking of this more as the next step on a road we started down a long time ago."

"This isn't a good idea," he said, even as his hands snaked around her ribs. "We're not thinking right. Not with sharing a room. Pretending."

"I'm not pretending now." She fitted herself more closely to him. The towel hadn't lied.

"Darce, it's been a crazy couple of days. We can't—"

"You're right." She nuzzled his chest. "But what if I told you that I've been thinking about this for a lot longer than the last couple of days?"

"You have?"

"Mmm-hmm." She stood on tiptoe, kissed the corner of his mouth. "And I think you have, too."

"God, Darce," he said, and there might have been more but his words were lost as she kissed him, really kissed him, all heat and need and melting into him. She gripped his shoulders and curled against him, kissing him again and again with absolutely no one watching.

"Darce," he said against her neck. "God, Darce, I've wanted you so long, but I didn't... I can't..."

"Oh, yes, you can."

His hands landed low, pulling her tight while his hips pushed against hers and the rush of need had her digging her fingers into his shoulders to keep herself upright.

"We should think this over," he said even as he molded her to him. "Get our heads clear."

"I've done enough thinking. I want to feel."

"What do you want to feel, Darce? This?" He nuzzled her breast through the thin cotton of her nightgown, the heat from his breath shooting straight through her. Some sound slipped from her throat. She was pretty sure it was a combination of "don't stop" and "yes, that," but when he laughed softly against her heart, she knew he'd found the right interpretation even if she hadn't.

He lifted his head and framed her face with his hands and kissed her eyelids. Lightly. Gently. His hands slid to her shoulders and he stepped back.

What the hell?

She opened her eyes. "Was it something I said?"

His thumbs caressed her cheeks. "Don't take this wrong, because you're driving me crazy six ways to Sunday and back. But we shouldn't jump into this."

"Jumping sounds pretty damned fine to me right now."

"Me, too, but neither of us—"

"Christmas."

He blinked. "What?"

"That story you told last night. About Christmas." She flattened her hands on his waist. All the better to hang on to him. "Cady was asleep and that rain poured down and I was about ten seconds away from attacking you before you vaulted out of the car. So don't you try to tell me that this is only because of what's happened the last couple of days, because I have been thinking and wondering and imagining and dreaming for at least six months, North." She hooked her thumb over the top of the towel and began a slow circle around his waist. "Haven't you?"

He closed his eyes and breathed in before nodding, short and tight. Her thumb slid forward.

"Darce, I'm not saying no, okay? I'm saying let's wait."

"Six months, North." Her free hand slid down his butt and crept beneath the towel. "I'm done with waiting."

"What about Cady?"

"She'll sleep for another half hour. And I put Lulu on the long leash outside with food and water."

"I don't want—"

She found the point where the towel was tucked into itself. He inhaled sharply.

"Okay. I've been wondering, too, okay? Longer than you think, and I don't want—"

"You keep telling me you don't want something."

She leaned forward and brushed her lips against his. "But from the way your towel keeps twitching, I think you do."

"Darce…babe…I don't want a quickie before Cady wakes up. I want to do this right."

Her hands stilled as his words sank in. He was very obviously primed and ready, but he was willing to wait until he could make things special? For her?

But she had waited so long already. And life could turn inside out at any time. She knew that better than anyone. What if this was their only chance?

"Ian North, you may not believe it, but those words alone just made this the most special and amazing time ever." Her fingers found the edge of the towel. She was one tug away from having him exactly the way she wanted him—naked—and two backward steps away from where she wanted him—on the bed, inside her.

His hand closed over hers. "I packed for a visit with my family, Darce. I didn't think to bring protection."

Oh.

For one crazy moment she tried counting days, but her brain cells were otherwise engaged. And while she was more than willing to take a chance on having sex with Ian, that was as far as her risk-taking would go.

They could step back.

But what if he changed his mind?

She could have a shower. Hit the drugstore. Spend the day in a buzz of anticipation.

But what if he spent the day thinking of a way to let her down easy?

She could wait a little longer, believe him when he said he wanted time to do it right, and then tonight, oh, tonight…

But thinking about the things they could do tonight had her knees buckling and her blood thrumming, and there was no law that said they couldn't still have tonight, and after all, she deserved a few minutes of happy after everything that had been tossed at her and…

The next thing she knew the towel was undone.

"All roads lead to Oz," she said. She wrapped her hand around that whole lovely length, and the switch was thrown. He growled something—her name?—and swung her in a circle, pressing her into the bed. Still in her nightgown, she arched against him, feeling the promise of everything that could be.

He yanked himself away, dropping to her side. She would have protested but his mouth was on hers and his hand pushed at her nightgown and why the hell had she worn underwear to bed? And then…then she was reaching and he was teasing and she was gripping and he was stroking and she was arching and he was licking and it was enough, it was good, it was building and sweating and heaving and then she was gasping against his shoulder while he shuddered within her grasp.

For a long moment all she could hear was ragged breathing—hers? his?—and the thudding of her heart. One bit at a time the world spun back into place, her senses returning.

It hit her that she was still in her nightgown. Sort of.

"Wow." She dredged up enough breath to laugh. "You know that saying about the most fun you can have with your clothes on? I think we just gave it a whole new meaning."

He hugged her hem back into place, smoothing it with a gentleness that sent aftershocks rippling through her.

"Probably better this way. If you'd been naked…" He stopped. Shook his head. And kissed her tenderly, lingering and nibbling while he pulled her close. She sighed and snuggled in, longing to yank off the sweaty nightgown but too limp to do it. Besides, he was right. Totally nude would be too dangerous in too many ways.

Her body was a lot happier than it had been for a long, long time. But she couldn't help but wish that she had felt all his skin press against hers, felt him deep within her. Couldn't help wishing that she could drift to sleep in his arms and wake up pressed against him to do this again, slowly.

Couldn't help but wonder if, in her need to take control of one bit of the roller coaster, she had ended up stranding them halfway up the Ferris wheel.

CHAPTER TWELVE

DAMN IT. HE KNEW he should have waited.

An hour after Darcy had kissed his nose and dragged herself away to tend to Cady, Ian was outside pretending to run. He shifted Lulu's leash to his other hand, dodged a giant thistle and stared at the river, seeing nothing. He had no illusions as to what had happened. He could tell himself he'd tried to hold back, but the truth was that his protests had been hollow. He could have walked back into the bathroom, asked her to leave while he put on some clothes, made a joke about not being dressed for company.

But her buttons had been undone, making him want to taste that bit of skin beneath his lips. She had given him that shaky smile and said she'd been wondering about kissing him. And then she'd tossed his Christmas story back at him, and even though he'd said all the right things, put up a show of self-control, that was all it had been. A show. After months of torturing himself, wondering and watching, he had checked his wish to do right by her at the door and handed over control to the wrong head.

"Don't believe anything a guy ever tells you, Lu," he said to the sniffing mutt. "We're all dogs."

She lifted her nose from the clump of grass she'd been inspecting and barked. He sighed.

"Sorry. No offense intended."

She waggled her rump at him. So much for that apology. He was blowing it left, right and center today.

"I'll give you an extra treat when we get back to the house," he said. "Ma showed me her stash."

At the word *treat*, Lulu bounded toward him, barking and leaping in a circle. He laughed despite his own idiocy and scratched behind her ears.

"Come on, girl. Let's run."

She picked up the pace, pulling at the leash while he stumbled in search of his rhythm. He used to do this path every day. Now every tractor rut and hillock of grass was an invitation to stumble. Between that and the way his muscles were still coming back from the deep post-Darcy relaxation, his so-called jog was more like one prolonged session of tripping.

He surrendered, flopping on his back on the grass. Lulu whined and poked her nose into his side.

"Sorry, girl. Today's my day to crash and burn."

He watched some clouds float overhead, listened to Lulu snuffling around his head and to the occasional deep blast of a tanker on the river. He thought about the morning again, reliving every kiss, every word, every touch.

Was it all bad? God, no. In fact, thinking about it had him wishing the day away, leapfrogging in his imagination to tonight, after he'd made a run to the store, when he'd have the chance to do things right. There had been some mighty sweet promise in those few minutes. He couldn't wait to see how it played out with more time and less desperation. In fact, there could be a silver lining to all this. He'd have a hell of a lot more control tonight, when he'd be operating after a few hours of waiting as opposed to a few months.

A few months…

He frowned, remembering things she'd said. About wondering for a long time. About thinking about him since Christmas. Every time she'd said something like that, he'd lost another bit of restraint. Not because of the reminders of how long he'd been wanting her, but because—

"Shit."

Because whenever she had pressed that body against his and whispered about time, it made him think of *her* last time. Of her and Xander.

He hadn't given in just because he was too far gone to resist her. He had wanted to claim her. Make her his. And that line about wanting it to be special? Pure and total bullshit. He had wanted it to be the best she'd ever had. To make sure he left

Xander in the dust. To drive himself into her and drive every memory of Xander out of her head.

You still think it's just biology, dumbass?

"Lulu, that thing I said about dogs? I'm sorry. Seems I was insulting you guys instead of the other way around."

DARCY FOUND IT easy to keep her worries at bay while she changed Cady and gave her a morning bottle. The shower was more of a challenge, what with the nakedness and the soaping of areas that were still tender and practically glowing, but singing kid songs at the top of her lungs helped. If anyone asked she would say they were for Cady, who was waiting impatiently in her portable crib with an assortment of toys.

Oddly, getting dressed proved to be the biggest threat to her concentration. She fastened her bra and winced at the pressure against skin scraped by stubble. Pulling on panties made her remember the way he'd yanked the other ones down, not all the way, just enough to let him work his magic. She'd gone from thinking they needed to be off her immediately to flying over the edge, all in the space of one *Oh, my God.*

She felt as if she should go home and offer flowers to his blacksmithing tools for helping him develop such amazing fine motor dexterity.

No, her body was very, very happy with the way

things had played out. It was just the rest of her that was unsettled.

Ian had an appointment at the dairy—another topic she didn't want to think about—so once he left, Darcy spread a blanket on the grass and settled in with Cady, Lulu and her laptop. Did she have any real hope of getting work done? No. What with the dog, the kiddo and the Topics That Must Not Be Named, she would call it a win if she could remember how to access her email. But if she had the equipment at hand, she wouldn't feel quite so conspicuous when Xander wandered by.

Which, as expected, happened about three minutes after they went out.

"Hey." He lowered himself to the corner of the blanket nearest Cady. "Mind if I join you guys?"

Better not to answer that one honestly. Nothing would be served by saying, *Actually, Xander, you're a very nice guy, but the more you hang around, the more I wish you hadn't shown up and blown everything to hell.*

None of this was his fault. He was doing exactly what her rational brain told her he should be doing. And if he hadn't reappeared, would she and Ian ever have gone from friends to, well, whatever they were now?

Play nice, Maguire.

"Be my guest. You can stand guard over the creatures while I work."

"Creature?" He made a horrified face at Cady. "Did Mommy call you a creature?"

"Compared to some of the things I said in those first insane weeks, this is nothing." Of course, the minute the words were out of her mouth, she realized how easily they could be misinterpreted. "But I always said it with love," she added quickly.

"Like when my mom used to call me a brat when I teased her."

Phew. He didn't seem to think she was a bad mother. At least not for this.

She frowned at the screen, all but impossible to read thanks to the glare. Not that it mattered. The laptop was more of a shield against unwanted conversation. She had to talk to Xander. She knew that. And yes, rationally, this would be a great time, with few distractions and no timetable.

But she was…befuddled. Ridiculously resentful. All twisted and cotton-brained, and for once she couldn't blame it on the lack of sleep.

"Hey, pretty girl, don't put that in your mouth."

Cady squawked as Xander gently tugged a piece of grass from her lips. Her big eyes filled with tears as she turned them to Darcy.

"Sorry, kiddo. I'm with…with your father on this one."

That was a step in the right direction, wasn't it? Someday she would be able to say *Daddy*. There was no law that said she had to do it right this minute.

It was a good thing she wasn't in a car. She couldn't find the proper speed for any activity these days.

"So, Darce." Xander leaned on one elbow and bounced Cady's stuffed puppy up and down, pulling a cautious grin from her. "You still working for your mom?"

Oh, goody, another of her favorite topics. At least if they were discussing Sylvie they wouldn't have to touch on the big things yet. "Not as much." She was tempted to leave it there, but as Cady's other parent, he probably deserved some details. And it wouldn't hurt for him to know that there were repercussions to parenthood. "Things got dicey for a while when I got pregnant. We had differing opinions over my ability to do the job with a baby in tow."

"But weren't you always flying everywhere?"

"Not always. And I would have managed. You know, brought a nanny along." True, it would have been harder than she had anticipated—her vision of parenthood had been a lot more rose-tinted in those days—but she would have worked it out.

"So what happened?"

"She hired someone else to take over everything that had to do with her travel and appearances. I'm still handling her books and website and a few other bits and pieces. It was a transition, but it worked out for the best," she added, bright and sunny enough to convince Xander with some perkiness left over for herself. "I branched out and do virtual assistant work for authors—help with social media, run contests, format ebooks. All those incidental things that eat up their time when they should be writing."

"It's all computer work?"

"Mmm-hmm. I like that. I work while Cady goes to day care in the mornings, then I bring her home for lunch and do more work during nap time and after she goes down for the night."

"How's it pay?"

"Well, between that and the rent money, I can support your daughter."

"No, I didn't mean… I was asking for myself."

She finally got a clue. "Oh, of course. Duh. I forgot that you're a—"

Crap. What was she supposed to say? *Computer whiz* didn't sound right but *hacker* might offend him.

Lucky for her Lulu chose that moment to stick her nose beneath the laptop in a desperate plea for attention. Darcy sighed and surrendered.

Was that what she had done with Ian? Pushed him to the point of surrender before she should have?

No. She needed to stop obsessing over that and focus on what mattered: keeping Cady's world steady.

"Maybe this would be a good time for us to sort out some things. About Cady, I mean."

"Oh. Sure." He pushed himself upright. Cady

grabbed his sleeve and pulled to her feet. He laughed and tapped the end of her nose.

Darcy curled her fingers deeper into Lulu's fur.

"Here's the thing, Xander. I know it's important for Cady to spend time with you. I'll do my best to make it as easy as possible. But I'd like to take this slowly—" *better late than never* "—to make it easier on her. Especially since you'll be, what, about four hours from Stratford?"

"Closer to three, I think." He pulled Cady's hand from his nose. "Is she always this aggressive?"

Yeah, and I think she gets it from me. "Be glad. It means she likes you."

"I'm honored."

She handed Cady a teething biscuit. "And I guess this is a good time to confess that I'm pretty independent. I've been on my own with this parenting thing since I figured out I was pregnant. So Cady isn't the only one who's going to need to adjust to having someone else in the picture."

"Except you already did that." At her blank look, he added, "With Ian."

"Right." Should she come clean now? Except, after this morning, were they really still pretending? "That was different. Very gradual, you know? He was there all the time and we kind of grew into the relationships. All of them."

"But I'm more like something that got dumped in your lap out of the blue."

Crap. Had he picked that up from her? She

wanted to protect her girl, but she didn't want to hurt him in the process.

"Okay. Total honesty here." At least in this one thing. "Yes, in some ways it would have been easier on me if you had never come back. Would it have been better for Cady? No." She held his gaze. "At least, not if you end up being the kind of father you seem to want to be."

He dipped his head.

Silence reigned for a second or two. Then Cady pulled the biscuit from her mouth and waved it in a wild arc, causing Xander to scoot back.

"Wow," he said with a laugh. "That thing's half gone already. Is she always this greedy?"

Are you always this greedy?

The early-summer sun shining down on Darcy didn't keep her from going cold.

Are you always this greedy?

She remembered those words. Xander had said them to her, that night. If memory served—not that she could trust it completely, thanks to the booze, but still—she was pretty sure that when Xander had said that, something inside her had broken. Because that was exactly how she had felt that night. Greedy. Desperate. As if everything had been yanked out from beneath her and she'd had to grab hold of someone while she could, because she hadn't known if she could face it all alone.

Kind of like this morning with Ian. Because if she was busy feeling him around her, she couldn't feel her breath turning to sharp points every time she thought of how her careful little world was slipping out of her control.

"Darce? You okay?"

She gave herself a shake, grabbed the toy puppy and danced it up and down on Cady's fat little arm.

"My dad died when I was seven," she said softly. "A drunk driver plowed into him. My mother… Well, she tried, and she certainly took care of me, but her focus was always elsewhere." Like on the Flavor of the Month. "Let's just say it's not like I had great role models. The closest thing I knew about how families were supposed to work was from visiting the Norths when I was a kid. But I read the books and took the classes, and I'm good at details and organization, so I figured I'd be okay."

"Looks that way from where I'm sitting."

"Thanks. But it's all because of Ian. Turns out you need to be more than organized to be a good mother. You need to be good at loving, and I kind of sucked at that."

Xander's eyes widened. He glanced from her to Cady and back, but kept his mouth shut. Smart man.

"I did love her. Desperately. But God's truth, Xander, at first, I didn't dare give in to it. I thought… I think I believed that if I let it show, I would…I would lose her."

"You know," he said, leaning back, "this makes sense. I always thought you were like a queen, wandering around with a smile and a welcome for

everyone, but still surrounded by a giant go-no-
further shield. Now it makes sense."

She wasn't sure that was a compliment, but she
decided to keep going.

"Ian had been doing things for me all along. You
know, running to the store, doing the yard work,
shoveling the sidewalk before I left in the morning.
But he always seemed so— Okay, don't laugh, but
I thought he was shy and reserved."

Now, of course, she knew the truth. He hadn't
been reserved. He'd been healing.

"After Cady was born, though, all that shyness
disappeared. He was always singing to her and telling her how amazing she was and just talking to
her like he really expected her to talk back to him.
I was walking around half-dead, obsessing about
schedules and feedings, and he would swoop in and
pick her up and treat her, well, like Lulu, honestly,
but more so." Her voice dropped. "And it worked.
She was more relaxed and happy with him than
she was with me. That was when I knew I had to
make a change."

Cady blinked up at Xander and clapped her
hands. He obligingly clapped back.

"So after I had this blast of jealousy and indulged
in a little pity party, I decided to treat him as my
personal how-to manual. I watched him and did
what he was doing." As Xander had been doing,
too. "It was scary at first, like I was daring the universe to come and get me. But I knew I wasn't giv-

ing her what she needed, so I made myself do it. Pretty soon I was singing to her and playing games and one morning I went in to get her and she looked at me with those eyes and, holy crap, five tons of love crashed all around me."

Cady must have felt that the interesting part of the story was over, for she wriggled free and began tugging at the grass on the lawn.

"Maybe I would have figured it out on my own," she said softly. "But I really feel like Ian is the one who taught me how to love Cady. And somewhere along the way, I kind of fell for—"

She stopped.

I kind of fell for him.

It couldn't be true. The part about Cady, yes. So much of her relationship with Cady was due to Ian's quiet, easy example. And of course she had grown closer to him as they spent more time together, shared more experiences. They were friends. More than friends after this morning. But only a step or so past the line. Right? Because she didn't...

She didn't.

Except maybe she did.

Maybe, while Ian had been showing her how to have a loving relationship with her daughter, he also had been teaching her how to love him.

IAN'S BODY WAS in Moxie's office, but his mind was far, far away.

"So that's how it looks right now. We'll get rolling as soon as you come on board, assuming you do. If not, I hear Kermit the Frog is looking for a new gig these days."

He blinked as the words sank in. Moxie pushed the last paper aside, folded her hands and fixed him with that *you don't fool me* glare. Across the table, Cash shot him a wink.

Oops. So much for thinking he could focus on business when his head was filled with Darcy.

"I... Sorry. Between Cady teething and...everything else, I'm not as sharp as I should be this morning."

Moxie snorted. "Ian, I've seen bricks that had more on the ball than you do right now. Why the devil didn't you man up and tell me you couldn't do this today? I have better things to do with my time than sit here yammering when you can't pay attention."

"Have I told you yet how much I've missed working with you, Moxie?"

She sniffed. "No. Can't say that you have."

"Good, because I'd hate to tell a lie."

Cash snickered.

"Right at this moment I'd have to say the feeling's mutual." Her face softened. "Lucky for you it passes faster than a bad burrito."

"Aw, Moxie. So tender. I'm going to start crying any minute."

"Oh, for the love of biscuits. Cash, take your

miserable excuse of a brother to his future potential office. Let him have a look around."

On impulse he scooted forward and kissed her powdery cheek.

"Okay, Moxie. I confess. I guess I've missed working with you after all."

"'Course you have." She patted his face. "And believe it or not, we've all missed you."

Some more than others, he was sure, but he was supposed to be looking forward not back.

The soft touch on his cheek turned into something more closely resembling a smack. "Now get going. I have work to do."

"Ma'am, yes, ma'am."

Cash hovered by the door. "Come on, Ian. Let's get you measured for your hair suit."

Cash took a sharp right down the hall leading to the executive offices. Ian followed behind, slowed by a mix of memories from the morning and questions about the future.

Striding down the halls he had walked since he was a child, surrounded by photos of the evolution of the dairy from its beginning to the hundredth anniversary, he couldn't help but feel as though he was slipping back into a place he belonged. Seeing these pictures again was like seeing his life in miniature. He was in a three-generation shot with Grandpa Gord and Dad and his infant self; scooping ice cream at the dairy bar, all teenage zits and grins; at the going-away party before he left for

Tanzania. And—oh, crap—there he was in the ridiculous garb they had donned for a celebratory dance performance during the anniversary.

In every one he was surrounded by family.

In all but the first and last ones, Carter was at his side.

"Here you go." Cash stopped in front of a door and gestured down the hall. "Right within yelling distance of Moxie. Lucky you."

"Like you're not?"

"Ah, but I have to be on the floor a lot, you know. Need to build those relationships so people know they can come to me when there's an issue." He winked. "At least that's what I tell Moxie."

"Right. Like anyone could put anything past her."

"I don't try to put anything over her. I tell her flat out that she's driving me 'round the bend and I have to get away from her." He opened the heavy door and gestured for Ian to enter.

"Bet she loves that."

"She tells me to get my sorry ass down there and do something constructive instead of getting snippy with an old lady. I just laugh and remind her that she's the snippy one."

"Fighting fire with fire. I like it." Ian stopped in the middle of the empty room and turned a slow circle. "Wasn't this Hank's office?"

"Yep."

"But he hasn't worked here for years. Why's

it still empty? Did Moxie think he was coming back?"

"At first, I think maybe. But once he and Brynn got married she saw the writing on the wall." Cash sat in the oversize leather chair and propped his feet on the desk. "I think it was around that time that she started talking about the foundation."

"You mean she's been planning this for almost two years already?"

"Yep."

"And the idea of me heading it up?"

"She never said anything, but if I were a betting man, I'd say that was part of the plan all along."

The wildest part was that none of this really felt like a surprise.

Ian squinted at his brother. "How have you managed to escape Moxie's manipulations all these years?"

"Who says I have?"

"True. But you're the only one who hasn't had any drama. It's unnatural. Are you sure you're not adopted?"

"Right. Because three boys weren't enough for Ma and she had to add a fourth."

"Didn't you get the memo? You were supposed to be the girl."

"Looks like I failed again."

There was a hint of something in Cash's voice that had Ian paying closer attention. "Not from what I hear."

"Ah, but you should know that there's usually a world of difference between the truth and what we're told."

Amen to that.

"In any case," Cash continued, but if he thought he was getting off this easy, he was doomed.

"Hang on. Ma said something the other night about you setting a new dating record around town. What's that all about?"

"How should I know?"

"Well, since you're the one she's talking about, it seemed like a logical assumption."

"You know Ma. World's most down-to-earth woman until it comes to us, and then boom. How many colds did we have that she was sure were first-stage pneumonia?"

He had a point. But...

"Nice job trying to throw me off course, but I'm used to following a toddler now, remember? You can't outrun me. So..." He crossed his arms over his chest and pulled up his best older-wiser-brother expression. "Aren't you getting a little old to be running around with half the town?"

"No. And don't try to look sage and experienced. It makes you look constipated."

"Pathetic," Ian said with a shake of his head.

Cash yanked open the bottom desk drawer and peered inside.

"Not as pathetic as being surrounded by people

who are all madly in *loooooove* and feel compelled to drag everyone else into the same boat."

"I'm not—" Just in time, he stopped himself from saying *in love*. Damn, this pretending had better end soon. He wasn't sure how much longer he could keep up with the story.

Especially when it had started feeling like such a damned good fit.

"I'm not trying to drag you into anything," he said to Cash. "Just saying, you know, there's something to be said for getting to know one person in depth instead of a lot of people on the surface."

Cash slammed the drawer and sat upright, all brisk and businesslike.

"I'll keep that under advisement. Meanwhile, it's lunchtime. I'm running out to Bits and Pizzas for a slice. Want to come along?"

"Thanks, but I promised Darcy I'd come home. I guess I'll see you Sunday."

"Saturday. Ma gave orders. We're all to show up and get things ready for the party."

"Aren't we just grilling outside and eating at the picnic table?"

"And this is why I will never get wrapped up in one woman. It leaves you blind to the rest of the world." Cash leaned against the desk. "She's invited half the town. Brynn's brother and his family, Taylor's folks, Uncle Lou and more. Basically she wants to be sure nobody could say they had to skip to spend the day with their own father, so she asked everyone who might be connected. Why do you think the pig roast truck is coming?"

"Jeez. She's really going all out."

"Yep. Every time we tell her to scale back, she does The Stare and asks if we don't think Dad is worth it."

Yep. Ian could totally see that.

He could also totally believe that his mother had invited a crowd to act as a buffer between him and Carter, just in case.

WHEN IAN GOT back from the dairy, he found Darcy in the kitchen feeding Cady. Xander and Lulu were nowhere to be found.

Privacy. Thank you, God.

She slipped a piece of banana between Cady's lips. "Xander said he wanted to go for a walk and Lulu was prancing, so I told him to take her along. Hope that was— No, Cady, Ian doesn't want yogurt in his hair."

"It's okay. I hear it makes great conditioner."

For the first time since he'd walked in, Darcy met his gaze. She laughed as he'd intended, but it felt almost as if she were forcing it. Did she think he was worried about the dog?

"Xander and Lulu—that's fine. It's not like he's going to run away with her. For one thing, his car is still out front. For another, if he did try to run away with her, I'm pretty sure that after ten minutes of her jumping around in the backseat, that bucket of bolts would surrender in the middle of the highway."

"Good point." She dabbed at Cady's nose with a washcloth, glanced out the window and said, "Um, about this morning…"

Oh, hell.

He didn't say anything but his reaction must have shown in his face, for she stopped and watched him as if she was waiting for him to say…what?

"I meant to stop on the way back from the dairy." He reached slowly, pushing her hair gently behind her ear. "To get you some flowers."

Her eyes closed. He could swear he saw the tension seeping out of her.

"I'm sorry I didn't listen to what you said." Her words were scarcely above whisper level. "I let myself get so— I mean, I'm not sorry that it happened. Don't think that for one minute, okay?" At his nod, she hurried on. "But later, when I could think again, I finally understood what you were trying to say. And do. And I just want to say, thank you, for having such—well, not honorable intentions. But you know what I mean."

He knew exactly what she meant. The fact that she was shouldering the blame didn't surprise him. Nor did the fact that hearing the catch in her voice, seeing the slight pink in her cheeks, only made him want to lure her upstairs for a slow, indulgent Round Two.

The clang of a baby spoon against a high-chair tray reminded him he needed to cool his jets a while longer.

"Listen to me." He framed her face with his hands, drinking in the uncertain brown eyes, the slight tremor in those lips that had haunted his morning. "When you said that I was saying one thing but meant another, you were right. I might have been playing noble, but trust me, that was a textbook case of token resistance." He stroked her cheek with his thumb. "The good news is that wasn't our only chance."

Some of her usual sass sparkled in her eyes. "You mean we might have to keep practicing until we get it right?"

"Yep. Over and over and over."

"Such hardship." She sighed and pulled him into a kiss. Or maybe he grabbed her. It was hard to be sure, and once she was tight against him, he decided it really didn't matter. Especially when her lips parted and a low, needy kind of sound slipped out of her as she wrapped her arms around him.

When the kiss wound down—slowly, lingering, leaving no doubts in his mind that Round Two would more than make up for the morning—she pulled back ever so slightly and smiled.

"So how did it feel to be back at the dairy?"

"Not as good as this." His hand traveled slowly

down her back. How many hours until night? "But yeah. It was almost like I'd never been gone."

"That must have made it easier." She peeked at Cady, busy dropping one Cheerio at a time to the floor, shook her head and returned her focus to him. "Speaking of which…was Carter there?"

"Maybe. I didn't see him." Was it his imagination, or did she have some kind of bee in her bonnet about him and Carter? "Darce, we're okay. It's gonna be awkward for a while, but we'll get through it."

"But shouldn't you—"

"Listen to me." He pulled her hand to his mouth and kissed her fingers—a much more attractive activity than talking about his brother. "You don't have siblings, so you might not get this, but believe me, we'll muddle through. It's going to take time, that's all."

"I don't know, Ian. Something like this goes way beyond, you know, stealing your toy when you were a kid. Taylor was your fiancée. You were engaged to be married. Don't you need to—"

"No. We don't need to do anything except keep moving forward." After all, that had worked when it came to getting over Taylor. It would work this time, too. "Did you and Xander have a chance to go over things?"

She gave his arms a quick squeeze as she slid out of them. "A bit," she called as she knelt to gather Cheerios. "Mostly we talked about Cady. I don't want to go into specifics with him until I get some legal advice, you know?"

That made sense.

So why did he get the feeling she was holding back?

CHAPTER THIRTEEN

IAN STAYED DOWNSTAIRS when Darcy took Cady up for a nap—partly because Darcy said she needed to work, mostly because he wasn't sure he could trust himself not to take advantage of a sleeping child, a quiet afternoon and an empty bed.

Tonight, North.

He'd brought work. He had a book. He could simply go outside with his sandwich and park his ass on the picnic table and watch the river for a while. He had plenty of things to do, and all of them appealed. Yeah, they would be better with Darcy at his side, but...

Xander ambled into the kitchen, caught sight of him and hesitated.

"Hey."

"Hey," Ian returned cautiously. Xander didn't seem like his usual laid-back self. There was an edge about him—almost as though he was braced for attack. From Ian, if the sidelong glances being shot his way were any indication.

Huh.

"How was the walk?"

"Fine." Xander opened the fridge and bent to

peer inside. "She tried to jump in the water, but I stopped her. Thought it might still be too cold for her."

"Thanks."

Something was up, that was for sure. Xander was awfully intent on staring at the bottles of ketchup and mustard. Ian wasn't in any hurry to be best buds with Xander again, but he didn't want to—

Oh, hell.

Every time it had been just them, Ian had gone on the offensive against Xander. True, the first time had been because Xander was demanding Lulu, and the second time, well, he had needed to see for himself that Xander had Cady's best interests at heart. But was it any surprise Xander was hiding in the fridge?

You know, there was a time when you would have invited me in and we could have talked this out over a beer...

Yeah. There had been a time when that's exactly what would have happened. Ian had been so busy defending what was his that he hadn't given much thought to Xander. Understandable at the time, but was that really how he wanted to go forward?

More important, was that what he wanted Darcy to see?

He was the one who had known Xander for years. He was the one who'd lived with the guy. Yet here he was keeping him at arm's length while telling Darcy it was okay to trust her *baby* to him.

It was time to put the caveman to rest.

"Hey. Xander."

Xander's shoulders tensed as he raised his head. Ian pulled the fridge door open.

"While you're in there, why don't you grab us a couple of beers?"

The quick light of gratitude that flashed across Xander's face made Ian feel like a first-class heel.

"Come on." He nodded toward the door. "It's sunny and the rest of the world is working. Let's sit outside and throw sticks for Lulu and make fun of all the slobs stuck in offices."

Which was exactly what they did.

There were more than a few false starts as they talked, more than a few topics that neither of them chose to address. But after a while it got easier. Stories from their university days turned into "Hey, did you hear what Mark is up to these days?" Which turned into Ian sharing tales of his work in Tanzania.

The laughs grew more frequent as the food and beer disappeared. When Darcy texted to say that Cady was awake and they wanted to go sightseeing, Ian was amazed to realize that a couple hours had passed.

This, he knew, was the best way to help Darcy adjust to Xander's presence in their lives. Not by telling her it would be okay, but by showing her.

"So Darce wants to go into town, walk around."

Ian shoved the phone back into his pocket and took a deep breath. "You want to come along?"

"Sure." This time when Xander hesitated, it was without the defensiveness that had been there earlier. "Listen, Ian. I've been thinking. Darcy said something this morning about you showing her how to take care of Cady. Not just the diapers and stuff, but how to be a mom."

He shrugged. "It was easier than she makes it sound. She knew what to do. She was just scared to do it."

"Yeah, well, she sure seems to appreciate it. But I was thinking…she's right. You're good at this, and you and Cady have something special. I thought, maybe, you could give me a hand, too. Teach me how to be a dad."

But I'm her dad.

The thought was so sudden, so strong, that it felt as though someone had yanked the picnic table out from beneath him. He wasn't Cady's dad. He knew that.

But for the first time he admitted that part of him was always going to wish he had been the one home that night Darcy had come knocking. Which meant that—damn—Moxie's line about protecting his family might have hit a lot closer to the mark than he wished.

No wonder Darcy wanted to slow things down.

"And something else," Xander continued. "The thing is I don't… I'm not an idiot, Ian. No one held a gun to my head to make me do the things I did. I don't want to screw up again, but I know things won't be easy. I could use a hand. I need someone who can see through my bullshit and yank me back if I start to screw up."

The meaning behind the words sank in slowly.

"You want me to be like what they have in Alcoholics Anonymous? Your sponsor? Mentor?"

Xander shrugged. "*Friend* sounds good to me."

Oh, hell. Xander thought Ian was going to be in Stratford. He assumed Ian was going to be a permanent part of Cady's and Darcy's lives.

What was that line about tangled webs when you deceive?

At heart Xander was a decent guy. He was probably a lot like Darcy had been about Cady. All he would need was a good word, a reminder that, yeah, you've got this. It would be complicated with Ian here and Xander in cottage country and Darcy and Cady in Stratford, but those were details. Darcy always said the details were the easiest part.

He could do this.

"Sure, Xander." He pushed off the table and stood. "Friends it is."

DARCY HAD BEEN upstairs for maybe twenty minutes when she heard the unmistakable sound of a doorbell. Not a problem, except half-asleep Cady heard it, too, and started to whimper.

Damn it. She'd heard voices a few minutes earlier

from down below and had peeked out the window in time to see Ian, Xander and Lulu headed to the river. They wouldn't hear the bell. And if whoever it was rang again, that would be the end of nap time.

She gave Cady a quick pat on the back, slipped out of the room and ran down the stairs as fast as her bare feet would carry her. She made it to the front door just in time to stop Taylor from hitting the bell again.

"Hi!" Taylor stood on the front step with a shopping bag at her feet and a bright smile on her face that faded quickly as her gaze ran over a slightly panting Darcy. "Oops. Did I drag you away from something?"

"Nothing exciting, trust me. But I just put Cady down. She can sleep through the bell at home no problem, but this one is different, so..."

"Got it. I'm sorry. Will she be okay?"

"I hope so. Did you need something?"

"Officially, I don't have your phone number, so I'm running here on my lunch hour to ask if you would like to help tomorrow when we make the desserts for the party. Unofficially—" she lifted the bag, sending the scent of something hot and delicious wafting through the air "—I'm here to ply you with food and get advice on surviving early pregnancy."

Darcy was pretty sure there was another agenda at play, and she wouldn't be at all surprised if it involved Ian and/or Carter. But her own lunch had been a scoop of peanut butter while dodging Cheerios, and her mouth was watering, and maybe she could weasel some information out of Taylor.

"Consider me plied. Let me run upstairs and grab the monitor."

"I'll meet you in the kitchen. Unless..." Taylor glanced over her shoulder. "I thought Ian would still be at the dairy, but I see his car."

Yep. This was definitely more than a getting-to-know-you call.

"He's outside with Xander. If we open the door, we could see them from the table, right?"

"You catch on quick."

"Motherhood lesson one, learn to think on your feet."

She padded back upstairs, peeked in on Cady— asleep, *yes*—and took a minute to run a comb through her hair and check her makeup. Did she believe Ian was over Taylor? Absolutely. Did some small part of her still wish she had pulled on something other than capris and a T-shirt proclaiming Shakespeare as her homeboy? Maybe.

Taylor had pulled cartons from the bag and was setting plates and utensils on the table when Darcy returned.

"I didn't know what you would like and I can't tell what's going to sit well these days, so I bought half the items on the menu."

No kidding. The table was covered.

"But we've got caprese salad, grilled artichoke

and chicken sandwiches, minestrone, a Monte Cristo and some quiche tarts. And I will tell you right now I'm calling dibs on the caramelized onion one."

"Fair enough." Darcy grabbed a piece of the monte cristo—when was the last time she had one of those?—made sure she had a good view of Ian and sat down.

On the other side of the table, Taylor forked up quiche and moaned.

"Oh, God. This is good. Everything tastes so gross right now, but this...this is working."

"How far along are you?"

"Seven weeks," Taylor said, and launched into a long list of her symptoms, her excitement and her plans for the nursery. Darcy figured her job was to listen, nod and keep an eye out for interlopers. She could do that.

"So." Taylor licked her finger and pressed it to the crumbs clinging to the side of the foil container. "Has Comeback Cove changed much since you were a kid?"

"I haven't seen a lot of it yet, so I can't really say."

"Has Ian talked you into moving up here yet?"

Ah, now they were getting somewhere. "Nope."

"Oh. I thought, maybe... It's just that he looks so happy now."

Considering that the last real time Taylor had seen him she'd been busy breaking his heart, that was no surprise.

"And seeing him with Cady, even though I know things are complicated with Xander and all, it's so clear that Ian worships the ground she walks on." Taylor plucked a cherry tomato from the caprese salad. "He was so eager to have kids. I used to joke that he wanted to be a father more than he wanted to be a husband."

"Well, that gave you a nice out, didn't it?"

Too late, Darcy slapped her hand over her mouth. Oh, *crap*.

"I'm sorry, I—"

Hang on. Why was she apologizing? Okay, yes, the comment had been rude. And yes, she was lying to his entire family. But compared to what Taylor and Carter had done…?

"I'm sorry for the way that came out." She made herself meet Taylor's gaze. "But I refuse to apologize for the sentiment behind it."

Taylor's cheeks reddened and her eyes grew wide, but after a moment's hesitation, she gave a slow nod. "I guess I can't fault you for that."

Damn straight.

"Look, Taylor. Ian told me how things played out. I understand that it was a lousy situation all around, and I do believe that everyone tried their hardest to avoid hurting him. But it still sucked. And even though I know that I wouldn't be here right now if you hadn't ditched him, part of me is still coming to grips with how badly he was treated. Especially by his own brother."

Taylor's eyes were wide but she managed a nod.

"I guess I don't have to wonder about hidden meanings behind things you say."

"Actually, I'm not usually this blunt." Darcy dished up some soup. "The weirdest thing is that even though I'm kind of furious with you, at another level it's like you do seem nice and I really do believe you tried to keep things from blowing up the way they did."

Taylor tipped her head the slightest bit sideways and seemed to be taking Darcy's measure. The tiniest hint of a smile tugged at the corners of her mouth.

"You know what's even stranger? I think I understand. Perfectly."

"Well, thank God one of us does, because right now I have this strange empathy for Dr. Jekyll."

Taylor burst into laughter.

"Oh, Darcy. I'm so glad Ian found you, because I think you're exactly what he needs."

Was she? Darcy didn't dare think about it. Everything was still so new and raw, and she was so rattled by what she may have stumbled over while talking to Xander that at that moment the only certainty was that if she didn't stop inhaling the soup, she would throw up.

Well, there was one other thing.

"Actually," she said, shoving the bowl aside, "there's something I think he needs even more. And you're just the person to help me."

Taylor glanced out the door. "Let me guess. You think he and Carter need to sit down and talk about what happened once and for all."

The part of her that liked Taylor smiled in relief.

"Exactly. Ian says it's fine. He's over it. He's over you—oops, no offense intended—"

"Not to worry. That's the best thing I've heard all day."

"And he keeps saying this is just what families do. They carry on and let time pass and then it's fine. I'm sure he's right about that working for most things, but my gut tells me this is bigger."

"I'm with you." Taylor eyed the remaining quiche before pushing it away. "Carter hasn't said much, but I think he would like to get this out in the open. It probably would be okay eventually, but my guess is that it will be a whole lot better a whole lot faster if they can just be honest with each other."

The mention of honesty made Darcy glance away. How would Taylor feel when she found out she'd been opening up to a woman who was pretending to be something she wasn't?

Taylor continued, "What Ian probably hasn't told you is that he and Carter were really close. They weren't just brothers. They were friends. Ian lost a lot when everything fell apart, and, honestly, I think that losing me was the easiest part of all for him."

"I agree. Again, no offense intended."

"None taken." Taylor leaned forward in her chair.

"Darcy, I'm going to go out on a limb here. Do you think it would be wrong if we—"

"If we orchestrated something to get them alone together?"

"You read my mind."

Darcy's pulse kicked up a bit. Did she have the right to do this? Heaven only knew. She wasn't really Ian's girlfriend, though the title was feeling less like a pretense with every kiss. Her own family life hadn't qualified her to give advice to anyone else, especially since Xander's arrival.

But she knew Ian. So much of what she had seen in him since he'd moved in made heartbreaking sense now that she knew the truth. The way he always chose his words carefully when he spoke of his family, the fact that he had never mentioned Carter's name, the way he stared wistfully at young brothers squabbling when they went to the playground—it all fit now. She was the only one who knew that side of him.

And at the core of it, she was his friend.

She checked the door once more and leaned forward.

"Tell me what you have in mind."

THE ADVENTURE IN town went off as smoothly as any outing involving a baby and a dog could probably go. They wandered leisurely, taking turns waiting outside stores with Lulu. Ian hadn't spent much time in Comeback Cove proper in the brief period between Tanzania and Stratford—there had been too many sympathetic glances and whispers for his comfort—so it was almost as if he hadn't been around for three years.

Of course, seeing the sights wasn't half as much fun as watching Darcy rediscover old haunts. Xander had volunteered for stroller duty so Ian and Darcy were free to walk slowly, hand in hand, him telling stories about the people he'd grown up with and her feigning resistance when he insisted that it was illegal to walk the sidewalks without buying fudge. In short, he didn't think he could have imagined a better reentry.

They returned to a driveway so crowded there was barely room for the Mustang.

"Six cars and one truck," Darcy said as she unbuckled Cady. "Are you guys opening a side business selling vehicles?"

"That's right. Everything must go. Well, except Xander's rust bucket," he said with a teasing grin, causing Xander to fake growl, which made Lulu yip and prance.

"The truck is Hank's, and the hatchback is Brynn's. So I'm guessing that it's either spoil-Millie night, or Hank couldn't keep Brynn from racing here to meet you any longer."

"Why do I get the feeling I'm the biggest thing to happen in your family in a long time?"

Ian started to put the diaper bag on his shoulder,

checked himself and handed it to Xander. "Here. The pink goes better with your shirt than mine."

Xander grimaced but shouldered the bag and fell into step.

"As for you and my family—" Ian slipped an arm around her waist and pulled her close "—you might not be the *biggest* thing to happen. But you're definitely the best."

They made it as far as the petunia bed before Hank and Brynn hurried down the steps, sweeping him into hugs and backslaps, shaking hands with Xander, chiding Ian over Darcy and switching to ridiculously high-pitched voices to talk to Cady.

They were making their way slowly to the house when the door burst open and a pint-size dynamo flew down the steps, her long hair flying behind her.

"Uncle Ian!"

"Mills!" Ian swept her into a giant hug, lifting her off her feet to twirl her in a circle, only to realize the town wasn't the only thing that had changed.

"Holy moly, kiddo." He lowered her to the ground with an exaggerated groan. "You're about twice as big as the last time I saw you. Has Brynn been giving you growing lessons?"

Millie giggled and sent a shy glance toward Darcy. "Mom says I had a growth spurt, but Brynn says that Daddy sneaks into my room and stretches me after I'm asleep."

"I can believe it." That did it. He was going to

have to make sure he got back to Stratford every other weekend. Cady was growing even faster than Mills at this age, and he'd be damned if he'd miss out on any of it.

He shook his head and tugged Millie forward. "Come meet Darcy and Cady."

"Grandma said Cady might be my cousin. Is that true?"

Lord, shoot me now.

"Mills…" Hank said with a groan.

"You know, Millie," Darcy rushed in, "Cady doesn't have any cousins." She bit her lip and sent a quizzical look to Xander, but point for him, he simply shook his head. "How about if we make you two honorary cousins for now?"

Millie scrunched her eyes tight behind her Harry Potter glasses. "Is that real or pretend?"

"It's as real as you want it to be." Just like what was happening with him and Darcy?

Millie broke into a heart-tugging smile. "Okay. I'm good at pretending. Once I told Brynn there was a snake in the basement, and she went down there with a flashlight and a broom, and she was gone for, you know, ages and ages hunting for it."

If the startled expression on Brynn's face was any indication, this was her first realization that Millie had pulled a fast one on her.

From the look on Hank's face, it would be the last time Millie got away with it.

Moxie appeared on the steps just then and ordered everyone inside before the food got cold. There came the predictable crush in the front hall, a few snorts of laughter and the shuffling of seats. Millie insisted on sitting beside Cady, and Brynn told Ian in no uncertain terms that he was to go hang with his brother so she could get to know Darcy.

"And by the way," she said, giving his arm a squeeze, "you are going to pay through the nose for keeping her a secret for so long, mister."

Damn, he had missed this.

The laughter flowed more freely tonight than it had the previous evening. He told himself it was simply because Brynn was a people person, and Millie could out-chatter the most awkward silence, and everyone else—his folks, Darcy, Xander— were more familiar with each other. He hoped those were the reasons. He didn't want it to be because last night everyone had been holding their collective breath at the sight of him and Carter at the same table.

But if it was, well, as he'd told Darcy, they needed time. Time and repetition. And maybe they could put Brynn in charge of reminding everyone to chill. He didn't know about Carter, but he was the slightest bit terrified of that woman.

Darcy, however, seemed to have no problem with her. Every time he checked on her she was either tending to Cady or deep in conversation with

Brynn, which didn't do anything to his radar until Hank elbowed him.

"Heads up, Ian. Looks like my wife is plotting something with Darcy."

He laughed away the twinge in his gut, peeked at Cady and felt the blood drain from his face when he saw that she had somehow got hold of a—

"Darce!" Ian jumped from his chair, ready to dive across the table if needed, but Darcy had already read his mind. She turned to Cady, paled and yanked the steak knife from Cady's hand as it sliced the air far too close to Millie's arm.

"Is she okay?"

"Mills, did you—"

Moxie's voice rang out above the hubbub. "For the love of God, people. Calm down before you set the child crying."

Cady, of course, was wailing in protest over losing her new toy. Darcy pulled her from the high chair and onto her lap, distracting her with a dancing spoon while she looked to Ian. The guilt in her face was unmistakable.

You okay? he mouthed. She took a deep breath, cracked a tiny smile and nodded.

That's my girl.

"Darcy," Dad said from his end of the table. "You don't remember this, of course, but once when you were not much older than that, your father brought you here and we took you kids outside to play. The twins were babies, so it was just you and Ian." He shook his head. "Our first mistake was in thinking we could put a grill together while watching a couple of toddlers."

Hank snickered.

"We were talking and hammering and trying to figure out the instructions, and then we looked up and you two had disappeared. We didn't think you could have gone far, but neither of us was really sure when we'd last seen you. I think we set provincial speed records racing all over the backyard hunting for you."

It was obvious there was a happy ending to this, so Ian had no problem laughing. Darcy listened with wide eyes, absently tugging Cady's hands away from her earrings.

"It felt like forever, but really we found you pretty quick. You were in the shed we had back there, the one where we stored the lawn mowers and gardening tools."

Ma jumped in. "The shed you were supposed to keep locked so the kids wouldn't get into it."

"Well, I did after that day, you can believe it."

"What were we doing?" Ian wasn't entirely sure he wanted to know, but from the way his dad was laughing, he didn't think it could have been anything too dangerous.

"Playing barber," Moxie said.

Thank God it was barber, not doctor.

"You'd found the pruning shears." Ma closed her eyes. "Half of Darcy's hair was on the ground."

Darcy made a small sound of surprise. "Wait. I remember... Not this, but my mother has one picture of me with this wild uneven haircut. Are you telling me it was Ian's fault?"

"Nah. Ian didn't do so bad, all things considered. The real problem came when Paul grabbed the shears himself and tried to make both sides match."

The rest of the table burst into laughter. Darcy, he noticed, bit her lip and frowned.

"But...wait. My mother always told me I did that to myself. Something about wanting to look like the little girl next door."

"Maybe it happened twice," Brynn suggested. Moxie laughed along.

"Was there maybe a few pictures with the shaggy look, Darcy?"

"I... Maybe. I don't remember. But that seems so, well, not like my dad."

Moxie snorted. "Child, your father worshipped the ground your little moccasins danced on, but when it came to the practical parts of being a father...well, put it this way. I will go to my grave remembering the day he showed up here with you in a snowsuit and boots with fuzzy pink socks on your hands because he forgot to pack you any mittens."

"Or the time you pranced in yelling 'Party on, Wayne,'" Ma said. "And he had to confess you fell asleep in front of the TV and woke up just in time for *Saturday Night Live*—"

"And he let you stay up and watch the rest."
Dad's eyes went from merry to melancholy in the
space of a breath. Ian's heart clenched at the sight.
He'd always known that Dad and Paul Maguire
had been buddies, but this was the first time it had
really hit home.

Maybe because this was the first time he had
been watching through Darcy's eyes.

CHAPTER FOURTEEN

WHEN DINNER WAS finished and the dishes done, when Hank and Brynn tore a protesting Millie away from Cady, Darcy handed Cady to Ian and slipped upstairs. Officially, she was setting up for Xander's first bath-time lesson. Unofficially, if she didn't get a minute alone she was going to start spinning.

It wasn't just the fact that Xander had been beside Ian at dinner, meaning that every time she saw one, she saw the other. It wasn't simply the plan she'd hatched with Taylor weighing on her conscience. It wasn't even the cumulative effect of the five million changes that had happened since Tuesday afternoon.

No, this time she needed a few minutes alone to process Robert's stories.

She gathered towels, laid out a fresh diaper and sleeper. She had loved hearing new tales about her dad. That was an unexpected bonus to this trip. But Robert's stories were so different from those her mother told that it was as if they were about two different people.

All her life she had been told that her dad was

a natural parent. Her own memories of him were filled with laughter and cuddles and, yeah, a few smacks on the behind. She certainly hadn't been a perfect kid.

But Robert's stories…

Not paying attention while she'd wandered off, she could understand. Kids moved fast. But chopping her hair with pruning shears to make it match on both sides? Forgetting mittens in the middle of a Canadian winter? Letting her watch an adult show at midnight?

None of it made sense.

On impulse she dropped the bath toys she'd been gathering and grabbed her phone. If luck was with her Sylvie would still be awake.

"Darcy." Sylvie had that brisk tone to her voice that meant Matteo was far away. "I'm finishing up a quick drink with the producer." Translation: she was talking business and didn't want to be interrupted. "Can this wait until morning?"

Darcy almost did the good-girl thing and said sure, of course. But to heck with that. This was her whole life they were talking about.

"I know this will sound crazy, but please humor me. Robert told some stories tonight about Daddy, and they were…well…"

Sylvie sighed. "Give me a minute."

Darcy heard her muttering something about *my daughter* and *time zones*. Nothing very compassionate, but on the other hand, Sylvie was excusing herself, so Darcy leaned against the headboard and gave thanks for small miracles.

"Darcy, I just walked away from something that sounded like the prelude to a position at the Old Vic. You have five minutes. If you can do it in less, that's even better.

"Right. Sorry, but I… Robert told these stories, very funny, but they made Daddy sound so…well… incompetent. Like about that really whacked haircut when I was around three that you always said I did to myself."

"Which is exactly what happened. I left for the theater one night with your hair in braids. The next time I saw you, it was all hacked off."

"But Robert sounded so certain. Did it maybe happen more than once?"

"Darcy, we're talking about something that happened almost thirty years ago." Darcy could almost see Sylvie in her favorite red satin after-performance dress, drumming her fingers on the wall of whatever alcove she was hiding in. "What exactly did Robert say?"

"That Ian North did it. With pruning shears. And then Daddy finished the job."

Stunned silence was followed by a peal of laughter. "And how much had dear Robert been drinking before he fed you this tale?"

"Nothing that I saw."

"Poor man. I always thought he would turn into a closet alcoholic. Darcy, I am your mother. I know

I wasn't always the best one, but I was there, and I remember being in awe of your father's abilities with you. He would never— Good Lord, pruning shears? No. Never happened."

Lulu padded into the room, surveyed the bed and gave a mighty leap. Darcy didn't have the energy to push her away.

"He never let me watch TV at midnight?"

"No."

"Never put socks on my hands because he forgot mittens?"

This time there was no mistaking the edge to Sylvie's sigh. "Darcy. Your father adored you. He would never have done anything to put you in jeopardy. He was a strict but fair parent, and you were blessed to have him, even if it was cut short. Now I really need to run."

"Of course. Thanks, Mom. I do appreciate it." She squeezed her eyes shut and sank her fingers into Lulu's fur. "Love you."

"Well, of course, and I love you, too. We'll talk tomorrow."

Sylvie was the first one to end the call. Darcy stared into space and let her phone drop to the mattress.

"Call me paranoid, girl," she said to Lulu, who sat up and tipped her head sideways. "But I grew up listening to her rehearsing and performing. And that laugh?" She shook her head. "Yeah. Pure and total acting."

WHAT WAS TAKING Darcy so long?

Ian forced himself to stay downstairs talking to Ma about people he'd gone to school with and Uncle Lou's latest antics while they chased Cady around the sunporch, but it was harder and harder to keep listening. Darcy had said she needed five or ten minutes, but it had been at least half an hour since she left. Xander was waiting outside—Ian could hear him talking to Dad—and Moxie had said something about taking a load off her feet. As far as he could tell Darcy was alone up there.

Maybe she'd had enough of his family and needed a break. He could understand that one. But for her to leave Cady for so long, especially with bedtime rapidly approaching, wasn't like her.

Ten to one she'd fallen asleep. He could go up and check on her. Or he could let Lulu out, grab Cady, take her up and either hand her over for the promised lesson or get her settled for the night himself, come back down, bring Lulu back in and then head up for real. As far as he could see, he would end up doing all of it anyway. The only difference was how many trips he would have to make up and down the stairs.

Since rumor had it he might have some far better ways to use his energy tonight, he opted for plan B.

He gave Cady a kiss, told Ma he'd be back in a minute, found Lulu on the stairs and lured her through the kitchen to the back door. So far, so good.

Then he turned around and came face-to-face with Moxie.

"Just the person I wanted to see."

"Sorry, Moxie. I'd love to stay and plot world domination with you, but I have to get Cady upstairs before she falls apart."

"I know. But this'll only take a minute."

Which meant it would be a good ten or fifteen, but arguing would only prolong the torture. He pulled out a chair and sat at the worn kitchen table. "Okay. What's up?"

Moxie opened the freezer and pulled out a carton of ice cream. "Don't tell your Darcy, but I just talked to Helene. She was able to change her flights so's she can be here on Sunday for the party."

"She's cutting her vacation short?"

"Eh. She had all the parts she wanted—the cruise, the glaciers, the polar bears. All she's missing out on is the day in Seattle, and she said if she wants to see people toss fish through the air, she can just go down to the river during the carp derby."

"Well, that's great. Darcy will be, uh, surprised."

"She'd better be a damn sight more than that."

"Now, Moxie…"

She waved a spoonful of something fluorescent orange in his face. "Don't you *Now, Moxie* me. Your girl is breaking my best friend's heart. I don't like it, and if I can help put a stop to it, you're darn tootin' I'm going to do it."

"You ever hear of live and let live?"

"'Course I have. But let me tell you, it's no kind of life when your last living family is turning her back on you."

"Darcy isn't—"

"Oh, I know she still talks to Helene. But it's not like it was. Those two used to be so tight, and then it all changed."

"And that couldn't possibly have anything to do with the fact that Darcy is now a self-employed single mother."

The spoon came perilously close to his knuckles. "Don't be an ass. Of course we know how busy she is. Paul's dad passed when he was just ten, so Helene knows all about being a mother alone. Besides, she said this started before Cadence was born."

In truth, Ian had a decent idea what had caused Darcy to pull back from Helene. The trick would be spelling it out for Moxie without having his head ripped off.

"Darce has never come out and said anything," he said slowly. "But from things she let slip, I get the impression that Helene wasn't too happy about Darcy getting pregnant without getting married."

"Huh." Moxie shoveled in another bite of the ice cream, pulled out the spoon and gave it a thoughtful lick. "I'll grant you, Helene and I are more old-fashioned about some things than other folks. And I know she was worried about Darcy going it alone.

But to say outright disapproved… I don't buy it. For one thing, Helene is the last person to tell someone else how to run their life."

A skill that Moxie's grandsons had fervently prayed she would learn.

"For another… Oh, Ian. There's never been a woman so excited about a baby coming. She might have been surprised at first, true. But she spent the whole winter knitting little sweaters and hats and the most beautiful christening blanket I have ever seen. She was making such plans. But Darcy… Helene says it was like someone rebuilt the Berlin Wall."

"Look," he said, only to be distracted by a ribbon of black in the middle of her ice cream. "Is that Tiger Stripe?"

"Yep."

"We stopped making that when I was a kid."

"We stopped selling it." Moxie spooned up another bite. "But every once in a while, I get a hankering for it. And what's the point of being head of a dairy if you can't get your favorite ice cream when you want it?"

There was that.

Dad wandered into the room. "Ian, your mother says she's not positive, but her bet is that Cady is about three minutes away from total collapse."

"Okay, I'll be right there. Can you tell Xander bath is canceled for tonight?"

Dad nodded, took the spoon from Moxie's hand, helped himself to a large bite and disappeared.

"I have to go. I'll talk to Darcy about Helene, okay?"

"Oh, that's rich. *You* giving someone a heads-up about not coming clean with someone they love?"

It was lucky for Moxie that Cady picked that moment to let out a wail that echoed through the first floor.

When the hell had life become so complicated?

DARCY WOKE TO DARKNESS.

At first, disoriented and groggy, she thought maybe the power had failed. Then other senses kicked in, slowly and sluggishly, and she figured out that the reason her nose was warm and her breath was moist on her own cheeks was because she was pressed tight against Ian's chest.

What the—

Crap. She remembered talking to Sylvie, dropping her phone, telling Lulu she didn't think Sylvie was telling the truth. Then she might have closed her eyes for a moment just to process everything and…

So much for her plan to spend the night making up for the hash she'd made of the morning. She'd fallen asleep fully dressed and— Oh, hell. Had he been stuck putting Cady down for the night?

She eased out of his embrace, pressed a kiss to his hand and then to his shoulder. Her fingers lin-

gered for an extra heartbeat, soaking up the almost-
forgotten mix of muscle and strength and heat that
was so male.

No. Not just male. *Ian.*

She checked the time—a little before three—and
slipped through the passage to peek in on Cady.
Sleeping soundly and obviously none the worse
for her mother's negligence. Not that leaving her
child in loving and obviously capable hands was
negligence, but...

She was almost out of the room, on her way back
to her own bed, when she stopped and returned to
the crib. She kissed her fingertips and touched them
lightly to her baby's cheek.

*I'm sorry, sweetness. I'm messing up everything
these days, but soon it will be just us again.*

Of course, even that was changing with Ian moving back home. How was she supposed to give her
child stability when the world insisted on turning
and throwing everyone around?

She tiptoed around Lulu and through the kitchenette. Ian had rolled onto his back. His face tipped
toward the door, almost as if he'd woken for a moment and looked for her.

She slipped into the bathroom and made a face at
herself in the mirror. Nothing like seducing a man
with her hair in spiky points and mascara smeared
across her cheek.

She shimmied out of her capris and ditched the
bra. Her T-shirt would suffice.

Wash face. Brush teeth. A dab of perfume. A smear of lipstick because even if it was dark she wanted to look her best for him, make this amazing for him. A smile and a shake of her hair, just enough to make it look as if it was ready to be rumpled some more.

Damn, she hoped he'd already brought the box of condoms upstairs.

She pressed one hand to her stomach, closed her eyes. *Savor this.* Much as she wanted to walk out of the bathroom and kiss Ian into wakefulness, she still wanted to hold this moment when her stomach jumped and her heart thudded and everything shimmered with promise.

One breath, two and then—

"Showtime."

Ian slept half under covers, one leg and arm on top of the blankets, one below. She watched for a moment in the soft glow of the bathroom nightlight. Where should she begin? The outstretched hand? The chest that she'd been facing when she woke? The mouth, oh, that mouth that had already ruined her for kisses from anyone else?

When she spotted the bit of hair falling over his eyes, she knew. *There.*

She slid into the bed and scooted close to him. Her fingers slipped through the misbehaving hair and pushed it back, smoothing it into place. He sighed softly.

Enough sighs. It was time to crank up the moan machine.

Heart pounding she scooted closer and kissed his eyelids, soft butterfly kisses that wouldn't wake him completely but would start things moving.

"Thank you," she whispered after each one. "Thank you."

His nose twitched, so she dropped the next kiss right there on the tip. His face tilted up the slightest bit as if inviting more, and the rush she felt at that simple reaction left her weak in the best possible way.

Hmm. If she was going to feel dizzy with every kiss, propping up on her arms simply wasn't going to work. She needed a sturdier position. Such as...

Before she could lose her nerve, she slid up and over. Hands on his chest, knees on either side of his hips and a whole lot of happiness tap-dancing between her thighs.

Every thought and wonder and temptation that she had pushed down over the past God knew how long rushed back to the surface. She closed her eyes and slid her hands up his chest, bracing and steadying while her imagination raced ahead and her hands shook and she curled forward, burying her face in his chest, her hair trailing across the muscles.

"So long," she whispered against his heart. "I've wanted this for so damned long."

Strong hands gripped her sides, sliding along her

ribs on a slow route north. A lingering route complete with some highly sensitive detours. When he reached her shoulders she curled down to kiss him, long, exploratory kisses, giving herself the chance to learn. To absorb. To savor and revel in Ian's taste, Ian's touch, Ian's voice whispering her name in wonder.

This was what she wanted. Not desperation. Discovery.

And discover she did.

She already knew about the light dusting of sandy hair on his chest, but she hadn't expected their crispness beneath her palms. She already knew about the scar on his collarbone—"The toboggan hit a tree," he'd said. "And Cash's boot hit me"—but she never would have guessed that a curve and a kiss lower, the brush of her lips above his ribs would start him shaking with suppressed laughter.

"Ticklish," he said with a snort, and she paused, but, oh, all that shaking beneath and against her had started the most amazing sparks fluttering. She dipped her head and—slowly, deliberately—licked that spot again. He sucked in a breath and arched against her, sending the sparks racing and playing momentary hell with her determination to take her time. But she had to do this right, so she pulled back the tiniest bit.

"I think I found your on button, North."

He laughed again, but since she was laughing,

too, the shaking was mutual this time. It pushed her higher, but still within her control.

She already knew the curve of the muscles in his arms: she found a bruise above his inner elbow and kissed it with a promise to make all his boo-boos better.

"All of them?" he asked, and she closed her eyes, thinking of the hurts he carried inside.

"Every single one."

"Glad to hear it." He pushed her shirt higher. "'Cause lately I've been having this weird ache, right around the scars where I was circum—"

She silenced him with a kiss but her giggles broke through. Or maybe he was the one snickering. Hard to tell who was leading and who was following when they were pressed so close that his laughter rippled through her.

He tugged her shirt over her head, slowly and lazily, holding it from his extended arm for a moment before letting it drop to the ground. Playing. As though they had hours.

As though they had a lifetime.

"Now we're getting somewhere." His voice had dropped about twelve octaves in the space of a few minutes.

"Such a man. Nothing counts until someone is naked." She scooted forward. Her perch was a lot more crowded than it had been when she'd first hopped on board. And, oh, she couldn't wait to feel that crowding deep inside.

Yes. She could wait. Could and would.

Though maybe if she were lucky, not too much longer. There was taking it slow and then there was cruel and unusual punishment.

"So, Mr. Typical Male. I know you paid a visit to the drugstore today."

"Mmm."

She wasn't sure if that was agreement or pleasure. Probably both.

"Tell me you made a highly significant purchase."

He appeared to be thinking. "Shampoo?"

"Wrong answer. Anything else?"

"A chocolate bar. I was hungry."

Okay, that was it. A girl could only take so much.

She leaned forward, kissing a soft line from his neck down his chest all the way to his belly button. Once there, she stopped. Nuzzled his navel. Let her hand drift lower, two fingers slipping beneath the elastic of his sleep pants. And then, in a move that would probably leave her abs protesting tomorrow, pushed herself forward again, back where she'd been at first.

"Darce…"

She made her way back down his chest. Once more, twice more. Each time she lingered a little longer, drew out her attention, pushed them each a little closer to the edge. When she made her third lunge forward he groaned, grabbed her arms and flipped her over.

"You always play dirty, Maguire?"

"I always play to win."

"Yeah? What do you get if you win?"

"You," she whispered, and the little word bounced around inside her.

You. Inside her, around her, at her side. Not just for tonight. Not just until he had to move back. But for that lifetime that this playful night promised.

She slid her hands down the muscles of his back. This time she didn't stop when she hooked her fingers through his waistband.

This time when he said, "Wait," against her neck, she held her breath and gave him the freedom to open the drawer of the bedside table.

This time when he took her in his arms, she didn't hesitate to open to him. To whisper encouragement as he finally, finally filled her. To find his rhythm. Laugh against his heart. To turn *slow and special* to *now, yes, now.*

And then to nestle deep within his arms, pressed against him skin to skin, and drift to sweet, sticky sleep.

DARCY TRIED TO think if she'd ever had a more perfect morning. The closest she could come was Christmas the year she had been six and got the Teddy Ruxpin she hadn't dared to think she could receive. Waking up to Ian was even better.

They stayed in bed until Cady woke, when—oh, the man was perfect—he hopped out, dealt with the diaper and pulled her in with them. For a few minutes it had been just the three of them laughing and cuddling together. For that hour or so they were the family she was beginning to hope they could be.

Ian had to go to the dairy in the morning, but they had arranged with Xander to pay a visit to Memorial Park in the afternoon. As soon as nap time was over they squeezed into the Mustang— three adults, one child in a car seat and the dog— and took off. Cady was in a good mood and Lulu wasn't too hyper, so they took the scenic route. Ian pointed out places he thought Darcy might remember from her childhood visits—the small family-owned grocery store where Helene still shopped, the church where Helene had shown her off to admiring friends, the ice cream bar run by the Norths. Bits and pieces of her childhood, all coming back.

They drove around until both Cady and Lulu had had enough and let it be known in no uncertain terms that it was time to get out of the car. She couldn't blame them. She shared that need to move and enjoy. The sun was shining, the breeze was calling and, as for her, she had spent the night making sweet love to Ian. It was the kind of day that made anything seem possible. When Cady let out an ear-piercing shriek as they pulled up to the park, Darcy was even able to make a joke about her getting her lung power from Xander.

Once Lulu was on her leash and Cady was in

her stroller and everyone had been given a drink, a snack, a coating of sunblock or all three, they set off.

"I remember this." Darcy lifted one hand from the stroller to wave toward the low curving walls circling the flagpole at the center of the park. Xander and Lulu walked slightly ahead of them, loose-limbed and carefree. "My father brought me here. I think there was music. And fireworks."

"Canada Day, probably. Or Victoria Day, or even the Rum Runners weekend. This is where the big things happen. Games, food and bands, and, yeah, fireworks at night."

Xander turned back and loped toward them, his half-buttoned denim shirt flapping in the breeze.

"Hey. This is a big area." He gestured toward Cady. "Could I maybe push her for a bit? Take her out of the stroller and walk with her?"

She bent to check Cady's hat, buying herself a second. It wasn't Xander's fault that she was deep in Ian-Darcy-Cady fantasy family land. If he wanted to have a few minutes alone with Cady, she needed to give them to him.

After all, once he started work she would only need to do this a few days each month. Surely she could handle that.

"Okay. She's more than ready to get out and move."

Xander squatted in front of the stroller, fiddled with the buckles and pulled the straps away with a triumphant laugh. "Got you, you suckers." He held out his hands to Cady. "Come on, baby girl. Let's explore."

Cady shoved her hand in her mouth and eyed him. Darcy's grip tightened on the handles. Ian's hand, warm and solid in the center of her back, was both a support and a reminder of how screwed-up this whole situation had become.

After a long moment, Cady leaned forward and took Xander's hands.

"That's right," Xander breathed. "That's my girl. Come to Daddy."

This was what was best for Cady. Wasn't it?

Cady's feet hit the ground. Xander maneuvered himself behind her and let her grip his fingers while she slapped one foot in front of the other. The wonder on his face made Darcy feel small and churlish.

"You kids have fun," Xander called over his shoulder as Cady veered toward a stand of trees.

"Make sure she stays in sight," Darcy called. "Just so, you know, she doesn't freak if she looks for me and I'm not there."

Ian's arm slipped around her waist. She leaned into him, grateful for his soft kiss at her temple. "You okay?"

"I've been better." She forced herself to smile up at him. "But I have to do this. It's only for a few days every once in a while, right? And if he wants to be her father, I have to let him."

He kissed her again, a little longer, a little deeper. Okay. Maybe there were *some* advantages to having someone else around to look after Cady once in a while.

Silver linings, right?

"Come on." He took her hand and led her toward the curved walls. "Time for your local history lesson."

"I remember some. This park is filled with things from the Lost Villages, right? The towns that were destroyed when the Seaway was being built."

"Right. Everything had to go." He tugged her off the grass and onto the paved circle within the embrace of the walls. Too late she realized that when he said everything, he really meant *everything*.

"Uh, Ian?" She gripped his hand a little tighter. "Are those *tombstones* in the walls?"

"Yep."

"So much for those tourist brochures that make this place sound like the home of sweetness and light."

"Are you kidding? Come here for Pirate Days sometime."

"Why, Mr. North. Is that an invitation to walk your plank?"

He probably was embarrassed by how easily she could make him blush, but she thought it was one of the most adorable things she had seen in ages.

"So anyway," he continued rather desperately, she thought. "All the buildings had to go. Some were moved. The rest were bulldozed, then everything was flooded. There are still some places where you can go out in a boat and see old roads under the water."

"That's creepy. So that's why this is called Memorial Park. Because of the villages?"

"Right. There are bits and pieces of the different towns all through the park. The flagpole came from Moulinette, the benches were from Mille Roches and I think that—" he pointed to a statue of a soldier on horseback "—was brought here from Woodlands."

She peeked over the low wall at first the statue, then at Xander duck-walking with Cady toward the slide. She bit her lip for a second before straightening her shoulders.

"You're lucky Comeback Cove wasn't lost, too."

"Part of it was. Not too much, maybe a block or two. Those buildings were all moved back. Kind of flipped the town around, Moxie says."

"This happened during her lifetime?"

"Oh, yeah. It was in the late '50s. If you ask her, she'll tell you some wild stories about watching houses being moved down the street, and all the dust and the mud and the noise. Just make sure you really want to hear it before you ask. And make sure you have plenty of time."

"Duly noted."

She drifted away, kneeling to read the inscription on one of the stones.

"I wonder how they did it," she said softly.

"Did what?"

"Stand by while everything changed. See the town you called home be wiped off the map, all in the name of progress." She traced a letter on the stone. "I wonder how they stood back and let things happen, knowing they had to make the best of it. Knowing they had absolutely no other choice."

He knelt beside her. "We still talking about the villages, Darce?"

"That obvious, huh?"

She tried to smile, but wasn't sure she pulled it off.

"All I want is to keep things steady for her. To give her a home where she can count on being surrounded by people who love her. A real family, you know? Like mine used to be." Though after Robert's stories even that didn't feel as solid as it once had. "Like yours always has been."

The lift of his eyebrows reminded her that his own family wasn't all sweetness and light all the time, either. But, smart man, he chose to ignore that. "She's going to have that."

"Is she? I'm doing my best, but I keep remembering what it was like for me after my dad died, when there was always some new boyfriend we had to work around." She kicked at a tuft of grass. "That does things to a kid."

"Darce. As long as she has you in her corner, and sees that you and Xander both want what's best for her, she's going to be fine."

"I don't know. Everything's been tilted sideways,

with Xander showing up and you getting ready to move and us coming here and—"

He touched the end of her nose. "May I remind you that some of those changes have been a long time coming? And frickin' amazing, to boot."

Now it was her turn to blush.

"You know, this might be a good time to start getting Helene more involved. To give Cady that feeling of continuity and family, I mean."

She couldn't hold back the snort. "Nonny made her disapproval obvious when I told her I was pregnant. You really think it will help to pull her in now that Cady's ex-con father is in the picture?"

"Darce," he began. "Did you ever think that maybe—"

"Hey, Darcy!"

She jerked back, swiveling to see Xander jogging toward them, reassured by the sight of Cady bouncing softly in his arms.

What now?

Xander halted before them. "Good news."

She seriously doubted it.

"I didn't want to say anything before in case it didn't work out, but once I found out about Cady, I started talking to folks to see if I could change the plan. It took some convincing and pleading, but I just got the official word." He tossed his hair from his eyes. "Long story short, that job I lined up in cottage country? Not happening. Instead, I've got the official go-ahead to set up permanent camp in Stratford."

CHAPTER FIFTEEN

THE RIDE BACK to the house was a lot quieter than Ian would have predicted just two minutes before Xander dropped his bomb. Sure, Cady laughed in the back while Xander played peekaboo with her, and Lulu barked every time they slowed for a turn, but in the front seat, silence was the name of the game.

Xander was staying in Stratford.

This wasn't going to be something confined and convenient, emails and Skype and occasional visits. This was going to be everyday life. Regular time together. Two bedrooms for Cady, two parents to share in her care and go to teacher conferences and cheer at her soccer games.

It was the kind of family that worked for a lot of folks. But it wasn't what Darcy wanted.

He hit the stoplight in front of the strip mall, swallowed down the sour taste in his mouth and checked on her. One hand reached back through the seats and gripped Cady's foot. She stared out the window, but he was pretty sure that this time around she wasn't seeing a thing. All he wanted was to make this easier for her, but, God, how?

The light turned green. He pulled forward and tried to think about what lay ahead. The details of integrating Xander into Cady's life—that, he knew, she could manage. There were airlines that could take scheduling lessons from her. It would take time, but she would find the right balance for all of them.

But emotionally...

"You guys okay up there?" Xander interrupted his game of backseat peekaboo to lean forward. "You're mighty quiet all of a sudden."

"Fine." This wasn't Xander's fault. For the love of Pete, the guy hadn't done anything wrong. Well, other than his little dance with felons, but when it came to stepping up, meeting the unexpected twist of instant parenthood, anyone would have to admit that Xander was behaving way above expectations.

Anyone except Darcy.

Xander wasn't going to be like those guys who had wandered in and out of Sylvie's life. He probably wasn't going to be the parental paragon Darcy thought her dad had been, but the more Ian saw, the more he believed that Xander would do right by Cady.

What wasn't going to help would be if Darcy continued to pay lip service to integrating Xander into Cady's life.

I keep remembering what it was like for me after my dad died, when there was always some new boyfriend we had to work around.

Unless—

Unless he himself was the one who might be in the way.

As soon as they pulled into the driveway, Darcy said something about a diaper, grabbed Cady and headed inside. Away from the drama and the worry and the reminder, each time Xander spoke, that everything was spinning away from her.

Away from everyone.

Alone in the bedroom, she locked the door and dropped to the bed. Cady, blissfully oblivious, let loose with a giggle as they bounced on the mattress. That small sound of delight was Darcy's undoing. She rolled to her back, Cady tight against her chest.

"You're mine," she whispered against the blond wisps that had escaped from Cady's hot-pink barrette. *"Mine."*

As if to make a lie of her mother's words, Cady wriggled against the tight embrace. Darcy loosened her grip just enough for Cady to rise up on her elbows with a drooly grin.

"I grew you." Darcy traced a line down Cady's nose. "I carried you and felt you kick and ate all that yucky kale to make sure you turned out perfect. I'm the one who went through labor and made milk for you and rearranged my whole life, and I would do it again, every single day, if it would keep him from…"

Stratford. *Permanent.*

She lifted Cady in the air, high above her. "Maybe we could run away," she whispered. "He probably can't leave the country, but we could still go somewhere, right? And come back for visits, because I don't want to keep you away from him totally. Well, I kind of do, but then the lawyers would get mad at me."

She curled up to kiss one chubby hand, dangling above her like the most delicious apple ever grown.

"What do you say we go to London, huh? My mom took me there a lot. She has a flat there. We could probably stay in it. Kick Matteo the boy toy to the curb and move in, just us. I could show you Winnie the Pooh's house, and we could watch the horses go *clop clop clop* when they change the guard." She emphasized the clopping with some extra bounces that made Cady giggle hard, the chortling kind of laugh that took over her whole body and made it shake.

"Okay. It's decided. London it is. We'll run away, just us, you and me and—"

Ian.

"Just us. No fathers who show up out of the blue and expect to be part of your everyday life." She bounced Cady up and down, pulling forth a squeal. "Ooh, hold on, turbulence! And don't give me that look. I know I'm not being fair. But this…" She swallowed. "We had such a good thing, Bug. You. Me. Ian. And now it's going to be all messed up, and Ian will be here most of the time, and Xander is going to be there all the time, and, damn it, sweetie. Why didn't I wait one more night to go knocking on Ian's door?"

Her voice finally gave out. So did her arms. She lowered Cady to her chest and wrapped her arms around her little girl and held on tight.

IAN PAUSED AT the edge of the passageway and listened to the soft voice coming from the bedroom, his heart twisting. Finding the main door locked hadn't been as much of a surprise as he should have expected. Finding the door to the nursery open was like being handed a second chance.

He'd been braced for ranting. Wailing. Anything other than these small hiccuping sounds that sounded so goddamned alone.

"Hey." He spoke softly as he entered. The last thing she needed now was to have the crap scared out of her. "Want some company?"

She didn't say anything. He was on the verge of retreating when one hand lifted from Cady's back and reached for his.

In an instant he was on the bed beside her, kissing her forehead and whispering encouragement and gently prying her arms from a squawking Cady.

"Shh," he said when she started to protest. "I'm not taking her away from you, babe. Just making sure you don't squeeze the breath out of her."

With that she let go. He *whooshed* Cady to the ground and helped her balance against the bed.

"There you go, Bug. Do some laps, okay? And here." He pulled his phone from his pocket, powered it down and handed it over. "Go wild."

Trusting that the phone would keep her occupied for a minute or so, he turned back to Darcy. She had pushed upright and watched him with an expression he couldn't read—maybe because he got the feeling she didn't want him to see what she was feeling.

"I thought I locked the door." Her voice was quiet but steady.

"You did. But the nursery was open." He made himself ask the follow-up question. "Do you want me to leave?"

"No."

The answer would have been a lot more reassuring if it hadn't been so slow in coming.

I keep remembering what it was like for me after my dad died, when there was always some new boyfriend we had to work around.

"You okay?"

She stopped herself in mid-head-shake. "Does it matter?"

Hell yes, it mattered. Everything about her mattered to him.

He laced his fingers through hers. "Will it help if I tell you I know you'll be able to do this?"

She shook her head.

"How about if I remind you that Cady is as much yours as his? And that right now, even if he's in the same town, he's in no position to ask for more than regular visits at your place?"

"You can't know that." But she sounded a little less lost.

"You're right. I'm no lawyer, and for that, I thank God every day."

Her tiny smile encouraged him.

"Darce. Babe. Think. Is this worse than when you found out you were pregnant?"

Her gaze followed Cady, doing her best to shove the phone into her mouth. "In some ways, no. That was so out of the blue, but in other ways… Oh, Ian. Now she's real, my whole world, and all I can think is that with him around all the time…"

"He's not like those guys your mother hung out with. And you're not your mom."

"No." Her voice was bitter. "I'm just the idiot who got drunk and messed up my baby's whole life."

It hit him then what he had to do—what only he could do to help her.

"I know him, Darce. And I promise you, he's going to be a good father."

"How—" she began, but he placed one gentle finger over her lips.

"I know you're scared," he said, slow and low, the way he would speak to a terrified child. "But just listen. Let me tell you about Xander, okay?"

He dug through his memory and pulled up every story he could remember. About walking into the dorm that first day, alternating between excitement and frickin' terror at all that lay ahead, and being greeted by his new roomie, who had seemed to have made friends with half the floor in the space of an hour. About the way Xander had plunged headfirst into university life, joining groups and signing up to tutor kids. About Xander's many exploits, yes, but about how he treated each new girl as if she were the most amazing thing to ever happen in his life. About how all his exes seemed to stay friends with him. About the night when Ian got the news that Grandpa Gord had dropped dead in the middle of the diner, when Xander had quietly and efficiently made arrangements for Ian to get home.

"That guy is still inside him, Darce. I know he went off track, but I promise, he's not that same guy who messed up. From the minute he found out about Cady, he's been… He's who he used to be. You don't know, but I do, and I swear on everything I hold sacred, he wants to do right by her. He's head over heels and I think— No, I know. I *know* he's going to be a good father."

"But the other day, when we found out he was coming here, you said you thought he was seeing her as his way out. That he was more interested in what she could do for him than—"

"Yeah, I said that. At the time, I believed it."

He ran a hand over her hair, brushed a kiss on her cheek. "I don't anymore."

She hiccuped. "Promise?"

How could one little word, barely audible, carry so much hope and fear and desperation?

"I promise."

She met his gaze then, searching his face. Hunting for any sign that he was simply saying things to make her feel better? He couldn't tell. But after a moment she nodded and curled against him.

He pulled her close and rocked her, kissing her hair, wishing to God he could make the promise he wanted to make most—that he would always be there to help her through.

Except the more he heard, the more he feared that his presence—not Xander's—was what would complicate her life the most.

SOMEHOW THEY MADE it through dinner.

Ian pulled up a smile for his parents' sake. Not that he fooled Ma. He doubted that even Darcy's mom could pull off an act that would get past Janice North when her radar was turned on. But she was focused on the party, chattering about the plans all through the night, interrupting herself to add things to her lists or place a quick phone call. She sent him and Darcy enough assessing looks that he started to wonder if she was related to Moxie by blood and not just marriage, but he could almost see her tell herself to let it go for the moment.

Dad was as oblivious as always, teasing Cady with a spoon and talking to Xander about making beer, of all things. And just when Ian had begun to have bad thoughts about the Almighty, God came through and sent Moxie to a card party at the Legion.

He and Darcy sat side by side, mostly quiet, mostly in their own worlds. Except every once in a while one of them would reach for the other's hand beneath the table and squeeze.

He wasn't sure if her touch made things better or worse. After a while he stopped questioning and decided simply to be grateful.

His litany of Xander's good points seemed to have helped her. She let Xander take over more of the dinner duties. When it came time to clear the table, she suggested that Xander take Cady outside for a walk around the garden. Xander was so busy racing to comply he probably didn't see the way Darcy bit her lip as he lifted Cady from the high chair, the way she turned sharply away when the two of them walked out the door.

This time, when Ian reached for her hand, it took a long time for her to let go.

Dishes. Bath. Songs and a bottle in the rocking chair, a few minutes assuring Ma that the weather forecasters knew what they were saying, that Moxie's dire mutterings about aching knees didn't guarantee weekend rain. Familiar routines that both grounded him, yet felt oddly surreal, probably because he was only halfway present. Even as he talked and teased and reassured, he was increasingly aware of a thread running beneath his thoughts like the steady beat of a drum, slowly getting louder, finally breaking through and claiming him when he took Lulu outside for a last walk before bed. He stood in the darkness of the backyard and let it roll over him.

The best thing he could do—for Darcy, for Cady, for everyone—would be to take himself out of that picture.

Not immediately, of course. He had to give notice, had to pack up and move and figure out a place to live here. More than that, he wanted to be there for Darcy during the first weeks of having Xander as a semi-regular presence in her life.

But once they got back to Stratford—once the party was over and Xander had been told the truth—they would have to go back to the way they were. Friends. Amazing friends, but no more.

Lulu ran up to him and let out a short, *what's up?* bark. He scratched behind her ear, sending her into a wiggling frenzy.

"You see the lights, girl?"

As the darkness grew deeper, more and more lights appeared. Watercraft out on the river. Stars overhead. And fireflies winking out from between tall leaves of the hostas and irises.

You know, North, Mother Nature might be try-

ing to give you a message. Lights that you can't see until dark and all that jazz.

Right. And according to Moxie, late at night, you could still hear music playing from the dance halls of the Lost Villages.

He scooped a stick from the ground, held it out for Lulu to bite. Time for a little tug-of-war.

"Here we go, girl. Here we go. Come and get it. Yeah, you think you're so strong, huh? Huh? Yeah, well, you're not the only one."

Because even though he knew he should talk to Darcy right now, he wasn't fool enough to think he could do it. Once they got back to Stratford he would do the decent thing. But not while they were in Comeback Cove. For as long as they were here, they could keep pretending.

"But tell me this, girl. Is it really pretending when I already love her?"

THERE HAD BEEN very few nights in Darcy's life that she'd wished would never end. When she opened her eyes Saturday morning, it hit her: if ever she could have chosen her own personal Groundhog Day, she would have picked last night.

Not because of the sex, as raw and needy as it had been. Not because of the moments after when Ian had pulled her close and stroked her arm and told her, without a single word, that he knew what she was feeling.

But because somewhere, in the sharing and the

holding and the understanding, she had found new hope.

Yes, Xander was going to be in Stratford, but she could still make this work. How many years had she spent protecting Sylvie? If anyone knew controlled access, it was Darcy.

So Xander would be in town. Okay. She could do this. Regular visits. A gradual transition to Cady going to his place, once he got one, and assuming it was child-safe, though he did seem to be very good about that. A routine. A schedule, clear guidelines, open communication.

And Ian to tell her that she was doing the right thing.

True, he wouldn't be around as much as she wished. But there was a highway and phones, text messages and Skype calls and emails. This wasn't *Little House on the Prairie*. She would never need to go more than a few hours without a word, a joke, a reminder.

She could make this work. *They* could make this work. Tonight she would tell him that he was right, that she could find a way to ease Xander into Cady's life so he could become part of a routine, not a disruption.

And then she would kiss Ian slowly and steadily and tell him that she loved him.

EVEN AN EXTRA-LONG run by the river wasn't enough to wipe out the *over-over-over* chant pulsing through

Ian's brain. Dripping and defeated, he let Lulu lead him across the yard and to the house.

One step at a time. Just like when things fell apart with Taylor. Just like when he found out the truth about Carter. One step at a time. Go upstairs. Shower. Get dressed. Come down and smile and don't let anyone figure out that pretty soon you're going to walk away from your own personal sun.

Lulu circled back and gave him a *get moving* bark. He dredged up a laugh for her.

"Thanks, girl. You want to come with me this morning, help load those picnic tables onto Hank's truck? I might need you to keep me on track."

Especially as Carter would be there. But Hank and Cash would be there, too—to lend muscle, Ma had said when she'd roped him into it—so surely this first brothers-only task would be survivable.

He dragged himself past the sunporch only to be stopped by a high-pitched squeal.

"Eee!"

Cady stood on Xander's lap, holding his hands and bouncing to her own unheard music.

"Morning!" Xander called over the shrieks, then turned back to Cady.

"You want Daddy to do the horse thing for you again. Don't you, pretty girl?"

Cady spotted the dog. "Ru! Ru!"

"Where's Darcy?"

"Upstairs. She asked me to look after Cady while she got dressed."

So they had a few minutes. This might be his best chance today to grab some time alone with Xander and propose the idea that had come to him as he'd run—an idea that both made perfect sense and made him wish he could yank his heart from his chest and lock it in a freezer so he wouldn't have to feel it break.

He dropped to the ottoman and sat on his hands to keep them from reaching for Cady. "Listen, Xander. You've probably figured out from the talk around here that I'm moving back to Comeback Cove."

"I heard things, yeah." Xander shot him a fast glance. "I didn't want to ask."

"Yeah, well, it's happening."

"So you and Darcy—"

God, get him through this. "We're still working out the details." At the swift panic in Xander's eyes, he rushed to add, "Look, this all happened before you came back, and everything's been so crazy since you showed up. Not your fault, just the nature of the beast. But, anyway, don't worry. Cady isn't going to leave Stratford the minute you get settled."

"That's good to hear. Not that it's all about me," he added with a laugh.

"Anyway, I was thinking." Ian said it fast, before he could change his mind. "With your plans getting rearranged and everything, you probably don't have a place to stay yet. So maybe you might want to talk to Darcy." He swallowed hard. "About renting the garage apartment."

"Your place?" Xander tore his eyes away from the bouncing baby long enough for Ian to see the surprise.

"Well, it's not like I've really been using it for a while now." And why the hell hadn't he figured that out earlier? "It would make a ton of sense. For you and for Cady. Probably the closest you all could come to that white picket fence thing."

Because even if Xander didn't need that, even if Cady didn't—Darcy did.

CLEAN, DRESSED AND as ready as she ever would be, Darcy set out to help with desserts. For the sake of everyone who would end up eating the food she was about to prepare, she hoped the recipes were written down in very clear language.

"Good morning!" Brynn all but sang the words as Darcy entered the kitchen. Taylor paused in the midst of setting out measuring cups, spoons and pans to offer a wan smile.

"Hi, Darcy." Taylor seemed a little more reserved than she had the other day. Given the paleness of her face, she might simply be having a particularly bad day of wrestling morning sickness.

Or it could be that her stomach, like Darcy's, was fluttering over the fact that—thanks to their plotting—Carter and Ian were about to find themselves alone together.

Brynn, who was in on the plan, pushed a bowl of pistachios toward Darcy. "Here. Put some of that nervous energy to work and shell these. We need them for the biscotti, and the store didn't have any of the naked ones."

"You sure you don't need me to cream something by hand, or punch some bread dough?" Darcy picked up a nut and squeezed. "It seems a shame to waste all this angst."

"You guys are wusses," Brynn said. "You're doing the right thing. Ian and Carter will be a little ticked off when they figure out they were hoodwinked, but they're smart enough to know this is for their own good."

"I hope so," Taylor said with a sigh. "I know Carter will be. Darcy, don't take this the wrong way, but he's been on edge ever since you guys arrived. I think he'll be glad to have this out in the open."

Darcy wasn't so sure that Ian would be as grateful. But there was nothing to be done about it now. He was already on his way to Hank's.

A pointed piece of shell poked her finger.

"How did you guys convince Hank and Cash to go along with this?" she asked.

Taylor's grin was a little bit more believable this time. "I called Cash and played the pregnant card."

"Shameless," Brynn said. "And clever."

"Oh, yeah? How did you convince Hank to play along?"

Brynn's blush was all the answer Darcy needed.

"Okay. We have to talk about something else or I'm going to freak out. So...how were you guys able to do this—" she gestured toward the bags and canisters "—without Moxie insisting on being part of the production?"

"Oh, that was easy," Taylor said. "Brynn promised we would stay out of her way while she made the salads if she left us alone to do this."

"You can do that?"

Brynn shrugged. "Here's the thing about Moxie. She's tough and smart and a little sneaky, but she's fair. If you are willing to negotiate, she's always willing to talk."

"Kind of like a hostage situation," Taylor said, and she and Brynn burst into laughter. Darcy couldn't help but join in.

Was this what it was like to have a family? Not just mother-father-kids, but the whole shebang, with cousins and aunts and uncles. To have something like this for Cady, for herself...

Ian *had* to patch things up with Carter. A family such as this needed to be preserved.

But thinking about what might be happening with Ian made her stomach twitch. She forced herself to focus on Taylor and Brynn and vanilla and flour, until she saw with a start that almost an hour had passed.

"I should probably check on Cady." She gave

her hands a quick wash. "Don't have too much fun without me, okay?"

With laughter echoing in her ears, Darcy went in search of Cady and Xander. She knew all was well. If not, Xander would have come hunting. But she still needed to see for herself. Not just to be sure Cady was okay, but to watch them in action together. To remind herself that Xander could bring things to Cady's life that she couldn't—at least one aunt, maybe more grandparents, maybe even cousins. She would love for Cady to have cousins.

She could handle this. It would be like…like when she started sending Cady to day care. That had been an adjustment. And, yeah, she had indulged in a pity party over the fact that finances wouldn't allow her to extend her maternity leave as long as most mothers got. But she had managed. She had organized and planned and learned to compartmentalize her life into Cady time and work time and—usually thanks to Ian—Darcy time. So now she would simply learn to add Xander time.

And, if she were lucky, maybe some regular, frequent Darcy-and-Ian time.

She found them outside tossing a ball with Lulu. Cady's welcoming squeal left her all gushy inside. Damn but she loved this kid.

Xander had a mildly frantic air about him, and there was no denying the relief that bloomed on his face at her approach, but she saw no evidence of either blood or tears on any of them, so she called that a win and pulled Cady into her arms.

"Hey. Sorry I was gone so long. I started working with Brynn and Taylor, and we got laughing, and, well, I guess I was more in need of a gabfest than I thought. Thanks for being a great babysitter."

"My pleasure. And I wasn't babysitting. I was playing with my daughter. Big difference."

She swallowed her flutter of panic. "Did you have fun, Buggy Boo?" She held Cady over her head and wiggled her back and forth. "Did you have so much fun with your—with Xander?"

"She led *Daddy* all over the yard. I probably know it better than the Norths do at this point. And remind me to tell one of them that there's a groundhog hole by that maple tree that they might want to fill in before the party."

"Sure. Listen, if you want to find one of them now, take a few minutes to recharge, you go ahead. I can put her in the high chair in the kitchen and give her a snack. She'd probably like that." She lowered Cady to her, nuzzled her nose. "For at least five or ten minutes."

"I think I'll take you up on that. I'm still building up my daddy endurance." He took a step toward the house, hesitated and turned back. "Darce, Ian said something this morning that made a lot of sense. Maybe I could…"

"What?" He seemed nervous all of a sudden, though she wasn't sure why. If Ian had suggested it, it was probably one of those ideas that would leave her smacking her forehead and asking why she hadn't thought of it herself.

"He told me about him moving back here, and not using the apartment over the garage. He thought it might be a good idea if…"

No. *No.*

"If I moved in there."

She pulled Cady close to her chest, folded her arms around her. "He came up with this himself?"

"Yeah. I never would've… And look, if you don't like the idea, I understand. This has been a lot all of a sudden, and if you don't want me to…"

No. No, I drew the lines, I talked myself into believing it would be fine as long as I colored inside those lines, and now Ian wants to erase them? Ian, who knows why I need them?

"It made a lot of sense to me. You know, make it easier for me to be a real part of her life, for us to share child care and, you know, everything. I'm thinking, in a couple of years, it might be nice for her to be able to run back and forth between us instead of me needing to set everything up ahead of time." His laugh was short and strained. "Hey, if we pull it off, it could end up being almost like a regular family. Right?"

CHAPTER SIXTEEN

IAN STOOD BESIDE Hank's beat-up old truck and scowled at the note propped on the windshield.

Sorry, guys. Millie needs school stuff and I have a big crew checking in today, so this was my only chance. The key to the truck is inside. Carter has the house key. I'll try to get back in time to lend a hand.

"Sure you will." Ian crumpled the note. The rough noise echoed the crowded sensation in his gut when he spotted Carter sitting on top of a picnic table in front of the Wolfe cabin, staring at the river as though he owned it.

"Hey." Ian shoved his hands into his pockets, shot Carter a fast glance, then decided to study the water himself.

"'Morning."

"Don't suppose Cash is showing up."

"Nope." Carter lifted the phone from the tabletop. "Just got a text. Twisted his ankle."

Despite himself, Ian snorted. "He never could lie worth beans."

"Moxie must have forgot to give him a full script."

"Oh, I'm not pinning this one on her." Memories tumbled through his head; lowered voices at the dinner table, Darcy asking if he'd seen Carter at the dairy, Darcy making an oh-so-subtle remark this morning about things being easier once they were out in the open. God, he was an idiot. "I think this was all Darcy and Taylor, with some help from Brynn."

"And they conned both the guys into going along with them?"

"Conned? No. Threatened, more likely."

"You're probably right." Carter leaned forward and rested his elbows on his knees, intruding into Ian's peripheral vision. "But since they went to all this work, maybe we should…"

Oh, no. No way in hell was he going along with this. Sure, for a minute there it had been almost like old times, almost joking around together again. That had been okay. But more than that? Uh-uh. Not going to happen.

Forward, North.

"Why are you just sitting there?"

"Huh?"

"We're supposed to be loading tables. Let's load. Unless your ass has developed magical powers and can do the job for you."

"I— Sure. Whatever." Carter pocketed his phone in obvious preparation for climbing off the table. Ian resisted—barely—the temptation to do the magician thing and yank it out from beneath Carter. He wouldn't mind seeing someone hit the dirt about now.

"Get it in gear," he said.

Carter frowned but complied, slowly circling to the other side of the table.

"On three." Carter grabbed his end. "One... two..."

Ian pulled the table toward him. Carter stumbled forward.

"Oops. My bad."

"Right." Carter brushed his shorts and took a deep breath. "Look, Ian. There's something I need to say."

Ah, shit. Not now.

"It looks like things are working out for you, and that's good. I mean, you could have knocked me over with a feather when you showed up with Darcy. But, hey, if you're gonna be surprised, better a good one than a lousy one, right?"

"Jeez, Carter." Ian held his brother's gaze. "You really think you should be the one telling me that?"

Dull red rose in Carter's cheeks, but like the stubborn idiot that he was, he plowed on. "I'm just trying to say, even though I know it's going to be... awkward...for a while, it's good to have you back. And I hope you take that job. I think it's a solid fit for you."

On that, Ian could agree. Not that he was going to, but it was the truth.

"So, I'm just saying, you and Darcy and Cady—I know things are messy, with Xander and all, but those things can be worked out. I'm just glad for you."

"Of course you are. It makes life a lot easier for you, doesn't it?"

Carter blinked. "What does that mean?"

Ian wasn't really sure. But something nasty had coiled itself in his stomach, something as poisonous as a snake, and he realized—too late—that he couldn't let it out.

What the *hell* had Darcy been thinking?

"It means exactly what you think it means. Now are you going to help me move tables, or are you going to stand there yammering?"

"Ian. Come on. We need to—"

For one sweet second, Ian let himself imagine how good it would feel to take the muscles he'd developed in his arms—muscles born of hours at the forge, long afternoons spent hammering away the pain of what had been done to him—and use them to shove his fist into Carter's face.

But he wasn't going to be the one to ruin Ma's party. "We need to get these tables on the truck, drive it to the house and unload them. That's it. That's all."

Carter held his gaze. A perverse part of Ian wished Carter would push this. He almost—*almost*—wanted to see what would happen if he finally let go.

Luckily or not, Carter let out his breath and lowered his eyes. "Fine." His voice was tight and clipped. "Whatever."

Ian grabbed the table and heaved. The sooner they got this done, the sooner they could get to the house.

And once he got there, he and Darcy were going to have themselves a talk.

RATTLED BY XANDER'S REVELATION, Darcy was barely focused on her actions when she took Cady to the kitchen. Which explained how Cady managed to dive-bomb the bowl of frosting. Which was how Xander finally got his first introduction to bath time in the middle of the day. Which was why he was now downstairs doing lunch duty, aided by a very willing Brynn and Taylor, while Darcy showered chocolate frosting out of her hair.

Of course, she wasn't sure what was creating more steam: the hot water or the thoughts bubbling in her brain.

Did it make sense for Xander to live in the garage? In theory, yes.

Did Darcy want him there? More to the point, did Ian—*Ian*—have any right to make that suggestion?

She snapped off the water, swore at the towel, snarled while she yanked on fresh clothes. She pushed the comb through her hair and tugged at the knots and froze when she heard familiar footsteps on the stairs.

Maybe the frosting fiesta hadn't been a total waste of time and sugar. At least now they would have some privacy while she set him straight.

The door opened with a bang. She lowered the comb, drew in her breath and went to meet him.

"Lock it," she said evenly.

"Already did."

And why the hell did he look so—

Oh. Yeah.

The Carter-Ian reunion had slipped her mind. From the way Ian's eyes were flashing, she was pretty sure it hadn't gone according to plan.

From the way her jaw was tightening, she was positive she didn't give a rat's ass.

They stared at each other. The words that had poured through her in the shower seemed to have been washed away. All that remained was the heavy, white-hot burn of betrayal.

"Why did you tell Xander to move into the apartment?"

He blinked, as if he couldn't believe she had to ask. "Because for one thing, I'm moving out and the lease says I can sublet with your approval. For another thing, it makes sense. Now." His eyes narrowed. "Who the hell thought it was a good idea to strand me alone with Carter?"

"It doesn't matter who thought of it." No way was she offering up Taylor to him. "You two need to talk, and since you were being too stubborn to do it on your own—"

"Hold on. I'm stubborn?" He leveled a finger in her direction. "What gave you the right to set me up that way?"

Love, that was what. Love and watching him hurt for two years and knowing in her gut that Carter had hurt him far worse than Taylor had, and that until he realized that, there was no way this family was going to heal.

But she'd be damned if she'd tell him she loved him when she was ready to toss him in the river.

"Your entire family sees how you're hurting. You want to move back here, fine. That's huge. But just being here isn't going to do a damned thing to get your family back on track if you won't admit—"

"I don't need to admit anything. I'm not the one who broke anyone's trust."

"Which is all the more reason—"

"But," he carried on as if she hadn't spoken, "I'm the only one who can see that dragging it out again will be like...like hauling something dead out of the ground. All it's gonna do is lead to a whole bunch of stink."

"That is so wrong." She tried to wall off her anger, but it spilled over anyway. "You think you can walk around and rearrange my life, mess up everything I'm trying to do with Cady and Xander even though you know how much I'm trying to give her a stable home. And then you get pissed off when someone dares to remind you that your stubbornness is going to hurt your family even more than what Carter did?"

"What the hell?" He scrubbed his hands over his face as though he was trying to wipe away the truth. "I don't know what you've been smoking, Darce, but you are so wrong—"

"You're right." At his blank look, she pushed on. "You're not stubborn. You're scared."

Something flickered across his face. Panic? Relief? But it was pushed aside by a mirthless laugh.

"Oh, God. You are so… I mean, jeez, Darce. You think because you're terrified to let anyone near Cady, that the rest of us are walking around like that? Jesus. Talk about the pot calling the kettle black."

"I'm not terrified to let Xander near her. I'm just trying to make it easier for all of us."

"And by *us*, you mean *you*."

"I mean—" Argh! Did *everything* have to spiral out of her control these days? She forced herself to breathe in, to back away. "Look, I know you must have felt…manipulated…when you saw you were alone with Carter."

"Congratulations. You finally said something true."

So much for stepping back. "Did you just say that I'm lying? Really, Mr. Let's-Pretend-We're-Involved?"

"Which you were only too happy to go along with, so don't act like you had nothing to do with it."

"Of course I went along with it! It helped me. It helped you." And even when it felt wrong, it never felt untrue.

"Yeah, well, guess what, Darce? I don't need your help."

"Because you're doing such a fine job without it."

"I am!" He punctuated his words with vicious jabs toward the floor. "This is my family, damn it. *Mine! I* will deal with them the way *I* know best, because in case you've forgotten, *you* are not really a part of it."

The words hit her like a shock wave. She stepped back, bumped up against the bed.

"You want the truth, Darce? Your mom isn't the only actress in your family. You did such a good job of pretending to be my girlfriend that I think you started to believe it yourself. So let me make it one hundred percent clear. You. Are. Not. My. Girlfriend. And you have no right in hell to act like you are."

She couldn't breathe. His cold, deliberate anger had frozen her, had sucked all the warmth and joy from her.

Oh, whispered a detached corner of her brain. *So this is how it feels to have your heart shattered.*

This morning she had promised herself that the time for pretending was over. She was going to tell Ian that she loved him, that with him at her side she knew she could make things work with Xander and Cady and the rest of her screwed-up life. That with him, she could build a family.

Dear God. She was such a fool.

"Fine." She walked a wide circle around him, aiming for the door.

"Where are you going?"

"Going to do what I should have done right from the moment Xander showed up at my door." She popped the lock and jerked the door open. "I'm going to tell everyone the truth."

HALF AN HOUR LATER, sitting in the sunporch surrounded by assorted slack-jawed Norths—Moxie, Ma, Dad, Taylor and Brynn, with Xander and Carter hovering in the door—Ian thought there was some seriously messed-up karma at play when it took an admission of massive dishonesty to get his family to shut up.

As she had the last time they'd pulled everyone together for a conference, Darcy did most of the speaking. Not that there was a whole lot to say after, "I'm sorry. We've been lying to you all along." But she did it swiftly, straightforward and without trying to make anyone feel sorry for her, and Ian could smack himself for admiring her ability to keep her cool while delivering the news that ripped his world apart.

Because there was no going back after this. Any shred of hope that there might be a way for them to be together, despite the distance, despite her fears...

Nope. This unemotional, just-the-facts monologue might as well be a sledgehammer slamming a brick wall.

And he was Humpty Frickin' Dumpty.

Moxie, of course, spoke first.

"All a lie, you say."

"That's right."

"Oh, Ian." Ma pressed her hand to her mouth. His heart twisted. "I never thought… I expected better of you. I can't imagine how hard it was for you to come home and face…everyone…again. But to think you had to pretend to be involved with Darcy, just to save face or make things easier for everyone else or…or whatever cockamamy reason you had. We didn't deserve to be led down the garden path that way."

It seemed it was finally his turn to talk. "We didn't plan it."

"Oh? You just spur of the moment looked at each other and said, 'Hey, let's make the trip more interesting by lying to everyone'?"

"Come on, Ma. Give us some credit."

"Give me an explanation and I'll tell you if you deserve it."

At that point, Darcy rose—none too steadily, he noticed, despite all her calm talk—and scooped Cady from the floor.

"I'm sorry to have dragged all of you into my drama. This might be a good time for me to start packing."

"You're leaving?"

He didn't mean to say it out loud. Didn't even know that he really had until all heads swiveled toward him.

Darcy shifted Cady from one shoulder to the other. "Yes."

"But the party," Ma began, and he closed his eyes against what his mind could see so clearly: all her hopes, her plans to show Cady off to her friends, her dreams for an afternoon of happiness and love. All yanked away from her by his own stupidity.

"I'm so sorry." For the first time, Darcy's voice wavered. "I never wanted to hurt anyone. But I... There's no need to pretend anymore, so I think it's best if we...if we go. That is—" She bit her lip. "Xander? Could you drive us back to—"

"Hold it right there, missy." Moxie didn't move. She didn't have to. Her voice was sharp enough that everyone in the room knew right away—one wrong move and they would be sliced, diced or even julienned.

"You're not leaving Comeback Cove. Not until tomorrow."

Cady was the only one who giggled.

"This isn't the Old West, Mom." Dad, as always, was the soothing voice of reason. "You can't keep the girl here against her will."

"Did I say she had to stay here? No, I did not."

Moxie answered her own question. "In fact, given the circumstances, I have to agree. It's best for her to move on."

Darcy's face and neck turned a deep, mottled red. But she stood her ground and looked Moxie dead in the eye. She didn't ask for an explanation, but her rigid back and raised chin made it very clear that she expected one.

He had to force himself to stop from springing to her defense.

Back away, North. No more pretending. It's better for everyone.

"You're not the only ones who've been keeping secrets." Moxie didn't seem the least bit embarrassed by her own transgressions. "Your grandmother's place is fine and dandy, and I have a key. And before you ask, I misled you because you're the light of Helene's life, and I wasn't going to have you staying all by yourself, no car, no company. So the house is empty and waiting. The three of you can stay there."

In case anyone might have missed her point, she pointed slowly from Darcy to Cady to Xander. Ian stared hard at the floor so no one could read the twisted feelings on his face.

"I hope you don't think we're going to come to the party. That would be pointless."

"Get over yourself, girl." Moxie's words cracked like a whip. "We're not going to be curled up in a ball sucking our thumbs because you won't be there. Though, truth be told, we will miss your little one. But you're staying in town because Helene has changed her flights to get back tomorrow morning, and, as God is my witness, if you break that woman's heart again I will hunt you down and drag you back here. Is that clear?"

Ian finally raised his head. Every set of eyes in the room was glued to Moxie.

Even Cady's.

"Nonny is coming?" Darcy shifted Cady to her hip. "But—"

"She'll be back at some god-awful hour of the morning. She's flying all night to see you and your babe, and I don't want to think about how much this is costing her. So you will march that cute little hind end of yours to her house, and you will stay there in the bedroom she has kept for you all these years." Moxie paused before adding, "And in case you're wondering, everything you need for the little one—a crib, high chair, changing table—it's all there. Been waiting for you since prit near the day after you said you were expecting."

There was no ignoring the rush of tears to Darcy's eyes. They spilled out and down her cheeks, probably faster than she even realized they'd formed.

He was not going to ache for her. He was not.

"Fine." For the first time, she spoke in a whisper. "I... Yes. We'll wait for her. At least, Cady and I will." She glanced at Xander, who offered a stiff shrug.

"It's Father's Day. I'm spending it with my daughter."

"Then that's settled." Moxie dusted her hands as if she'd been dispensing a royal blessing rather than threatening Darcy with kidnapping and kicking her out of the house. "I'll take Cady so's you can pack. The rest of you, show's over. Janice has worked her heart out for tomorrow and none of you are going to do anything else to ruin it for her."

The room emptied out. In a matter of seconds it was just Ian and Moxie left, him alone on the love seat, her jiggling Cady up and down.

"You know, Ian," she said, her voice oddly robbed of its usual starch, "there was a time when I could have cheerfully taken a belt to your brother for what he did to you and this family. I finally let it go, though, because I could see he was hurting almost as much as you were. He never set out to cause you pain. And I know you don't believe it, but if I hadn't told him to get his arse in gear, he would have let Taylor slip out of his fingers, all to keep from making things worse for you."

She wiped a bit of drool from Cady's chin, kissed the child's forehead and turned back to Ian. "But mark my words, Ian. If this family comes apart at the seams now, it's not Carter who's going to bear the blame."

HE HAD NO place to go.

Darcy was the one leaving, but Ian was the one wandering. He couldn't go upstairs. He was pissed, he was aching, he didn't know what was right anymore. But one thing was clear: he couldn't watch Darcy gather her things and walk away. Because this, he knew, would be the end.

Sure, he would still have to go back to Stratford, give his notice, pack up his things. He would see her. He should apologize, because already he knew he'd overreacted and blamed her for way too much of what he'd been feeling. After everything they'd had, he hoped they could end as friends.

But the rest of it—that was done. And God help him, but he wasn't going to walk up those stairs to watch the funeral.

But when he went into the kitchen, the chatter—muted though it had already been—came to an abrupt halt. In the dining room, Ma glanced up from the papers spread across the table, gave him a tight-lipped shake of the head and returned to her phone call. Carter and Dad paused in their hauling of tables to watch him let Lulu out. Neither of them raised a hand.

So he hit the river.

He sat on the dock, feet dangling, and stared at the islands on the horizon—places he had known since he was a kid. Funny how they could look the same when everything he knew had gone to hell and back in the space of a few minutes.

The minutes slipped past. Voices rose and fell. He never turned, never looked. Not when a car door slammed. Not when an engine flared to life. Not when it clanked out of his hearing.

Footsteps sounded on the dock, the footfalls vibrating through him. Each one seemed to jostle one jagged bit of his self-control against another. Pretty soon all the pieces would slide up against each other and slice through him.

"Not now, Moxie," he called over his shoulder.

The footsteps continued. Figured.

"You made it all perfectly clear in the house. Save your breath. Energy. Whatever."

She kept coming. Damn it to hell and back. Why did his family have to push themselves into everything?

Maybe he could jump into the river and swim out to the closest island. He'd done it before. And if it bought him a few minutes of peace—

"Don't even think of it," came Taylor's voice as his hands hit the dock, ready to push off.

Damn it. Moxie was one thing. Taylor was another.

"Not a great idea," he said as two bright blue sandals landed beside him.

"Well, since the crappy ideas are flying all around today, one more shouldn't make a difference."

She kicked the shoes out of the way, grabbed his shoulder and lowered herself to the dock. Two seconds later, she was sitting at his side, her feet swinging beside his, waving a sleeve of saltine crackers in his face.

"Want one?"

He was pretty sure lunchtime was long gone, but even a cracker was too much for him right now. "No, thanks."

"Figured. Here." She pulled a can from her pocket and handed it over. "Sorry. I know you prefer bottles, but this was right there in the door of the fridge, and if I had tried to poke around the shelves with all those smells…" She shuddered and pulled a cracker free. "It wouldn't have ended well."

"Darcy went for pretzels."

Now, why the hell had he let that slip? He might as well have waved a flag and told her to start her engine.

"Speaking of Darcy…"

"We're not."

The cracker pointed in his direction. "Tough. You have to accommodate me. I'm pregnant."

"Congratulations, by the way."

"Sorry?"

He popped the tab, listened to the slow, welcome hiss. "I never congratulated you. On the baby, I mean. I'm glad for you."

"Really?"

One word. Six letters. About four hundred hopes and fears and worries.

"Yeah, really. We had a good run, Taylor, and even though the ending sucked…"

Should he say it? Yeah. He should. If the honesty bandwagon had started rolling, he might as well keep going with it.

"You were right. Right to end it, and right about...about why it had to end."

"And why was that, Ian?"

He risked a glance in her direction. What he saw took him by surprise.

"Holy crap. You have it already."

"Have what?"

"The mom look. Like you can see right through me."

"Considering half this kid's genes will be coming from your family, I think I'm going to need it."

"Can't argue with you on that one."

She bumped against his shoulder. Casual. Friendly. Sisterly.

"Ian. You know that you and I would have ended even if Carter wasn't in the picture."

Did he?

Yeah. Yeah, hard as it was to admit it, he did.

"But that doesn't excuse what he did."

"No. It probably doesn't. Though might I remind you the only thing that happened before I ended things with you was a lot of talking and the proverbial river of tears."

There was that.

"Today wasn't Darcy's idea, in case you were wondering. I was the one who had that brainstorm."

Okay. That one took him by surprise.

"Not your usual style."

"Yeah, well, I'm thinking for two these days." She bit into a cracker. Tiny crumbs floated down and settled on her denim skirt.

He helped himself to a long draw on the beer. "Thanks for telling me, but it's all kind of irrelevant anyway, okay? You were there. You heard us. It was all pretend."

"Ian Tyson North, if you try to tell me—*me*, of all people—that you two aren't in love, so help me, I will knock you off this dock and into the river. And you know damned well how cold it is this early in the season."

Whoa. Taylor, making threats? Taylor, talking to him about love?

"I'm going to have to pee again in about five minutes, so I don't have time to listen to your nonsense. Let's cut to the chase." She waved the sleeve of crackers like a sword. "You are so obviously head over heels for her that it's a miracle you aren't doing permanent cartwheels. Her and Cady. The three of you together—it's like looking at the sun. You can't do it directly because it'll burn the heck out of your eyes."

"I—"

But for the life of him, he couldn't deny it anymore. Maybe it was because someone else had put it into words. Maybe it was because, even though it hurt like hell, a part of him desperately wanted it to be true. Maybe because this was Taylor, the woman who had once heard all his dumbest thoughts and wildest dreams. But just like that—at least for the moment—he was tired of pretending.

"Okay. You got me. I fell for her."

"Congratulations." She patted his hand. "Believe me. I couldn't be happier for you."

"Really? 'Cause from where I'm sitting, it doesn't make a whole lot of sense."

"Why?"

"Well, for one thing, I'm here and she's at her grandmother's. For another, I'm moving back here and she's staying in Stratford. For another…"

Huh. The words felt trapped somewhere in his chest.

"For another…?"

He shook his head.

"Ian." A soft hand gripped his chin and she turned his face in her direction. "Ian, this is me. Not Moxie. Not your mother. Me. So talk."

Shit.

"She wants to make things right. For Cady, I mean. Wants to give her a nice, solid home and family. Without, you know, some guy messing things up by only being around part-time, wanting her to move. Stuff like that."

"She actually said that?"

"What? Oh, God, no. She thinks Xander is the one who's gonna mess everything up."

Taylor's brow crinkled. "Then what exactly is the problem?"

"Tay. Xander is Cady's *father*. He needs to be there. I...don't."

She stared at him, her eyes narrowing, then opening wide as she seemed to get what he was trying to say.

"Let me get this straight. You're in love with her. But because she is confused—not that anyone could possibly be confused by the things she's had tossed at her the last few days, oh, no—you have decided that the best course of action is for you to walk away so she doesn't have to worry about life being too complicated and confusing for Cady."

"It's not that simple."

"Oh, yes, it is. And you want to know what else it is? It's stupid. Also, it's such a...a *martyr* play that I might have to toss you in the water after all."

"I am not a martyr."

"Right. And when Carter and I said we would be the ones to leave Comeback Cove so you wouldn't have to be separated from your family, you said, 'No. That's fine. I'll just go off by myself and take my halo with me.'"

"I didn't... Look, the dairy was already running without me. It made sense—"

"The *dairy* would have coped, no matter what happened. But you sure got to pat yourself on the back for being the noble one, didn't you?"

"I..." But once again, the words refused to come. He didn't want to think about that too closely.

"Look, I'm not saying you didn't have good reasons to leave. A fresh start in a new place after something like that… Yeah, that's legit. But you can't make me believe you didn't console yourself sometimes by congratulating yourself." Her voice dropped. "Just like you can't make me believe that you're not terrified of what could happen between you and Darcy."

"Nothing is—"

"Cut the crap, Ian. I know you. You're scared silly to talk to Carter because you're afraid if you open that can of worms, you'll never get it to close again. You're scared beyond silly to be with Darcy because you're afraid you're going to wind up having your heart broken again, so you're grabbing any virtuous excuse you can to walk away before that happens."

He would sell his soul for her to be wrong.

"Here's the thing, Ian. Maybe the can of worms won't get closed, but at least if you open it, nothing's going to explode." She patted his hand. "And maybe you think you're doing what's best for everyone, but from where I'm sitting, it looks like you already failed at that whole avoiding another heartbreak thing. So what the heck do you have to lose?"

CHAPTER SEVENTEEN

THE MEMORIES REACHED out to claim Darcy even before she unlocked the door to Nonny's log cabin.

She saw the ghost of her dad in the shadows from the wall of black walnut trees lining the driveway; heard the echo of his laugher in the muted babble of the creek at the edge of Nonny's property; felt his arm around her, strong and supportive, in the branches of the weeping willow that trailed across her shoulders as she walked up the stone steps.

"Nice place." It was the first thing Xander had said to her since they'd left, other than asking for directions. "Peaceful."

"Good way to describe it." She fitted the key into the lock. "Of course, when I was a kid, all I could think was that it was lonely."

Especially after a visit to the North home, which always had overflowed with noisy, sticky life.

Xander lowered Cady to the floor and helped her walk into the house. Darcy let them go on while she drank in the sights of the most unchanging piece of her childhood.

The living room was shadowed, as always, despite the floor-to-ceiling windows on the south wall. Even the brightest summer sunshine came in filtered by the abundance of trees around the house. The stone fireplace, the fuzzy brown sofa, the coffee table made of a cross section from a fallen maple—they were all there, lifted straight from her memory.

She checked on Cady, cruising her way around the sofa with Xander hovering over her, and then moved to the fireplace. Her heart, already wiped out from trying to keep up with what had happened with Ian, took in the parade of photos of Cady and twisted painfully. Some of them were ones Darcy had dutifully sent. Most, though, were the candids she had posted on Facebook—Cady in her splash pool, Cady grabbing Lulu to haul herself upright, Cady asleep on, oh, God, Ian's shoulder.

A low whistle sounded behind her. "Someone has a serious case of Cady love."

She wrapped her arms around herself. "Nonny hates the computer. She makes herself use it, but she complains the whole time. For her to figure out how to get these off Facebook and print them… For you or me, it would be nothing. For her…"

For Nonny, it would be an act of love.

Dear Lord, did I totally blow that one, too?

She couldn't do anything about it at the moment. Nonny would arrive tomorrow. In the meantime, she had practical matters to consider—unpacking, finding food, making a place for Cady to take her overdue nap before she fell apart.

"Could you get the portable crib from the car, please? I want to get it set up before someone starts wailing."

"Sure. But Moxie said there was one here."

"Right, but I doubt it's put together."

"Probably not. But it'll only take a second to look."

He clattered up the stairs before she could point out that he was wasting time. She sighed, popped Cady on her shoulder and felt the familiar weight of her little girl sinking into her. Yep. Definitely nap time.

"Hey, Darce," Xander called. "Check it out."

"Don't tell me," she said to whatever smirking angels might be watching. "I was wrong about this, too."

Cady let loose with a quick butt squeaker. Just in case Darcy had missed the message, probably.

She ascended the stairs, walked down the hall lined with photos of the trees, of Dad, of Darcy through the ages, past Nonny's room and the room Daddy used to use, to the room Nonny had let her redecorate when she had been all of fifteen. She had a feeling the purple-and-teal decor she'd chosen probably hadn't aged with grace.

She stepped into the room and winced. Damn. The one time she wouldn't have minded being wrong...

But all was not lost. For there, tucked into the corner beneath one of the many posters she'd stuck to the walls, was a white four-poster crib. A smiling teddy bear danced at the top of each post and across the front of the change table sitting beside it. Sheets on the crib and a carton of wipes on the table were further proof that Moxie hadn't been kidding.

"Oh, wow."

"Looks like we're good to go." Xander pointed at the poster. "Though I don't know how I feel about her sleeping under a picture of Hanson. Tell me you're not going to teach her the words to 'MMMBop.'"

"Of course not." Only because she had never been able to understand them. "I think she's tired enough to fall asleep in a strange place, but I should probably— No, wait, there's a monitor right there." Guiltier and guiltier. "Maybe while I'm getting her settled you could bring in the things. And then I should probably look through the kitchen and send you to the store for some essentials."

"No problem."

Thank heaven. She was desperately in need of a few minutes alone, of some time without an audience, to let down her guard and—

And what? Feel all the hurt and bewilderment and guilt and worry?

"On second thought, maybe I should be the one to go."

"Whatever." But as she checked Cady's diaper— dry, good—he continued.

"You know that sooner or later we're going to have to talk about it."

She closed her eyes. "I know."

"I don't appreciate being lied to, Darcy. I know you must feel like you're barely treading water, but if we're going to make this work—"

"I know." The irony of an ex-con lecturing her about honesty wasn't lost on her.

She held Cady toward him for a kiss, which he bestowed gently.

"Have a good nap, pretty girl. We'll play when you wake up."

A soft whimper was the only reply.

Xander slipped out of the room. Darcy hit the lights and grabbed the monitor, but instead of turning it on, she sat in the rocker wedged into the spot where her guitar used to live.

Alone in the shadows, she rested her head against the back of the chair, closed her eyes and rocked.

But unlike a scraped knee, she could not rock away this hurt.

IAN SPENT THE REST of the day avoiding his family as much as possible.

He stayed down on the dock until the mosquitoes came out. Then he dragged himself back to the house, slapped some peanut butter on bread and took himself to the sunporch. Tucked off to the side of the house as it was, the room gave him the perfect spot to turn everything over in his head while remaining undisturbed. He heard the repeated creak of the screen door and the slam as it closed behind folks. He heard footsteps and voices and the soft clink of bottles each time someone opened the refrigerator. He closed his eyes, letting the sun warm his face as he listened to muted voices and silverware jangling and always, always the laughter. Sometimes it was short, sometimes low, occasionally loud and hearty. But almost every trip into the kitchen included at least one person laughing.

God, he'd missed that.

He'd always associated his family with laughter. It hadn't always been appropriate—witness the way Carter and Hank had fallen into a silent snickering fit at Grandpa Gord's funeral when the minister had stumbled over the word *clock*—and yes, sometimes it had been cruel and used against each other. None of them had been above lobbing a well-timed insult or a mocking sneer while they had been growing up.

But most of the time the laughter had been the kind that mattered most, shared and supportive. The kind that drew people together instead of driving them apart. The kind that had gone missing from his life two years ago until he'd found it again with Darcy.

And now he might have lost it all over again.

He roused himself long enough to take Lulu out for her last call of the night. Once she was done, he crept back inside and considered his choices.

Climbing the stairs to the bedroom would be a waste of energy. No way could he sleep in that bed without Darcy.

"Guess we might as well hit the hay here tonight, girl."

He tossed an ancient blanket on the floor for her, then stretched out on the gilder and covered himself with an afghan. It was a lousy fit, but what the hell.

"It's not like I'm going to get much rest no matter where I am. Right, Lu?"

A cold nose nudged his hand. His throat tightened.

"Thanks."

He stared into the darkness, reliving his own idiocy over and over in his head like a song stuck on replay. All around him, the house settled into quiet. Lulu sent up some soft doggy-snores. The refrigerator hummed through its cycle, and outside an occasional splash reminded him that life on the river was still flowing.

He dozed on and off, always jerking awake with a horrible sensation of falling that had nothing to do with the narrowness of the glider. After about the fourteenth such episode, when the sky was beginning the shift from inky black to pearly gray, he hauled his cramped self upright and stumbled off to the bathroom.

When he came back, Moxie was sitting on his so-called bed.

"So this is where you decided to hole up." She

ubjected him to a slow and thorough scrutiny. "You sulking or hiding?"

"Neither." As soon as he said it, he knew it was a lie. "Maybe hiding."

"Figured as much. Folks'll be waking up soon. If you really want to lie low, this might be the time to head upstairs."

No, thanks.

"That's okay. I think I'm done with it."

"You talking about now or the last two years?"

This time he knew enough to consider his answer before blurting it out. "Sometimes hiding is your best chance at surviving."

"No one said it wasn't. The trouble comes when you get yourself so hidden that you can't find your way back again."

His brain was too fogged to come up with an answer for that one. Not that he could have figured it out if he had been wide-awake, but it was as good an excuse as any.

He settled for sitting beside her. The glider swayed softly beneath them.

"We got our first glider when you were little," she said. "Probably no more than four or five. For the first week or so it seemed every time we turned around you were out here. You would grab a blanket and hang it from the top to make yourself a little fort. You had this castle, and you would set it up here with all the knights and horses."

"I think I remember that. There was a cannon or the top, right? That sent plastic boulders flying?"

"That there was." A soft chuckle escaped her "There was nothing quite like walking in here and hearing a little voice yell, 'Fire in the hole!' righ before something hit the side of the blanket."

"Wasn't there another set like that? A Wild West town? I have this memory of plastic cowboys and a— I guess it must have been a saloon. You know, with the swinging half doors."

"Right. Right." Her voice lost some of its lilt. "That was Carter's."

And there it was.

"Ian...what I said to you yesterday, about blaming you if this family fell apart...that was wrong of me."

If he'd had more energy, he would have been floored. Had Moxie just admitted to a mistake?

"I know you think we're all sticking our nose in where it doesn't belong. I can see why you'd feel that way. You're wrong, but I still can see it."

And the earth resumed its proper rotation.

"Taylor talked to me about it. Not about yesterday, so much, but back then. It helped."

"But you still blame Carter."

Did he? Really? Now that he had firsthand experience of the way love could sneak up and bite you in the ass when you weren't looking, could he keep dumping the guilt on Carter?

"I guess I don't really blame him," he said slowly. "But I'm still angry."

"That's about what I figured."

"I don't know if I can forgive him." He'd never said the words, barely even let himself think them, but something deep in his gut told him that if he wasn't honest now, there was no way back. "It doesn't make sense. I don't love Taylor anymore, so why can't I forgive him?"

"Because you're not thinking about Taylor. You're thinking about you. Carter betrayed you more than she did, and even though we all know it wasn't deliberate, it happened anyway." She patted his knee. "And brothers aren't supposed to do that to each other."

"So what am I supposed to do?"

"I don't know, exactly. But here's one thing I'm sure of. This silent thing with you trying to push it all under the rug and carry on like nothing happened... how's that working for you?"

Crap.

"You ever think about not being right all the time, Moxie? Maybe letting the rest of us have a little secret superiority once in a while?"

"Nope. Suck it up and deal with it."

As if he had a choice.

"Okay, then, Yoda. Answer me this one. My gut tells me that the mess with Carter and the mess with Darcy are connected, and not just because she set me up to be alone with him. The thing is, I'm not sure how they go together."

Moxie was uncharacteristically silent for a few seconds. The soft creak of the glider and a sleep-whimper from Lulu were the only sounds.

"You done with trying to convince yourself that everything between you and her was make-believe?"

"Yeah."

"Good. 'Cause you might have forgotten that my room is right underneath that nursery, and let me tell you, there were a couple o' times I thought the only way I was going to get any sleep was if I headed up there with a can of WD-40."

Could he be lucky enough that there was still sufficient darkness to hide his blush? Probably not.

"The thing is," he said when he trusted himself to speak again, "when we got here, we weren't, um—"

"You were still dancing around each other?" At his nod, she made a soft *tsk*ing sound. "I thought it seemed mighty suspicious. But I have been known to be wrong once in a millennium, so I thought I'd give you the benefit of the doubt." She sighed. "I shoulda known better."

"So why'd you put us in the same room, if you weren't sure? Trying to force the universe's hand again?"

"I'm a churchgoing woman. Does that sound like something I would do?"

Hell, yeah.

"Here's what I think about you and Carter and Darcy and your gut. I think maybe you need to listen to it. Maybe what it's telling you is that you have to fix the family you have if you want to have a shot with the one you want to make."

"But what if I'm wrong? What if I wrecked everything?"

"Could you be any more miserable than you are now?"

"Probably not."

"Then this is what I think about that."

He braced himself.

"Surely a blacksmith knows that the only way to make things turn the way you want is to shove them into the fire."

DARCY'S TALK WITH Xander didn't happen.

His quick run to the grocery store turned into a long afternoon of frustration when his car refused to start in the parking lot. Darcy had food for Cady, but Nonny's pantry was sparse. By the time Xander got the car straightened out and made it back to the house, Darcy was well into the evening routine. Bath, bottle, blankie, boom—and Cady wasn't the only one who was exhausted.

"I know I promised we'd talk," she said as she wolfed down a grilled cheese sandwich. "But honestly, Xander, I don't think I could even remember my name at the moment."

His standing as a father went up about seventy points on her chart when he hesitated only briefly before nodding. "Tomorrow, then."

"Tomorrow," she agreed, and showed him how to jiggle the temperamental handle in the bathroom before dropping into her bed. Her second to last conscious thought was that Cady's father was sleeping in her dad's room.

Her last thought was to wonder if Ian was alone in the bed they'd shared, reaching for her the way she already found herself reaching for him.

She slept the sleep of exhausted motherhood, deep and dreamless, and didn't open her eyes again until she was pulled awake by the sound of Cady bellowing. She was glad for both the rest and the hours of not thinking. But snoozing late meant she wasn't showered and dressed when Cady woke her, which meant she was already five steps behind all morning, which meant she was still in her nightgown, about to press Xander into duty, when Nonny walked in.

And with that first glimpse of the beloved tight silver curls and brick-shaped body, Darcy fell apart.

It was as though some giant permission switch had been thrown. One moment she was on the steps juggling Cady, and the next her head was buried in Nonny's shoulder and she could scarcely breathe for the sobs clawing their way out of her.

Nonny was here. In some small corner of her

brain she was aware that she had questions and confusion, but right now, Nonny was here.

At some point they moved to the sofa and sat down. She was vaguely aware of Cady pulling up on her knee and whimpering until Xander appeared, mumbled a rough "'Morning" and stumbled outside with her. With that she leaned into Nonny's embrace and cried even harder, all while Nonny did nothing more than rub Darcy's back and hand her tissues.

When Darcy was able to speak, she wiped her eyes and blew her nose and managed a choking kind of laugh. "Welcome home."

"Believe it or not, it truly is." Nonny's groan as she patted Darcy's hand and pushed herself off the sofa was the kind guaranteed to inspire guilt of the most extreme kind.

"I didn't mean... I didn't think I would..."

"Darcy Elizabeth, don't you dare apologize for being human and needy." She pushed the hair from Darcy's damp face. "Believe you me, I'd rather have you crying all over me than ignoring me."

"Oh." Darcy squeezed the ball of damp tissues in her hand. "Nonny, before anything else, I'm sorry. I... When I told you I was pregnant, I got the feeling that you, well, didn't approve. Because I wasn't married, or, you know, even with Cady's father. Not that I bothered telling you who he was. But don't feel bad about that, because I didn't tell anyone."

"I don't—"

Darcy shook her head. "Wait. The thing is…it didn't really matter what you said or did. Because *I* was the one who was disappointed in myself and angry with myself. So when you didn't fall all over me with excitement, well, it was a lot easier to tell myself that you disapproved than to admit that I was reading what I wanted into it." She frowned. "Did that make any sense at all?"

"Enough for me to follow, even after flying across three time zones. And don't you try to apologize about that, either, because I would have had to make the flight sometime. I would much rather do it knowing that you and my great-granddaughter were waiting for me."

"I can't believe I wouldn't let myself turn to you for so long," Darcy said as she wiped her eyes. "Of all the boneheaded things I've done…"

"It would only be boneheaded if you kept at it once you knew the truth."

"You're being way too understanding."

"Darcy, these days, my friends are dropping like flies. I can't afford to hold a grudge. There might never be time to make things right again." She paused before adding softly, "That's something better learned early than late. Not that I have any particular reason for mentioning it, of course."

Darcy closed her eyes. "You talked to Moxie this morning, didn't you?"

"Yeah. The minute we landed and I turned on my phone, it went crazy with messages. She gave me the whole lowdown." Nonny cracked her familiar grin. "I have to say, much as I don't like trying to keep up with all the gadgets and such these days, it's mighty nice to be able to get the gossip while you're still taxiing to the gate."

It was the first laugh that felt real since she'd been in the kitchen with Brynn and Taylor.

"Come on." Nonny headed for the kitchen. "I don't know about you, but I could use some coffee. Didn't dare drink any before I left the airport, 'cause then I woulda had to stop every half hour, but I'm way past due."

"Sounds good."

"Should I make some for— It's Xander, isn't it?"

"Yes." Too late, Darcy saw the situation through her grandmother's eyes. "Nonny, you know that Xander and I never— Well, yes, once. That's why Cady's here, but we're not together."

"Breathe, girl. Moxie told me that part, too. I'm looking forward to really meeting him, but for now…" She peered through the window to the backyard. Xander lay facedown on the grass and Cady crawled over him. "For now, I think we'll leave him be while I finish talking to you. So, what's this about you and Ian telling everyone some story that turned out to be true?"

Even if Darcy had wanted to answer, she couldn't have. Her throat tightened to the point where no sound could emerge.

Nonny sighed. "That's about what I thought."

She forced herself to breathe, hating the sound that accompanied her inhalation but unable to stop it. "This wasn't supposed to happen."

"I wouldn't be so sure." Nonny looked slightly shamefaced. "Moxie and I might have had some thoughts about this when we told him to rent your apartment."

"Wait. What? You were trying to set us up? When he had just been dumped, and I was still with Jonathan?"

"We weren't trying to force anything. But the hope was always there. Not a big hope, mind you, but it was there."

"I'm sorry we let you down." Darcy bit her lip before moving to the stove and pulling out a frying pan. "I haven't eaten yet. Have you?"

"I could use an egg. And who's to say you let us down?"

This laugh was nothing like the last one. "Well, I'm here, he's there, and after the things we said and did…"

"You mean you had your first fight?" Nonny sounded so completely not dismayed that Darcy had to double-check to ensure she'd heard right.

"I guess you could call it that. But we…" She pulled the carton of eggs from the fridge. "The thing is, I thought I knew him. Better than anyone else except maybe you and Mom and Cady. And then he went behind my back and told Xander he should live in the apartment—"

"And you're upset over that? It sounds like a capital idea to me."

"I— Okay. Now that I've had time to think about it, he's right. It is. But he shouldn't have done it without talking to me first."

"Does he love Cady?"

"Absolutely."

"Did you ever have a talk with someone and think of something and blurt it out before you should have?"

"Okay, now I really feel like an idiot." She cracked the egg against the pan. Oops. One yolk, busted. "But it's not just that. I've been thrown by everything that happened with Xander showing up, and I'm trying to put the brakes on, not to stop things but to slow them down. But meanwhile, Ian has been pushing me to accommodate Xander, and I feel like someone threw me in the washing machine and hit the spin cycle."

"I can see how that would leave you feeling extra flustered. But here's something you need to remember, Darcy. He grew up in that big family. He's used to juggling lots of people and demands. You, not so much." Nonny poured water into the coffeemaker. "Nobody's saying you need to start moving at light speed, and when it comes to Cady, yes, you need to be cautious. But it might not hurt to take some lessons from him."

Darcy stared at the eggs, her own misery snapping in time with the hot butter in the pan. "You're saying I blew it."

"I'm saying you had a hell of a week and you wanted to stop the spinning, but you maybe grabbed the wrong thing."

"I could buy that. Except—" she peeked out the window in time to see Cady and Xander sticking their tongues out at each other "—it almost always feels that way, you know? Ever since she was born. Not just the busyness. I get that. But I never feel like I'm doing it right."

"And you honestly believe there's ever been a parent who feels they are?"

"My head tells me, no, of course not. But some folks just seem so natural at it. You. The Norths. My dad. I do a good job with Cady, but it never feels like I just know what to do. Some things are automatic now, thank heaven, but there's so much I don't know. And it's not the stuff like when she should stop having a bedtime bottle. It's the big things."

"Like whether or not her father should be around?"

"Like whether I can give her a solid life, like I had when Daddy was alive." She poked at the eggs with a spatula. "Or whether having a family where Mommy lives here and Daddy lives here and Daddy's friends are all on parole and Mommy really wants to be—"

But it didn't matter what Mommy wanted. That had been lost in a flood of angry words.

"Darcy." Nonny sat at the small white table with a muffled groan that sent Darcy's guilt level soaring. "When it comes to building a family, no one knows what the hell they're doing. And that's okay. Half of being a good parent is pretending you're not scared out of your tree."

"Let me guess. The other half is love?"

"Nope. Though, of course, that's important." Nonny grinned over her mug. "The other half is stubbornness or persistence or whatever you want to call it. Refusing to give up when things are rough. Hanging in there because you're pretty sure it's going to get better. Knowing that these people are your life, and that being with them, no matter what it takes, is better than being without them."

"Are you saying it doesn't matter if I make a mess of things with Cady?" She frowned at the uneven, broken eggs in the pan. "Like a worse mess than these?"

"Of course it matters. But the thing is, child, the good Lord gave you a head, a heart and a gut. As long as you're listening to all of them, you're going to do okay." She forked up a bite of egg from the plate Darcy set in front of her. "I know you want to give Cady a wonderful life. Every parent does. And by the way, no matter what your mother tells you, Paul was not a perfect father, and your world wasn't all hunky-dory before he died."

Darcy's butt hit the chair a bit more forcefully than she'd intended, probably due to the sudden wobble in her knees.

"I know she's told you stories about him and the things he did with you," Nonny said. "Most of it has some truth. But she's… Well, I won't say she's twisted things. But she's definitely working from a script that I wouldn't recognize."

"But why?"

Nonny snorted, then coughed and thumped her chest. "Huh. Darcy, your mother and I come from very different worlds. I never understood her, not even when Paul was still with us. I hoped things would get better after you arrived, but I never did warm up to her, so I'm not the one to get inside her mind, you know? She made Paul happy. That was all I cared about. Drove him half out of his head most of the time, too, but it's like I said—for him, being with her was worth it."

"Then why—"

"Hang on, girl. I'm getting to that part." She sighed and forked up more eggs. "Sylvie is a story-teller. It's not just her job, it's how she gets through her life. She and Paul were like gas and matches, but she did love him. After he died…I'm not sure, but I think she wanted you to remember him in the best way possible. So she told you stories. And stories need a good guy, right? So that's what he became." She sighed. "You think you don't know what to do? Sylvie had you beat, hands down. I think that when she told you things about Paul, it was her way of figuring out what she should be doing. And since it was her, she needed everything to be as perfect as she could make it."

Oh, yeah. That sounded like Sylvie.

"Did Daddy really cut my hair with pruning shears?"

"Ha! Who told you about that? Was it Moxie?"

"No. Actually, it was Robert."

"That makes sense. Yep, he did it. It was your last day here, and there wasn't time to get you to the hairdresser and fix it up before you went back home. Sylvie wasn't happy." Nonny's shrug was evidence of how little Sylvie's opinion meant to her. "It was just hair. It grew back. And, Darcy, that's the thing about being a parent, or a friend or even a wife. There are very few things that can't be fixed, no matter how scary they look at the time."

Darcy let the words seep into her while staring out the window. At Cady...at Cady's father...and at the empty space where Ian should have been standing.

"I know you want to make her life as strong and wonderful as you can, Darcy." Nonny's hand covered her own. "But the rest of the world isn't steady and perfect, you know? You can try to protect her from all the hurt and confusion. Or you can teach her how to find her own steadiness no matter what life throws at her."

"And how do I do that?"

"By living that way yourself."

CHAPTER EIGHTEEN

DARCY CARRIED THE MUG of coffee across the back-yard, moving slowly to avoid slopping it onto her hand. She'd be damned if she'd made it this far only to be stopped by a rogue burn.

"Is that for me?" The hope in Xander's eyes was almost pathetic.

"Indeed. Here. You sit and enjoy. I'll take Bug watch."

"Darce, don't take this the wrong way, but right at this minute I really love you."

"Since that was how I felt when you appeared in the middle of my sobfest, I think you'll understand when I say that the feeling is mutual."

She reached into her pocket and grabbed the spoons she'd tucked in there, handing them to Cady as she sat beside her.

"Why are your pants wet?"

"The grass hadn't dried when we first came out. Cady needed someplace warm and dry to climb."

She remembered him lying prone while Cady clambered all over him. "You didn't have to do that."

"Yeah, and maybe someday I won't be that dense

again. But I was still half asleep and she needed something to keep her happy while you weren't around. So I got a little cold." He shrugged. "Nothing that can't be fixed with a hot shower and some excellent coffee."

If she'd had any lingering doubts over what she was about to say, those words blew them out the window.

"I want you to move into the garage apartment, Xander."

The sputtering sound was so unlike his usual cool that she couldn't keep from snickering.

"Seriously?" It came out in three gasps and a gulp.

"Very seriously. And before you aspirate any more coffee and we have to rush you to the ER, let me explain everything."

He blinked and nodded. She mock-tugged one spoon from a giggling Cady.

"We didn't set out to lie to you," she began, taking him through the entire course of events. Well, everything except how she and Ian had managed to turn make-believe into reality, at least for a little while. She would need to share many things with Xander in the years ahead. This wasn't one of them.

When she was finished, he spent long seconds studying the clouds in his coffee.

"I'll be honest, Darce. I wish you'd been up front from the start. We're going to have enough of a challenge to do right by her as it is without throwing mind games into the mix."

"You're right."

"That said, I can see where you're coming from. In your shoes, I might have done the same thing." He paused before adding gently, "And in Ian's shoes? Yeah. Absolutely."

"Thanks." Gratitude thickened her voice. "That's probably more than we deserve."

"Yeah, well, you gave me something pretty amazing. I figure I owe you."

"Um, I didn't exactly give Cady to you," she said with a laugh. "I'm pretty sure you had almost as much to do with her being here as I did."

"Darce. You gave me a chance. You might have been dragged into it kicking and screaming, but you're doing it. You'll never know how much that means to me."

"You're giving me too much credit, Xander." She pulled the spoon from Cady's mouth. "Ian is the one you need to thank for that."

"Oh, paying him back is gonna be easy. All I have to do is let him keep Lulu." He tickled Cady's tummy with his toes. "And make sure he knows that I'm not trying to replace him in Cady's life."

Loneliness cut her, sharp and deep. "Well, the problem with that is I'm not so sure he wants me in his life anymore. Cady, probably. But me?" She traced a slow line down Cady's nose. "I'm not so sure."

"What the hell? Darce. You ever stop and ask yourself why it was so easy for you guys to make us all believe you were a couple?" He leaned forward and delivered two quick raps to the top of her head. "Hello. It's because it was true."

"But we weren't—"

Xander slid off the table and down to the ground, where he took Cady's outstretched hands and helped her stand. "Cady girl, what are we gonna do about your mama, huh? She thinks she was fooling everybody else, but the only one she was fooling was herself."

Could it be true?

"Oh, Xander. I don't know. The things we said…"

"Good God, Darce. Did *you* dump a dog on him and leave? Did *you* hide things from him and end up in jail? Did *you* come back unannounced and expect to pick up where you left off?"

"No, but—"

"Darce. Someone who can get past all that from a friend—a friend who hasn't done much lately to deserve the title—well, someone who can get past all that isn't going to just walk away from someone who loves him."

"He walked away from Carter."

"Yeah, he did. But then he came back."

"For everyone else, yes. For Carter?"

"Carter's part of the parcel. He knows that better than you ever will." Xander grabbed one spoon and clanked it against Cady's, sword-fighting style.

"Maybe he didn't handle it the way you would have, but come on. He's a guy. He's not complicated. If he's here, talking about moving back, then yeah. He wants to make things right with Carter."

"So I should have stepped back and let him do it his own way."

"Hey, I'm not saying he couldn't use a swift kick. I'm just saying... Damn. I don't know anymore." He lowered himself onto his elbows. "Cady, you are going to have one screwed-up family."

Funny. He didn't sound the least bit worried about that. In fact, he sounded pretty happy at the prospect.

Maybe she should take a hint.

"Screwed up, maybe, but still workable." She tugged Cady's blond wisps, then gave a soft tweak to the thicker head of hair that was the perfect match. "Happy Father's Day, and welcome to the family...Daddy."

IAN NEVER WOULD have believed it, but for the first time in memory, talking to Moxie had left him more settled rather than less. Which was damned unnerving in its own way, but he'd take it.

The glider had felt too confining after she left. "Into the fire," he'd said to Lulu, and dragged himself upstairs. There had been one bad moment when he'd rolled over and his head had hit Darcy's pillow, filling his lungs with sex-scented memories. But after that first slice of pain he had pulled the pillow close and decided it was like when he had been in Tanzania and Ma had sent care packages filled with Millie's drawings and newspaper clippings and boxes of Kraft Dinner. It left him longing, true, but it also comforted. More than that, it gave him hope.

And hope was enough to let him close his eyes.

He woke with a start and a cold nose in his hand.

"Damn it, Lulu!"

He couldn't believe he'd fallen asleep.

Or how bright the sunlight was for this early in the morning.

Or how much laughter was floating up the stairs.

He grabbed his phone, squinted at the display and let out a word that would still make Moxie wash his mouth out with soap.

How the hell had he let himself sleep past ten?

Pushing his barely awake body from the bed, he hobbled to the window, pulled back the curtain and checked the driveway. Yep. Everyone was here, probably hard at work setting up for the party. Not only was he not helping, he was going to go down there and steal another pair of hands from the preparations. He was never going to hear the end of this.

Lucky for him, once folks figured out why he was doing it, they might agree that in the long run, it would be worth it.

Wake up, brain. We have work to do.

One cursory shower later, he hit the stairs faster than he had since the morning after the infamous trig all-nighter. He followed the trails of conversations, listening for that one voice he needed right now.

It wasn't in the kitchen, which had been taken over by people who were either caterers or thieves.

It wasn't in the sunporch, where Ma was on the phone apparently trying to make some poor soul swear there would be no high winds or rain.

Nor was it in the dining room, where Millie, Brynn and Taylor were singing some song about fireworks and doing something with ribbons and glittery stars. But at least they might have an idea of where he should look.

"Taylor. Where's Carter?"

That was one way to bring the music to a crashing halt.

Taylor glanced at Brynn. Cautious hope dawned on both their faces.

"He's outside with your dad and Hank and Cash. Moxie decided the backyard looked bare, so she went out and bought a helium tank and balloons. They're blowing things up as we speak."

"Backyard. Right." He turned on his heel but wasn't fast enough.

"Ian? Why do you need him?"

Once again, he asked himself why he had been so insistent that he had to come back here. But he knew it was a purely rhetorical question.

"You'll find out soon enough," he said, and set off for the back door. He didn't have to look back

at the women to know what must have been happening: the quick exchange of glances, the scissors
hitting the table, the race for the door. He should be
hearing footsteps in three—two—one—

"You know, I don't think I've ever actually seen
a helium tank in action." Brynn linked her arm
through his. "This seems like as good a time as
any."

"Nope. Bad idea. Go back to your glitter."

"Sorry, but I have a sudden and severe glitter
allergy. I'll be sneezing all through the party if I
don't take a break. Multicolored, sparkly sneezes.
Your mother would not be pleased."

Thank God they had reached the door. Maybe
he would feel less as if he was being shanghaied
once they were outside.

The good thing was there was no backing out
now. Not with this crew in attendance.

One side of the yard had been taken over by the
tent, where the pig-roast people were sending some
smells into the atmosphere that made his stomach
remind him he should eat. Preferably soon.

Carter and Dad and the others huddled around
one of the picnic tables. Moxie was tying a bunch
of multicolored balloons to the end of another. He
would have to remind her to leave one or two of
the tables bare. Balloons were a choking hazard,
and he didn't want Cady—

Oh, yeah. No Cady.

Brynn squeezed his arm. "You can do this, buddy."

Divine intervention in the form of his take-charge sister-in-law?

"Remind me to tell Hank that marrying you was the smartest thing he ever did."

"Will do. But don't worry." She winked. "I make sure he hears it all the time."

She released his arm. Behind him he heard Millie whisper something, followed by Taylor's low answer and a muffled gasp.

It seemed he didn't need to bother working his way over to Carter and issuing a private invitation.

"Carter." His voice didn't crack. More proof that the Almighty was in his corner. "You have a minute?"

A frustrated groan sounded behind him. Ma. "Now?"

"Yeah, Ma. Now."

"Fine," she said, and he could so clearly hear her war within herself that he had to peek over his shoulder.

"I promise I'll only be a few minutes. And when we're done, I'll do the work of ten Grinches plus two, okay?"

She offered a faint small and a slightly stronger nod.

Carter placed the scissors he'd been holding on the table. "Yeah. Sure."

Dad scooted sideways to give Carter room to move. Cash offered a slap on the back. Hank shook his head.

"Some people will do anything to get out of work," he said, but the grin he sent toward Ian was pure encouragement.

At the side of the table Moxie rubbed her hands together before blowing on the fingertips. Ian frowned, not sure what she was doing, until it hit him. She was pretending to warm her hands over a fire. A blacksmith's fire, hot and glowing and waiting for him to jump in.

"Come on," Ian said to Carter, jerking his head toward the dock. "If we go out there, we can keep an eye on the jackals, make sure they don't come too close."

Carter nodded. Ian slapped his thigh and Lulu came running. They crossed the lawn in silence. Well, other than Lulu's excited panting.

"Ma says you guys have a dog now, too."

Carter shoved his hands into the pockets of his jeans. "Yeah. Taylor gave him to me for Christmas."

"What kind?"

"A black Lab. We named him Vader."

Ian looked at Carter for the first time since they'd set out. "You named your dog after Darth Vader?"

"You know, all that shiny black hair, the long floppy ears, the kind of square face—it works."

"If he ever sires puppies, will you name them Luke and Leia?"

"Jeez, Ian, he's just a baby. Don't make me think about that stuff yet."

"Yeah? Well, get used to it. Things change faster than you think."

That topic exhausted, they stared at the water. Ian kicked off his shoes and sat on the dock. Lulu stretched out at his side, a furry barrier between the men. Carter followed a moment later.

"Everybody watching?" Ian asked.

"Yep."

"You didn't look."

"Don't need to."

This was true.

"So," Ian said when it all became too weird. "I'm not sure where to start."

"Ian, if you're not ready... I know you've been trying to keep your distance, and I know they set us up yesterday. I admit, I was kind of glad when I figured out what had happened because I want to get this behind us, but if you're not—"

"Don't know if I'll ever really be ready. But I think I'm readier than I'll ever be."

"I guess that makes sense. After what happened with Darcy, that is."

"You know, this isn't really for— Okay. In some ways it is. But—" and he was surprised to realize it was true "—I'm mostly doing this for me."

Carter's eyes widened. "Didn't expect to hear that."

"Didn't expect to say it."

"And I never expected to fall in love with my brother's fiancée."

There it was. The truth, shining and waiting for Ian to seize it.

"I know. I mean, I'm not sure I believed it back when it happened. But I know it now."

"That's good to hear."

"It doesn't mean..." He watched a sailboat dip and sway. "It still hurts. Not the part about losing Taylor, okay? I don't want you to think that I look at her and think...anything. That's over."

"I figured that out the minute I saw you with Darcy. And yeah, I know, that was all supposed to be an act, but honestly, Ian, the only time any of us thought you were lying was yesterday when you told us it was all pretend. So that should tell you something."

It told him that he needed to make his peace with Carter—well, the first steps—so he could go to Darcy with a clear conscience. But there was something that still needed to be said.

"What if I hadn't shown up with Darcy? If I'd been solo? Would you have been so trusting then?"

Carter stayed silent long enough that Ian knew he'd hit a nerve.

"I'd like to say yeah, of course." He breathed in, slow and deep. "But honestly? It probably would have been there in the back of my mind."

"But you were still on board with me coming back."

Carter shrugged. "Yeah. That was never a question."

"Never?"

More silence. Ian wasn't exactly sure why he was pushing this, but his gut told him it was important.

"I guess… I guess I did feel more…welcoming… when I saw Darcy. And I guess that before she turned up, if I thought about how it would be to have you back here, even though I absolutely trust both of you, maybe…" His voice dropped. "I guess maybe, if it bothered me, then it was no more than what I deserved."

Was it wrong to feel a little pleasure at that confession?

"Carter."

"Yeah?"

"No matter what happens with Darcy, you won't have anything to worry about. Not because I'm such a noble guy or anything, but because Taylor never loved me the way she loves you."

When Carter spoke, his voice was thick. "I thought I would be the one doing the apologizing and explaining today."

"So did I." He scratched absently behind Lulu's ears. "Guess I'm just full of surprises."

"There's an understatement."

This time the silence that fell between them was almost comfortable.

"So what happens now?" Carter put voice to the question rolling around in Ian's head.

"Don't know exactly. But I think maybe this is the point where we give things time."

"I'm good with that." Carter hesitated before adding, low and fervent, "I don't want to lose you, Ian. I know it probably can never be the way it was, but I hope…you know, maybe with working together again and living in the same town and everything…maybe we can find a new way."

A new way to be brothers?

Well, hell. Almost every other relationship in his life was changing. What was one more?

"I can get behind that." Before he could second-guess himself, he added, "But so help me, if you ask Moxie to plan what we should do, all bets are off."

Carter took only a second to break into loud laughter. When Ian joined in, he could almost feel things begin to shift inside.

"Come on." He pushed to his feet, gave Lulu a soft nudge. "Want to watch me make Ma go ballistic?"

"You're gonna throw me in the river, aren't you?"

"Tempting, but to be honest, that wasn't what I had in mind. Remember I told her I would help work once I was finished with you? I lied."

"Planning to go over to Helene's place?"

"Yep."

"No need." Carter pointed to the knot of people gathered just out of earshot. "She's already here."

DARCY HADN'T EXPECTED to have to run a gauntlet of Norths to get to Ian. But that was sure how it felt.

She had wanted to drive over as soon as she finished talking to Xander, but Nonny convinced

er that showering and dressing were in her best
nterests,

"After all," she'd said, "families don't have to be
erfect, but they run a whole lot smoother if every-
ne smells good."

With the essentials out of the way she had headed
or the car only to find Nonny, Cady and Xander
vaiting.

"You are not all coming along for this."

"Oh, yes, we are." Xander fastened Cady into her
ar seat, which he had already moved to Nonny's
3uick. "We'll let you talk in private, but this is going
o impact this whole family, Darce. We want to know
vhat's happening as soon as you do."

"But—" Darcy began, only to have Nonny de-
iver the ultimate nonnegotiable point.

"Lord have mercy, girl. It's bad enough I've had
o hear everything else from Moxie. I didn't fly all
night to miss out on this."

The closer they got to the house, the more her
heart sped up. By the time they pulled into the
driveway she wasn't sure if she could walk, what
with the way everything was jumping and clang-
ng and shaking.

"I haven't felt like this since I was in labor," she
said to Nonny as she pulled herself out of the car.

"Well, seeing's how this will be another kind of
beginning, that seems right to me." Nonny patted
her cheek. "It'll be fine, Darcy. I promise."

Her head knew that Nonny couldn't really mak that guarantee. Her heart settled the tiniest bit.

A quick walk through the house confirmed tha the entire family had either been kidnapped b aliens—Xander's vote—or gone outside. But it wa still a shock to walk out to the backyard and fin the bulk of the Norths huddled together halfwa down the lawn, staring at the two men on the dock

"Taylor?" Darcy squeezed in beside her. "Ar they…"

"Yeah." Taylor never took her eyes off the broth ers, but she reached over and gripped Darcy' hand. "Yeah, I think they are."

Moxie bent and peered around Janice and Rob ert to glare at Darcy. "Have you apologized yet t your grandmother?"

"Oh, Moxie, stifle yourself," Nonny said indul gently. "You have enough worries with your ow family. You don't need to take over mine, too." Sh elbowed Darcy. "Even though I have my finger crossed that pretty soon we're going to be relate by marriage."

"Will you two hush?" Janice whispered. "It' hard enough to try to figure out what's going o without—"

Cady broke in with an excited, "Ru! Ru! Ru!"

Sure enough, Ian and Carter had risen and wer headed back to the voyeurs. Lulu bounded ahead of them.

Darcy and Taylor stepped forward.

"Back, you two," Moxie said. "Let them come
us."

Darcy looked at Taylor, who raised her eye-
rows and nodded. Together, they took off across
e grass, Brynn's laughter spurring them on.

Carter kicked up his own heels and met Tay-
r halfway. Darcy heard him say, "It's good, it's
od," followed by Taylor's sobbing kind of laugh,
it Darcy wasn't stopping to get the details. She
eded to get to Ian.

Except he wasn't coming any closer.

She went a couple more steps before slowing.
he needed to be near him, to read his face, but
e wouldn't look at her. Instead he was looking
ast her.

"Ian?"

"I can't— I don't want to do this with everyone
atching."

"Oh." The word slipped out, bewildered and
mall. A perfect match for the way she felt.

But with that, he finally turned to her, panic and
nderstanding dawning in his face.

"No. Darce. It's not— God, I'm such an idiot.
m making a mess of this, but I really don't want
have an audience the first time I say—"

"I love you."

She couldn't keep it in any longer. And if she'd
aid it a bit too loud, trying to be heard over his
lood of words, and if the sound had carried to the
thers, well...

"I love you," she said again, louder this tim
"And I don't care who hears it. Even if you thin
I'm a total idiot, because God knows I've been :
stupid about Xander and Cady and everythin;
even if you say you don't want to ever come bac
to Stratford, I love you."

"God, Darce," he whispered, then at last he wa
crossing the lawn, gathering her close, framin
her face with his hands while he kissed her an
pushed her damned hair away from her mouth an
kissed her again, slower and fuller and as if h
never wanted to stop.

"Are they cheering?" she whispered when sh
came up for air.

"Yeah." He nuzzled her nose. "Guess I was drean
ing when I thought we could do this in private."

"Well, they've been there for everything else
Why not this?"

"You have a point." He ran his hands down he
arms, laced his fingers through hers.

"You were right. About Carter. I didn't want t
do it, and yeah, I was frickin' terrified, but yo
were right. We don't know how we're going to d
it yet, but we want to make this work again."

"I'm so glad. But—" she bit down on her li
and bumped his nose lightly with her own "—
shouldn't have pushed you. That was the kind o
thing you should have done for yourself, not be
cause I made you. I'm so sorry I didn't hear wha
you were trying to say."

"Yeah, well, the thing is, I was so busy talking I never bothered listening to myself. Turns out that once I shut up, I wasn't nearly as pissed anymore as I thought I was."

"I don't know if I followed that."

"Not a problem. I'm planning on having a whole lifetime to explain it."

She needed to kiss him again. No matter that they were still being watched, she was pretty sure that if she didn't kiss him in the next, oh, twenty seconds, she couldn't be held responsible for what might happen when she finally tasted him again. But there were things she had to say first.

"Xander is moving into the apartment."

His eyes clouded. "Ah, Darce. I—"

"No. Listen. It makes perfect sense, and if I had thought of it myself, I would have been walking around beaming over how clever I am. But—"

"But you'd already had a hell of a week and you'd already been pushed into more than you'd had time to process. I know."

"Those are all true. But let's not forget that I was stubborn and rigid and so busy making up stories about what I thought a family should be that I almost forgot the most important part." She let herself kiss his jaw then, a soft brush of her lips against his bristles that only reminded her how much she wanted him. "But I think that's another topic that we're going to have to spend a lifetime figuring out."

"Did I tell you I love you, too?"

"I think it was implied." She tipped back, smiling up at him. "You'd better say it again, though, just so I'm clear.

"I love you, Darce. So much more than I ever would have believed." His gaze scooted past her again. "But it's going to be complicated."

"Complicated. But worth it."

"Listen to me, okay? I want the whole nine yards, Darce. I want to build a life with you, have a home and maybe get another dog and make some brothers and sisters for Cady. I want that with everything that's in me." He breathed in, slow and ragged. "But I want to do it right."

"I've heard that line before." She nuzzled his chin. "This time, I'm going to be smart enough to listen."

"I want to be sure I know what I'm doing. Not about you." He laced his fingers through hers. "You're the one thing that's certain. But I have things I need to work out. With both of my families. The one in Comeback Cove." He kissed her, soft and swift. "And the one in Stratford. You. Me. Cady. And, God love him, even Xander."

"Meet the Teacher nights are going to be interesting."

"*Everything's* gonna be interesting. I need to be here, and I know you need to be there."

"But what do you need from me?"

"Weekends?"

She lifted her face to his, laughing. "Weekends?"

"Long ones. Once we're all on more solid footing I hope I can convince you and Xander to move up here—"

"Speaking for Xander, I think he's half anticipating that already. Speaking for myself, I thought you'd never ask."

"I'm slow sometimes, okay? In the meantime, I convinced Moxie to let me do a four-day workweek."

"Oh, I bet that was difficult."

"Being family has its advantages."

"*Having* a family has advantages, too," she said, remembering how grateful she had felt to Xander just a few hours earlier. "Like grandmothers who might want to babysit when Cady and I come up here to see you. Or a father who might eventually be able to do daddy-daughter weekends, so you and I could have some time alone. If we want to give Cady a brother or sister, we should probably spend some time working on our sibling-making technique."

"Do you have any idea how much I wish I could make them all disappear right this minute?"

"Pretty sure," she said cheerfully. "But since we can't, how about we put them out of their misery and give them the good news?"

"I'm ready if you are."

"More than ready."

She slipped her arm around his waist as, to-

gether, they moved forward. Just before the lov
ing horde descended, he gave her a squeeze.

"You think it's crazy that we never started tel
ing each other the truth until we started lying t
everyone else?" he asked.

"You forgot what I told you." She rested he
head against his shoulder, snuggling even close
into him. "The best lies are always based in truth.

* * * * *

LARGER-PRINT BOOKS!

GET 2 FREE LARGER-PRINT NOVELS PLUS

2 FREE GIFTS!

HARLEQUIN®

Romance

From the Heart, For the Heart

YES! Please send me 2 FREE LARGER-PRINT Harlequin® Romance novels and my 2 FREE gifts (gifts are worth about $10). After receiving them, if I don't wish to receive any more books, I can return the shipping statement marked "cancel." If I don't cancel, I will receive 4 brand-new novels every month and be billed just $5.09 per book in the U.S. or $5.49 per book in Canada. That's a savings of at least 15% off the cover price! It's quite a bargain! Shipping and handling is just 50¢ per book in the U.S. and 75¢ per book in Canada.* I understand that accepting the 2 free books and gifts places me under no obligation to buy anything. I can always return a shipment and cancel at any time. Even if I never buy another book, the two free books and gifts are mine to keep forever.

119/319 HDN GHWC

Name	(PLEASE PRINT)	

Address		Apt. #

City	State/Prov.	Zip/Postal Code

Signature (if under 18, a parent or guardian must sign)

Mail to the Reader Service:
IN U.S.A.: P.O. Box 1867, Buffalo, NY 14240-1867
IN CANADA: P.O. Box 609, Fort Erie, Ontario L2A 5X3
Want to try two free books from another line?
Call 1-800-873-8635 or visit www.ReaderService.com.

* Terms and prices subject to change without notice. Prices do not include applicable taxes. Sales tax applicable in N.Y. Canadian residents will be charged applicable taxes. Offer not valid in Quebec. This offer is limited to one order per household. Not valid for current subscribers to Harlequin Romance Larger-Print books. All orders subject to credit approval. Credit or debit balances in a customer's account(s) may be offset by any other outstanding balance owed by or to the customer. Please allow 4 to 6 weeks for delivery. Offer available while quantities last.

Your Privacy—The Reader Service is committed to protecting your privacy. Our Privacy Policy is available online at www.ReaderService.com or upon request from the Reader Service.

We make a portion of our mailing list available to reputable third parties that offer products we believe may interest you. If you prefer that we not exchange your name with third parties, or if you wish to clarify or modify your communication preferences, please visit us at www.ReaderService.com/consumerchoice or write to us at Reader Service Preference Service, P.O. Box 9062, Buffalo, NY 14240-9062. Include your complete name and address.

HRLP15

LARGER-PRINT BOOKS!

HARLEQUIN

Presents®

GET 2 FREE LARGER-PRINT NOVELS PLUS 2 FREE GIFTS!

PASSION
GUARANTEED
SEDUCTION

YES! Please send me 2 FREE LARGER-PRINT Harlequin Presents® novels and my 2 FREE gifts (gifts are worth about $10). After receiving them, if I don't wish to receive any more books, I can return the shipping statement marked "cancel." If I don't cancel, I will receive 6 brand-new novels every month and be billed just $5.30 per book in the U.S. or $5.74 per book in Canada. That's a saving of at least 12% off the cover price! It's quite a bargain! Shipping and handling is just 50¢ per book in the U.S. and 75¢ per book in Canada.* I understand that accepting the 2 free books and gifts places me under no obligation to buy anything. I can always return a shipment and cancel at any time. Even if I never buy another book, the two free books and gifts are mine to keep forever.

176/376 HDN GHVY

Name	(PLEASE PRINT)	
Address		Apt. #
City	State/Prov.	Zip/Postal Code

Signature (if under 18, a parent or guardian must sign)

Mail to the **Reader Service**:
IN U.S.A.: P.O. Box 1867, Buffalo, NY 14240-1867
IN CANADA: P.O. Box 609, Fort Erie, Ontario L2A 5X3

**Are you a subscriber to Harlequin Presents® books
and want to receive the larger-print edition?
Call 1-800-873-8635 today or visit us at www.ReaderService.com.**

* Terms and prices subject to change without notice. Prices do not include applicable taxes. Sales tax applicable in N.Y. Canadian residents will be charged applicable taxes. Offer not valid in Quebec. This offer is limited to one order per household. Not valid for current subscribers to Harlequin Presents Larger-Print books. All orders subject to credit approval. Credit or debit balances in a customer's account(s) may be offset by any other outstanding balance owed by or to the customer. Please allow 4 to 6 weeks for delivery. Offer available while quantities last.

Your Privacy—The Reader Service is committed to protecting your privacy. Our Privacy Policy is available online at www.ReaderService.com or upon request from the Reader Service.

We make a portion of our mailing list available to reputable third parties that offer products we believe may interest you. If you prefer that we not exchange your name with third parties, or if you wish to clarify or modify your communication preferences, please visit us at www.ReaderService.com/consumerschoice or write to us at Reader Service Preference Service, P.O. Box 9062, Buffalo, NY 14240-9062. Include your complete name and address.

HPLP15